"DELANEY, BEHIND YOU!"

A huge birdlike shape plummeted down out of the darkness. Even as Delaney spun around, it struck, clipping him with its wings and tearing the bow out of his grasp. They caught a quick glimpse of a large, avian body, about the size of a man's torso, with huge talons and a leathery wingspan of at least twenty or thirty feet.

"Harpies!" Jason cried. "They are demons! They are the very Furies themselves, sent by the gods!"

They stood with weapons drawn, waiting for the next attack. It came quickly. They heard the whoosh of something moving with incredible speed and Andre cried out as talons sank into her shoulders, lifting her off the ground ...

7 TIMEWARS

THE ARGONAUT AFFAIR

SIMON HAWKE

ACE BOOKS, NEW YORK

for Dave Mattingly
with thanks

This book is an Ace
original edition, and has never
been previously published.

THE ARGONAUT AFFAIR

An Ace Book / published by arrangement with
the author

PRINTING HISTORY
Ace edition / August 1987

ISBN: 0-441-02911-6

Ace Books are published by
The Berkley Publishing Group,
200 Madison Avenue, New York, New York 10016.
The name "Ace" and the "A" logo
are trademarks belonging to Charter Communications, Inc.
PRINTED IN THE UNITED STATES OF AMERICA

10 9 8 7 6 5 4 3 2 1

A CHRONOLOGICAL HISTORY OF THE TIME WARS

April 1, 2425:   Dr. Wolfgang Mensinger invents the chronoplate at the age of 115, discovering time travel. Later he would construct a small scale working prototype for use in laboratory experiments specially designed to avoid any possible creation of a temporal paradox. He is hailed as the "Father of Temporal Physics."

July 14, 2430:   Mensinger publishes "There Is No Future," in which he redefines relativity, proving that there is no such thing as *the* future, but an infinite number of potential future scenarios which are absolute relative only to their present. He also announces the discovery of "non-specific time" or temporal limbo, later known as "the dead zone."

October 21, 2440:	Wolfgang Mensinger dies. His son, Albrecht, perfects the chronoplate and carries on the work, but loses control of the discovery to political interests.
June 15, 2460:	Formation of the international Committee for Temporal Intelligence, with Albrecht Mensinger as director. Specially trained and conditioned "agents" of the committee begin to travel back through time in order to conduct research and field test the chronoplate apparatus. Many become lost in transition, trapped in the limbo of nonspecific time known as "the dead zone." Those who return from successful temporal voyages often bring back startling information necessitating the revision of historical records.
March 22, 2461:	*The Consorti Affair*—Cardinal Lodovico Consorti is excommunicated from the Roman Catholic Church for proposing that agents travel back through time to obtain empirical evidence that Christ arose following His crucifixion. The Consorti Affair sparks extensive international negotiations amidst a volatile climate of public opinion concerning the proper uses for the new technology. Temporal excursions are severely curtailed. Concurrently, espionage operatives of several nations infiltrate the Committee for Temporal Intelligence.
May 1, 2461:	Dr. Albrecht Mensinger appears before a special international conference in Geneva, composed of political

leaders and members of the scientific community. He attempts to alleviate fears about the possible misuses of time travel. He further refuses to cooperate with any attempts at militarizing his father's discovery.

February 3, 2485: The research facilities of the Committee for Temporal Intelligence are seized by troops of the TransAtlantic Treaty Organization.

January 25, 2492: The Council of Nations meets in Buenos Aires, capital of the United Socialist States of South America, to discuss increasing international tensions and economic instability. A proposal for "an end to war in our time" is put forth by the chairman of the Nippon Conglomerate Empire. Dr. Albrecht Mensinger, appearing before the body as nominal director of the Committee for Temporal Intelligence, argues passionately against using temporal technology to resolve international conflicts, but cannot present proof that the past can be affected by temporal voyagers. Prevailing scientific testimony reinforces the conventional wisdom that the past is an immutable absolute.

December 24, 2492: Formation of the Referee Corps, brought into being by the Council of Nations as an extranational arbitrating body with sole control over temporal technology and authority to stage temporal conflicts as "limited warfare" to resolve international disputes.

April 21, 2493:	On the recommendation of the Referee Corps, a subordinate body named the Observer Corps is formed, taking over most of the functions of the Committee for Temporal Intelligence, which is redesignated as the Temporal Intelligence Agency. Under the aegis of the Council of Nations and the Referee Corps, the TIA absorbs the intelligence agencies of the world's governments and is made solely answerable to the Referee Corps. Dr. Mensinger resigns his post to found the Temporal Preservation League, a group dedicated to the abolition of temporal conflict.
June, 2497– March, 2502:	Referee Corps presides over initial temporal confrontation campaigns, accepting "grievances" from disputing nations, selecting historical conflicts of the past as "staging grounds" and supervising the infiltration of modern troops into the so-called "cannon fodder" ranks of ancient warring armies. Initial numbers of temporal combatants are kept small, with infiltration facilitated by cosmetic surgery and implant conditioning of soldiers. The results are calculated based upon successful return rate and a complicated "point spread." Soldiers are monitored via cerebral implants, enabling Search & Retrieve teams to follow their movements and monitor mortality rate. The media dubs temporal conflicts the "Time Wars."
2500–2510:	Extremely rapid growth of massive support industry catering to the exacting art and science of temporal con-

flict. Rapid improvements in international economic climate follows, with significant growth in productivity and rapid decline in unemployment and inflation rate. There is a gradual escalation of the Time Wars with the majority of the world's armed services converting to temporal duty status.

Growth of the Temporal Preservation League as a peace movement with an intensive lobby effort and mass demonstrations against the Time Wars. Mensinger cautions against an imbalance in temporal continuity due to the increasing activity of the Time Wars.

September 2, 2514: Mensinger publishes his "Theories of Temporal Relativity," incorporating his solution to the Grandfather Paradox and calling once again for a cease-fire in the Time Wars. The result is an upheaval in the scientific community and a hastily reconvened Council of Nations to discuss his findings, leading to the Temporal Strategic Arms Limitations Talks of 2515.

March 15, 2515–
June 1, 2515: T-SALT held in New York City. Mensinger appears before the representatives at the sessions and petitions for an end to the Time Wars. A ceasefire resolution is framed, but tabled due to lack of agreement among the members of the Council of Nations. Mensinger leaves the T-SALT a broken man.

November 18, 2516: Dr. Albrecht Mensinger experiences total nervous collapse shortly after being awarded the Benford Prize.

December 25, 2516:   Dr. Albrecht Mensinger commits suicide. Violent demonstrations by members of the Temporal Preservation League.

January 1, 2517:   Militant members of the Temporal Preservation League band together to form the Timekeepers, a terrorist offshoot of the League, dedicated to the complete destruction of the war machine. They announce their presence to the world by assassinating three members of the Referee Corps and bombing the Council of Nations meeting in Buenos Aires, killing several heads of state and injuring many others.

September 17, 2613:   Formation of the First Division of the U.S. Army Temporal Corps as a crack commando unit following the successful completion of a "temporal adjustment" involving the first serious threat of a timestream split. The First Division, assigned exclusively to deal with threats to temporal continuity, is designated as "the Time Commandos."

October 10, 2615:   Temporal physicist Dr. Robert Darkness disappears without a trace shortly after turning over to the army his new invention, the "warp grenade," a combination time machine and nuclear device. Establishing a secret research installation somewhere off Earth, Darkness experiments with temporal translocation based on the transmutation principle. He experiments upon himself and succeeds in translating his own body into tachyons, but an error in his calculations causes an irreversible change in his sub-atomic structure, rendering it unstable. Darkness becomes "the man who is faster than light."

November 3, 2620: The chronoplate is superceded by the temporal transponder. Dubbed the "warp disc," the temporal transponder was developed from work begun by Dr. Darkness and it drew on power tapped by Einstein-Rosen Generators (developed by Bell Laboratories in 2545) bridging to neutron stars.

March 15, 2625: *The Temporal Crisis*: The discovery of an alternate universe following an unsuccessful invasion by troops of the Special Operations Group, counterparts of the Time Commandos. Whether as a result of chronophysical instability caused by clocking tremendous amounts of energy through Einstein-Rosen Bridges or the cumulative effect of temporal disruptions, an alternate universe comes into congruence with our own, causing an instability in the timeflow of both universes and resulting in a "confluence effect," wherein the time-streams of both universes ripple and occasionally intersect, creating "confluence points" where a crossover from one universe to another becomes possible.

Massive amounts of energy clocked through Einstein-Rosen Bridges has resulted in unintentional "warp bombardment" of the alternate universe, causing untold destruction. The Time Wars escalate into a temporal war between two universes.

PROLOGUE _____

The creature slept standing up, its head lowered, the upper half of its complex, jointed spine bowed forward. Its breathing was deep and regular. Technicians had attached sensors to various portions of its body and a robot scanner was completing a slow holographing run of the creature's torso. A civilian veterinarian had been called in to consult with the team of army doctors. The atmosphere inside the lab was one of tense, barely restrained excitement. It was the first time anyone had ever seen a real live centaur.

From the waist up, it was an extremely well-muscled man, naked, with long, thick, manelike white hair—pure, albino white. The centaur's skin had an alabaster sheen and the pupils of its eyes were a deep red. From the waist down, it was a snowy Arabian stallion, only with tufted hoofs, like a Percheron's. Its muscles were taut and sleek, exuding a sense of explosive power. Its equine torso was over eighteen hands high, tall for a horse, but above its animal torso was the upper body of a man, a man who dwarfed the people in the laboratory. The arms were huge, the shoulders broad and powerful. The stomach muscles looked like cobblestones. It was an imposing looking creature, yet the most compelling thing about it was its most human feature—its face. It was the bearded face of an ancient, scored by time, yet free of sagging flesh. The features were lined, but firm and sharp, giving the same impression of great age that an old marble statue might convey.

Finn Delaney shook his head slowly in amazement. His black base fatigues looked as if they had been slept in. In fact, he had been asleep when the call came and his thick, dark red hair was still in a state of disarray, but his eyes, bleary with drink from the previous night, had cleared instantly when he beheld the centaur.

"It's grotesque, yet at the same time, beautiful," said Andre Cross. Unlike Delaney, who had a cavalier disdain for such trifles as reveille, she needed little sleep and was an early riser. By the time first call had blown at six A.M., she had already risen from bed and worked out pumping iron for two hours. Her straw blonde hair was still damp from her shower. She stared with wonder at the centaur. "I can hardly believe it's real."

Moses Forrester grunted. "My sentiments exactly. What's your impression, Dr. Anderson?"

The veterinarian could barely contain himself. "General, I've never seen anything like it! This is an amazing organism! It has two hearts! One in the human portion of its body and one in the equine half. Both organs are incredibly strong. The performance of its equine heart is superior to a thoroughbred's and its human heart is in better condition than a marathon runner's. I estimate this creature is at least ninety years old, yet despite its age, there is no evidence of cardiovascular degeneration at all, no signs of atherosclerosis, no calcification whatsoever. Its circulation is tremendous.

"It has two sets of lungs, as well," the vet continued, excitedly. "The equine lungs are about average for an animal of this size, but its human lungs are at least twice the normal capacity. Both sets of lungs are interconnected by a complex system of sub-bronchials, with valves, no less! The human lungs seem to be the primary respiratory system; the equine lungs apparently act as a sort of turbocharger. The stamina of this creature must be almost boundless. Its digestive system is basically similar to ours, but larger and more complex, with a wider variety of enzymes. The creature is omnivorous, but judging by its stool, its recent diet has been primarily vegetarian. The spinal cord is the most interesting part, however, incredibly complex, with the tensile strength of—"

Forrester cut him off. "I can well understand your fascination, Dr. Anderson, but what I'm primarily concerned with is the creature's ability to withstand a psychological conditioning procedure. It's imperative that it has no memory of this experience, but I don't want to injure it in any way if I can help it."

"There's nothing in a psychological conditioning procedure that should cause it any physiological damage," Anderson said. "However, I'm not really qualified to venture an opinion on how well its cognitive processes would stand up to such an operation. I'm not a neurosurgeon or a cyberneticist. You'll have to consult with Dr. Hazen."

"Capt. Hazen?" said Forrester. "A moment with you, please?"

The officer in charge of the army medical team turned away from the monitor screens and approached Forrester. "General," she said, with a curt nod.

"What's your prognosis on the debriefing and conditioning procedure?" Forrester asked.

"I would say it's feasible," said Dr. Hazen. "The creature's brain seems normal by our standards, but I can't speak with absolute certainty, because we've obviously never encountered an organism like this before. We haven't had any experience with horses, much less a complex hybrid such as this one, which is why I asked to have Dr. Anderson here to assist. I don't anticipate any major problems, but we're going to proceed cautiously, taking the debriefing and conditioning procedures in very easy stages. We've had good success with the trial debriefing run. The centaur has remained essentially unconscious, yet has answered all questions we put to it."

"We were able to communicate perfectly through an interpreter," said Dr. Anderson. "It speaks classical Greek! General, this creature is intelligent. In a sense, it's even human. We have an unprecedented opportunity here for research that would—"

Forrester cut him off again. "I'm sorry, Doctor. This is a top security procedure and I'm afraid you're not authorized to conduct any sort of extensive observation. Besides, it would be pointless. The moment my psych team is through with the centaur, they'll start on you."

Anderson stared at him. "You're joking."

"I'm afraid not, Doctor."

"You can't *possibly* be serious!" Anderson said with disbelief. "This is *outrageous!* You . . . you have no right! What you're talking about is a flagrant violation of—"

"I'm less concerned with your civil rights, Doctor, than with security," said Forrester. "In the event of a national emergency, the rights of civilians on a military base are governed under the Wartime Emergency Powers Act. Admittedly, I am interpreting them rather loosely. My actions may not be justified in a court of law, but it will prove difficult for you to bring suit against me if you have no memory of the incident."

Anderson was stunned. "General, do you realize what you're *saying?* What you're talking about is a *felony offense!*"

"Only if I'm caught," said Forrester. "I'm sorry, Doctor. I have my responsibilities. You'd probably thank me if you understood the full implications of what's happening here. Fortunately for you, you'll be spared that knowledge. It will enable you to sleep nights. Frankly, I envy you that luxury."

Creed Steiger had never liked politicians. Politician, he knew, was not the term of proper protocol at the Council of Nations. They preferred to call each other delegates. But they acted just like politicians, he thought, right hands constantly raised to make a point of order, left hands covering their asses, at least when "proper protocol" didn't go completely by the boards and they started shouting at each other like traders at a commodities exchange. Perhaps delegates was a good term for them after all, thought Steiger. What they did best was delegate responsibility and the commodities they traded in were lives, his own among them. He hadn't cared muct for their "proper protocol" at all, something he had demonstrated in a dramatic manner, by firing three copper-jacketed hollowpoints into the ceiling of their meeting chamber.

The revolver was a 20th century antique, but it was in excellent condition. Steiger had brought it from its time of origin to the 27th century. It was a treasured part of his collection of antique firearms, but it was seldom fired. On this occasion, he had fired it three times into the ceiling of the Council chamber, bringing down a small rain of debris and achieving the desired effect of shocking the members of that august body into silence.

They had asked to see a "delegation"—how they loved that word!—of historical adjustment specialists, temporal agents. They wanted to hear from the front-line troops, to solicit their views concerning the best way to handle the temporal crisis they were facing. The request had been submitted through the Director General of the Referee Corps to the Deputy Chief of the Temporal Army Command. General Moses Forrester had bumped the request down to his executive officer, Col. Creed Steiger. It was a chance to meet face to face with some of the most powerful government officials in the world and Steiger wasn't about to pass it up. He had a few things he wanted to get off his mind.

The Council had been impressed by his appearance. He had the right look for a high ranking military officer of the Temporal Corps. For a change, it was the way he *really* looked. Having his own face back was a relief after the numerous cosmetic surgeries necessitated by his undercover activities as a former field agent of the T.I.A. His flaxen blond hair was parted casually on the side and fell over his forehead to a point just above his pale gray eyes. His features were Germanic in their squared regularity, only his nose was rather Semitic, sharp and hooked like the beak of a predatory bird, giving him a hard, cruel appearance. His frame was large and well muscled and his bearing was just short of textbook military, with the casual, relaxed-yet-controlled motions of the seasoned soldier. Yes, he looked like the sort of man they wanted to hear from, but the format Steiger chose for his presentation wasn't quite what the Council members had expected.

It was the first time any of them had ever heard gunfire. The Council Security Force had not appreciated Steiger's demonstration, either. None of them had any familiarity with lead projectile weapons and the gunshots gave them a bad turn.

"What you don't know can kill you," Steiger had said into the stunned silence occasioned by his blasting away at the ceiling. He held up the nickel-plated gun for all to see. "This is a Smith & Wesson 25-dash-5 .45 caliber revolver chambered for the "Long Colt" cartridge. It fires a hollowpoint lead projectile with a copper jacket, propelled by gases generated by the explosion of the powder in the shell casing. This projectile, called a bullet, expands on impact and tears through everything in its path, shredding organs and pulverizing bone. It's a primitive weapon, centuries out of date. But that doesn't make it any less effective.

"As a covert operative of the Temporal Intelligence Agency, I've had to face weapons such as this one and others even more primitive, though no less deadly. You people were the ones who put me there. Well, now that I've got your attention, I'm going to tell you what the result of that has been and why I don't think you're qualified to make any operational decisions concerning the resolution of this crisis. I know what I'm talking about. I suggest you listen carefully."

They had heard the explanations and the theories of the scientists, but Steiger went over it again, presenting the situation to them in simple, laymen's terms, without technical asides and theoretical conjectures. Another universe had come into congruence with their own and the convergence of two separate timelines had resulted in a confluence effect which rippled through both timestreams, causing them to intertwine like a double helix strand of DNA. The integrity of each depended on the disruption and possibly even the complete destruction of the other.

No one knew the exact cause of the phenomenon, whether it was a result of temporal contamination brought about by the actions of the Time Wars or chronophysical misalignment caused by clocking massive amounts of energy through warps in timespace known as Einstein-Rosen Bridges. The fabric of time and space had ruptured or shifted in some way and reality now had an alternative—one that was no less real.

The congruence of two separate timelines was causing an instability in the flow of temporal inertia. The timelines were apparently not dissimilar enough to set up crosscurrents in the timeflow which would manifest themselves in temporal discontinuities. Instead, the result was a surge in the inertial flow at points of confluence, where the separate timestreams converged like two powerful rivers. The Laws of Temporal Relativity attempted to compensate for the instability. The greater the number of confluence points, the stronger the inertial flow. Eventually, if unchecked, the increased flow in temporal inertia would overcome the rippling effect caused by the congruence and cause both timestreams to merge into one timeline. The only way to keep that from happening, it seemed, was to maintain the temporal instability caused by the congruence, to keep working against the surge in the inertia flow. Yet, maintaining temporal instability meant almost certain temporal disruptions. To avoid a catastrophe, they had to invite disaster. It was a Hobson's Choice of the lesser of two evils.

The Council could no longer afford the expedience of using time travel to resolve international conflicts. It had been a convenient form of warfare. It had absolved the world powers of facing the harsh realities of war in their own time. It was so convenient and so beneficial to international economy that the least little disagreements were often quickly escalated into fullscale "arbitration actions" with temporal soldiers being clocked back to fight and die in ancient wars. Now fear had finally done what reason previously failed to accomplish. A ceasefire in the arbitration actions had been called and the Council's member nations were forced into uneasy unity against a common enemy—their doppelgangers in the congruent universe.

Now they want to listen to the soldiers, Steiger thought. Tell us how to fight the war, they said. Tell us how to win. The best answer he had to give them was that he did not know. His best advice was more direct. "Leave it to the professionals," he said. "Stay the hell out of our way. You can't legislate temporal combat. More wars than you can count have been lost by inept politicians telling experienced generals what to do." Diplomacy had never been his strong suit, but then it was a bit late for diplomatic answers.

As the robot shuttle crossed the plaza of the Pendleton Base Departure Station, Steiger sat silently, lost in thought. The soldiers he had chosen to accompany him had been content to let him do most of the talking. When questioned, they had answered briefly and politely, but they were veterans of the Temporal Corps and felt it was a waste of time trying to educate a bunch of politicians. Steiger hoped it wasn't. Time was a valuable commodity.

As the shuttle crossed the plaza, Steiger saw soldiers in every type of costume imaginable milling about in the Departure Station, waiting to clock out to their assignments. A ceasefire had been called, but at Pendleton Base—as at other military bases—things seemed not to have changed at all.

In fact, there were profound changes, though they were not readily apparent. These soldiers were not clocking out to fight in arbitration actions. They were being sent back to other time periods as scouts. Those about to leave had already been re-trained for their new duties by the Observer Corps and there were thousands more in the process of retraining.

Their mission was twofold—to be on the alert for temporal disruptions and to find points of convergence where the time-stream intersected that of the congruent universe and a confluence existed. The confluence effect was unstable. A convergence could occur and a confluence point exist for a timespan as brief as several seconds or as long as—no one knew for certain. The result was massive temporal instability. Both timestreams were rippling, although not in any manner that was immediately noticeable—unless one stumbled into a confluence point and crossed over from one universe into another. If these points of confluence, however ephemeral, could be pinpointed and logged, then it was possible for them to be patrolled. At least, that was the theory they were operating on.

Already, there had been a brief and furious battle between the commandos of the First Division and soldiers of the Special Operations Group from the congruent universe. The greatest threat was that a force from the congruent universe would locate an undiscovered confluence point and cross over undetected to create a temporal disruption, as they had attempted to do in the Khyber Pass in the year 1897. The enemy was operating on the theory that increased temporal instability would serve to diminish the confluence effect or even elimin-ate it by creating a timestream split. Chaos, thought Steiger, was an understatement for what was going down.

The tension was evident on the faces of the soldiers in the plaza. In the Time Wars, the mortality rate had always been very high. Death could come from a spear thrust or a bullet. Oblivion could arrive with the rupture of a spacesuit or the ex-plosion of a land mine. For a soldier of the Temporal Corps, there were a thousand ways to die. Now there was one more.

None of these soldiers about to clock out on long term as-signments in the past, in Minus Time, knew what to expect. They had been briefed as fully as possible, programmed through their cybernetic implants with the languages, customs and histories of the periods to which they were assigned, but if by chance they happened to clock back into the past at the exact location of a confluence, the odds against their ever coming back were astronomical.

No one had yet crossed over into the congruent universe. The theory was that if a confluence point could be discovered and a crossover achieved, then returning would be a "simple" matter of retracing one's steps exactly. Turn a corner, Steiger thought, and you're in another universe. But if you were to clock directly into a convergence, with no physical reference for the confluence point, how would you find the corner? Once in the congruent universe, clocking backwards or forwards would only result in time travel *within* that universe. Because of the confluence effect, every temporal transition would now be even more uncertain.

Until now, Steiger had found his duties as a T.I.A. agent challenging enough. Now, General Forrester was considering a new type of mission for them. If a confluence point could be located, one the people in the congruent universe were unaware of, then Forrester meant for them to attempt a crossover. The object of such a mission would be to disrupt the temporal continuity of the congruent timestream. Their job had always been to prevent historical disruptions. Now, they would be trying to create them.

"We've got to do it to them before they do it to us," Forrester had said during one of their regular briefings. "It's as simple as that. They're apparently working on the assumption that if they create a massive temporal disruption in our timeline, the resulting timestream split will overcome the confluence effect at our expense. For all anybody knows, they may be right."

"Dr. Darkness doesn't think so," Steiger had said, referring to the scientist whose experiments with tachyon transition had altered his subatomic structure, making him the only human who was faster than the speed of light. Dr. Darkness believed it was equally possible for a timestream split to compound the confluence effect, resulting in multiple timestreams intersecting, but the only way to prove that was the hard way, something no one was anxious to do.

"I know what Darkness thinks," Forrester had said, "and I'm inclined to listen to him. However, the trouble is we have no choice. The alternative would be fighting a purely defensive action, something we just can't afford to do. If we disrupt their timestream, then our counterparts in the congruent universe will have to conduct their own historical adjustment missions to compensate for what we've done. If we can keep them busy doing that, they'll have less time to interfere with *our* history.''

"So we cause disruptions in their timestream which they'll have to adjust and they'll do it right back to us," Capt. Finn Delaney said. "It's madness. Where does it all end?"

"Who knows?" Forrester said, wearily. "The Time Wars have been escalated into a new dimension. Literally. Nobody knows how it will end. We'll just have to ride it out."

The shuttle arrived at the entrance to the Headquarters Building of the Temporal Army Command. As Steiger entered the spacious lobby, he paused before the Wall of Honor, which listed the names of soldiers of the First Division who had died in action. Steiger stared at the most recent name added to the wall, that of his predecessor, Lt. Col. Lucas Priest.

Before the Temporal Intelligence Agency had been merged with the Temporal Army Corps, Steiger had been the T.I.A.'s senior field agent, code named Phoenix. Lucas Priest had been his counterpart in the First Division of the Temporal Corps, the elite commando unit assigned to deal with temporal disruptions. The temporal adjustment team of Lt. Col. Lucas Priest, Lt. Andre Cross and Capt. Finn Delaney had the most impressive record in the corps. Now that the First Division and the T.I.A. had merged, Steiger was the ranking officer after Moses Forrester, replacing the late Lt. Col. Priest as the exec. It was a large pair of boots to fill.

He snapped to attention and saluted the wall, according to tradition. Priest had given his life to preserve the past. Now those left living in the present would have to risk their lives to save the future.

1

The mission team sat in the darkened briefing room, watching the holographic presentation. The three-dimensional laser image of the centaur slowly revolved before them as the recorded voice of Dr. Hazen dispassionately described the examination procedure. At the appropriate moment in the briefing, the image of the centaur dissolved to the scanner graph recording, showing the interior organs and the skeletal structure. At the point where the recording switched to the psych team's debriefing session, Forrester allowed it to continue for a few moments, so the agents could have an opportunity to see the centaur, in its conditioned state, responding to the questions put to it in ancient Greek. The he switched the projection off and brought the lights back up.

"The centaur's name is Chiron," he said. "A check with Archives Section reveals that the name first appeared in old Greek legends. Its earliest recorded mention is reported in a story told by Apollonius of Rhodes, one of the librarians of Alexandria. According to the story, which was reputedly based upon actual exploits of seamen of the Mycenaean Bronze Age, Chiron was half-man, half-horse; a teacher who lived in a cave on Mount Pelion centuries before the time of

Christ. The young boys who were brought to him for instruction became the greatest heroes of the ancient legends, among them Jason, Theseus and Hercules. The centaur confirmed this information during the interrogation session."

"*Confirmed* it?" said Delaney. "But those are all mythical figures!"

Forrester made a wry face. "Indeed they are, Captain. As are centaurs, I believe."

Under other circumstances, the exchange would have been funny, but no one laughed.

"What we are apparently confronted with," Forrester continued, "is our first example of how the congruent universe differs from ours. The centaur came through a confluence, appearing in our timestream during the year 219 B.C., at the beginning of the Second Punic War. It caused a considerable amount of excitement among some of Hannibal's troops before our Observers on the scene were able to capture the creature and clock back with it. I won't bother speculating whether our happening to have Observers on the scene was pure dumb luck or a manifestation of the Fate Factor, magnified by inertial surge in the presence of a confluence. I'll leave that brain bender to the scientists. Zen physics only gives me headaches. I'll simply concentrate on what this creature's appearance in our timestream means to us.

"The centaur provides us with our first piece of hard evidence supporting the theory that the physical laws of the congruent universe might not be the same as ours. There is also the question of the temporal focus of the centaur's appearance in our timeline. It came through in the year 219 B.C., but according to Archives Section, the story which mentions the creature dates back at least six centuries before the time of Christ. Either the chronology of the congruent universe is radically different from ours or the congruence has caused an even more pronounced ripple in the timestreams than we realized."

"Excuse me, sir," said Andre Cross. "Does this mean a confluence point which occurs at, say, the 18th century in our universe might lead to another time period entirely in the congruent universe?"

"Quite possibly," said Forrester. "We don't know exactly what that means, though. It's possible that crossing over through a confluence point which occurs in our universe during the 18th century, to follow your example, might bring you to the 20th century, in the congruent universe, or the 25th or the 14th or any other century. But we still have no knowledge of what those time periods in the congruent universe are like. We *believe* the congruent universe is a mirror image of our own, but we now think it's a sort of funhouse mirror. Distorted, by our standards."

"Which means anyone going through would be going in blind," said Finn Delaney. "There would be no temporal reference. And we wouldn't have any idea what time period we might end up in."

"Correct," said Forrester. "However, we've already taken steps to work within those parameters. I've incorporated most of the former T.I.A. field agents now under my command into a new type of Pathfinder unit. This new unit has been designated as the 1st Ranger Pathfinder Division. Their function will be to go through confluence points as advance scouts for a mission team. They will be equipped with full battle kit, with orders to avoid unnecessary contact with locals if possible, but to engage any enemy decisively if they encounter hostility. Their primary responsibility will be to gather intelligence. However, if they are placed at risk, their secondary mission will be to conduct a quick guerrilla strike, inflict as much damage and as many casualties as possible and then get back fast so they can neutralize any hostiles coming through into our own timeline. Obviously, it's preferable to gather intelligence which allow a mission team to go through and conduct a covert operation designed to achieve maximum temporal disruption, but failing that, better to conduct a quick blind strike which may or may not cause significant temporal damage than to lose any of our people.

"The breakdown for this type of operation will be as follows: one, as soon as a confluence is pinpointed and logged, a commando unit will be clocked back to set up an outpost, providing security on our side of the confluence. A unit has already been dispatched to cover the confluence point through which the centaur came into our timeline. Two, a Ranger unit will effect crossover into the congruent universe for the purpose of gathering intelligence. If they do not encounter immediate resistance, they will utilize available local resources to blend in and gather whatever intelligence they can. If feasible, they may be directed to capture locals and bring them back for interrogation. Three, a mission team of adjustment specialists will effect crossover with instructions, based on intelligence gathered by the Rangers, to conduct a covert operation aimed at creating a significant historical disruption in the congruent universe. Four, units of the newly organized Temporal Counter-Insurgency Strike Force based in Galveston will stand by on alert status in the event hostiles attempt to effect a cross-over into our timeline.

"Needless to say, this does not cover all contingencies. We are still vulnerable in the event that hostiles from the congruent universe discover a confluence point we are unaware of and send units through to cause disruptions in our timeline, as they did in the Khyber Pass. We were lucky that time, but we need to guard against something like that happening again. For this reason, all available temporal divisions are being broken up and reorganized, converted to Observer squadrons. We clearly cannot begin to cover all of recorded time. Nevertheless, we have to try. We can only hope that between mobile Observer squadrons looking out for temporal anomalies and members of the Temporal Underground providing unofficial intelligence support, we can spot disruptions and clock out adjustment teams to effect repair before the damage becomes permanent. Word has been unofficially leaked through channels that will reach the Temporal Underground so far as that's concerned. They'll cooperate. They have no choice, since their existence is at stake, as well. So if you want to be optimistic, you might say it's business as usual, only more intensified. Much more. And that, ladies and gentlemen, is the overview. Now, we get down to the specifics of this case.

"The appearance of the centaur brings up an interesting question. As Capt. Delaney pointed out, centaurs are mythical beings, yet here we are confronted with one in the flesh."

"Horseflesh," said Delaney. Forrester ignored him.

"The debriefing session with the centaur produced the names of individuals who, according to *our* history, are also mythical figures. Jason, Theseus, Hercules and others. Yet there is some question about that. There is, for example, evidence showing Theseus actually lived. He was described in Plutarch's writings. We don't know for certain about some of the others, such as Hercules. There exist a number of versions of the story of Jason and the Argonauts and there are a number of irreconcilable details. Reconciling those details would require a mission in itself and it would only give us intelligence about what happened in our timeline. What happened in the congruent universe could be something entirely different.

"Archives Section feels this situation has raised a number of fascinating questions. For example, is it possible that our mythology, to a certain point, is *their* history? And does that then suggest that *our* history is their mythology? Or are we confronted with some sort of metaphysical trans-temporal contamination? In other words, is our mythology the direct result of the situation confronting us today? Has the congruence of the two timelines resulted in a sort of trans-temporal psychic leakage to which esper-sensitive individuals are susceptible? When Apollonius of Rhodes wrote his *Argonautica*, was he actually subconsciously picking up images and impressions from the congruent universe? If this is the case, then we might have a basis for gathering intelligence about the congruent universe from the mythology of our own history. Archives Section is particularly anxious for information which might corroborate this theory."

"I think someone in Archives Section has gone right around the bend," said Finn Delaney.

Forrester heard the not quite *sotto voce* comment. "Perhaps, Capt. Delaney. But what if going 'around the bend,' as you put it, leads to the congruent universe?"

Delaney grimaced. "That's what I love about zen physics," he said. "The more you understand about it, the less you know."

"The important thing is that you understand what our priorities are," said Forrester. "First and foremost, we need to safeguard the integrity of our own timeline. Only after we've made certain no hostiles can cross over through a confluence, either intentionally or by accident, can we contemplate sending a mission team through. These teams will be kept small, as in historical adjustment situations, in order to maximize covert flexibility and minimize the chances of discovery before the mission can be completed. We don't want to risk a mission team blowing its cover and falling into the hands of S.O.G. interrogation teams. The first mission will, assuming it's successful, teach us a great deal about how these operations should be conducted. Consequently, I'm sending in our best team. Capt. Delaney and Lt. Cross, you will report to mission programming immediately following this briefing. Since you have already had experience working in the field with Col. Steiger, he will be joining your team, replacing the late Lt. Col. Priest. The rest of you will provide mission support on this end. You will clock out to reinforce the outpost team

stationed at the confluence point. With the exception of the
mission team, you will draw full battle kit in addition to
period ordnance and report for mission programming. The
crossover team will carry period ordnance only. Any questions?"

"Just one, sir," said Finn Delaney. "What exactly *is* our
mission?"

"You will cross over into the region known as Mount
Pelion," said Forrester, "located near the kingdom of Iolchos
in Thessaly. There you will make contact with Jason, son of
the deposed King Aeson of Iolchos. Your orders are to gather
intelligence and create a historical disruption in the timeline of
the congruent universe."

"Sure," Delaney said, wryly. "We'll infiltrate the argonauts and steal the golden fleece."

"Interesting idea," said Forrester. "If, in fact, they do find
the golden fleece, see if you can bring it back with you. I'd like
to see it."

The mission briefing was unusual, to say the least. According to the legend, Phrixus and Helle were brother and
sister, the children of King Athamas of Minua. Their mother
was the cloud nymph Nephele, but Athamas also had two
children with a concubine named Ino. It was Ino's belief that
if the children of King Athamas were dead, she would be able
to convince him to adopt her own children as his heirs. When
famine came to Minua, Ino's intrigues came to fruition. She
convinced Athamas the gods were angry with him and that to
regain their favor, he had to make a sacrifice. He had to give
them that which he loved best. Ino insisted that if Athamas
gave Phrixus and Helle to the gods, their anger would be ap-
peased.

Driven by the effects of the famine on his kingdom and by
Ino's ravings, Athamas ordered an altar built and tearfully
sent word for Phrixus and Helle to be brought to the high
priest. But Nephele learned of the peril to her children and
refused to stand by and let them die. The god Hermes had
given her a present of a flying ram and Nephele took Phrixus
and Helle, set them on the ram's back and had the ram fly
them to safety, forever out of reach of Athamas.

When Athamas learned that the ram had flown off with his
children, he realized the gods had never intended for them to
die and he went mad. In a fury, he killed one of Ino's children

and Ino, escaping from him, leaped off a cliff with her other child in her arms. She fell into the sea and turned into a dolphin that would swim the waves forever, crying with its offspring at its breast. The people of Minua drove out their mad king and he was forced to wander miserably until he came to the Oracle of Delphi. The Oracle told Athamas his fate would be to wander in penance for his sins until wild beasts would feast him as their guest. Mad and sorrowful, Athamas wandered starving through the wilderness until one day he encountered a pack of wolves. So fearsome was his appearance, the wolves ran off at the sight of him, leaving their kill. Athamas, desperate with starvation, threw himself upon the carcass of the sheep which they had left behind. In this way, a feast was provided for him by wild animals and the prophecy was fulfilled. Athamas recovered from his madness, founded a new settlement and eventually became a king again.

As to the fate of his two children, the ram flew far from Minua with Phrixus and Helle on its back. Helle became exhausted and lost her grip. She fell into the sea near Thrace and drowned. From that day on, the place where she fell bore the name of Hellespont. The ram flew on with Phrixus over the Euxine Sea to Colchis, on the Circassian coast. There it landed, spent, and promptly died of exhaustion. In recognition of the ram's heroic feat, the gods turned the ram's fleece into gold. Phrixus settled in Colchis and gave the golden fleece to King Aietes of Aea in exchange for his daughter, Chalciope, in marriage. In celebration of the union, Aietes hung the golden fleece upon an ancient beech tree in the sacred grove of Ares. It became the greatest treasure of his kingdom, a relic of the gods.

Phrixus did not have many years to live happily and peacefully in Colchis with his wife. When he died, his spirit had no rest because his body was buried far from his native land. Thereafter, he appeared often to the heroes of Minua in dreams, pleading with them to bring back the golden fleece so that his spirit could return with it and find rest.

Aeson of Iolchos was a cousin of Phrixus. He had a stepbrother named Pelias, who was said to be a nymph's son. When he was an infant, Pelias was abandoned in the mountains where he was meant to die, but a shepherd found him, nursed him back to health and raised him. When he became a man, Pelias returned to Iolchos and drove out King Aeson, who escaped to the mountains with his young son, Jason. At

Mount Pelion, the deposed King Aeson encountered Chiron
the centaur, a teacher in the arts of music, healing and warfare. Aeson gave his son into Chiron's care so the centaur
could prepare him for the day when he would return to Iolchos
and reclaim his birthright.

Jason grew up with Chiron and his other young students
and remembering the wishes of his father, he learned his lessons well. He became accomplished in all Chiron had to teach
him and he lived by the principles which Chiron preached. He
vowed never to speak harshly to any soul whom he might meet
upon his travels, to give his help to all in need of it and always
to stand by his word.

When he grew into a young man, he left Mount Pelion and
traveled back to Iolchos to reclaim the throne. On his journey
home, he encountered an old woman on the banks of the river
Anaurus. Frail and weak, she begged his help to cross the
swiftly flowing river. Remembering his vow, Jason did not
refuse her. He took her on his back and started to cross the
river.

Halfway across, his foot became wedged between two rocks
in the riverbed. In freeing his foot, he broke his sandal, which
was swiftly carried away by the current. Jason was upset
because he would have to enter Iolchos with one foot bare,
looking like a beggar, but the old woman whom he had helped
across the river was actually the goddess Hera, Queen of the
Immortals on Olympus, in disguise and though he lost his sandal, Jason gained her favor.

When Jason came to Iolchos and arrived for an audience
with King Pelias, the king was greatly disturbed. The Oracle of
Delphi prophesied that he would lose his kingdom to a man
who came to him wearing only one sandal. Thinking to rid
himself of Jason, Pelias promised to relinquish his throne if
Jason would bring back the golden fleece to Iolchos, thereby
proving his worth to rule. Pelias knew such a quest would be
hazardous and he was convinced Jason would never return
from it.

Jason went to the Oracle of Delphi and asked for guidance.
Speaking with the voice of Hera, the Oracle told him to seek
out Argus, the shipwright, and to have him build a galley with
fifty oars, then to send out a call for heroes to accompany him
upon his quest. Then the Oracle told him to cut down the
Speaking Oak of Dodona and give Argus the trunk to carve
into a figurehead which would guide him on his voyage. Jason

did as he was told and while the ship was being built, the call went out across the land for heroes to sail with him. When the ship was finished, it was named the *Argo* in honor of its builder. The crew, calling themselves the Argonauts, set sail from Iolchos on their quest for the golden fleece. . . .

The programming run ended and Finn Delaney sat up, massaging his temples. Cybernetic programming always left him with a slight headache. He glanced over at Steiger, lying back in the contoured chair with his eyes closed. Andre Cross sat up and frowned.

"That was the strangest mission programming session I've ever had," she said. "Gods who walk with mortals, oracles that see into the future, flying rams, monsters, supernatural events . . ." She shook her head. "If I hadn't seen the centaur for myself, I'd swear someone played a joke and slipped in a fake program."

"I was thinking the same sort of thing," Delaney said. "It's impossible to take the story seriously. It's an ancient fable, after all. Still, there's the centaur . . ." He glanced at Steiger, still lying back with his eyes closed.

"Creed?" said Delaney.

Steiger grunted in reply.

"What's wrong?"

"I'm thinking," Steiger said.

"That could be dangerous," said Delaney, grinning.

Steiger opened his eyes, but didn't smile.

"It was a joke," Delaney said.

"I got that," Steiger said.

"Right," said Delaney. "Apparently what you don't got is a sense of humor."

"Everybody has their own way of breaking the tension just before a mission," Steiger replied. He glanced at Delaney. "Some people make jokes. I guess I'm not one of those people."

"How do *you* handle the tension?" Andre said.

Steiger swung his feet down onto the floor and stood. "I don't get tense."

Andre shook her head as she watched him leave the room, heading for the Ordnance Section. "I don't quite know what to make of him," she said. "We've been involved on several missions together, yet I still can't figure him out."

"He's been out in the cold too long," Delaney said. "Field

agent Phoenix, man of a thousand lives. We've seen only two of them—Temporal Corps deserter Barry Martingale and Pathan warlord Sharif Khan. Both very different personalities. We haven't seen much of Creed Steiger yet.''

"You make him sound schizophrenic,'' Andre said.

"That's one of the reasons I've always had a hard time working with T.I.A. people, especially field agents,'' said Delaney. "The best of them have never been too tightly wrapped. Remember our old friend, Carnehan, agent Mongoose? He was an excellent case in point.''

"That doesn't sound like a promising analysis of our new partner,'' Andre said.

"Maybe it's not,'' Delaney said. "But on the other hand, he's a survivor. The fact that he made bird colonel in Temporal Intelligence speaks for itself. And don't forget we wouldn't be here now if it wasn't for his help on our last two missions.''

"Do you really think he doesn't feel the tension?'' Andre said.

"I don't know. I sure as hell do. Every time. Maybe he internalizes it. Some people just don't seem to get tense. They don't feel fear; they never panic.''

"There's a word for people like that,'' Andre said.

"What word is that?''

"Crazy.''

The outpost was located in the 2nd century B.C., high in the Alpine range overlooking the Po Valley. Several miles to the west was the pass through which Hannibal would take his 26,000 Carthaginians to meet with the Roman consul Scipio at the Battle of Trebia. The three temporal agents materialized in the heart of the small outpost, which was well concealed in the rocks high above the valley.

Beneath their coveralls, the three agents wore lightweight chitons, the knee-length universal garment of the ancient Greeks. Made from wool and sometimes embroidered with borders covered by geometrical designs, chitons were rectangular one-piece garments worn draped over the left shoulder, leaving the right arm and shoulder bare. The chitons were sometimes pleated and usually fastened at the waist by girdles, little more than cords encircling the hips. They wore chlamys with their chitons, lightweight woolen capes or mantles which were fastened at the shoulder or the throat by brooches or fibulae, metal clasps resembling safety pins. Their warp discs were disguised as heavy silver bracelets.

They were met at the transition point by Major David Curtis, the officer in command of the outpost. He wore one-piece, lightweight battle fatigues and a plasma sidearm. "All clear on this end," Curtis said. "Are you straight on S.O.P.?"

Standard Operating Procedure called for them to program the transition coordinates for the other side of the confluence as soon as they went through, checking them with the outpost unit to make certain the coordinates were consistent with the confluence point on the other side. They would then have a temporal reference for the location of the confluence, which would enable them to return to precisely the same place and time when they completed their mission.

Curtis and two of his Rangers accompanied them on the short hop to the confluence point location, at the foot of the Alpine range. "We go on foot from here," said Curtis. "We don't want to make a transition anywhere close to the confluence point itself. We don't know yet how warp disc fields might interact with a temporal convergence. Orders are to play it safe."

"What's the temporal range of the confluence point?" said Steiger.

"It's a short one," Curtis said. "Three days. We've mapped it backwards and forwards to make absolutely sure. The centaur came through yesterday, Present Reference Time, and we'll synchronize temporal coordinates to have you coming through tomorrow, P.R.T., on completion of your mission."

"That doesn't give us much timespace," Delaney said.

"True, but it works for us as well as against us," Curtis replied. "We've got one day either side of Present Reference and then the rippling effect displaces the convergence and the confluence dissipates. No way to track it; it doesn't shift and move on, it just disappears. That means the opposition probably won't find it unless they luck out like we did. Even if they do, we've got it covered throughout its duration."

"Where are the Carthaginians at this point?" Andre said.

"On their way through the pass," said Curtis. "We shouldn't be encountering them if we keep to the mission timetable. We don't want to hang around in this area very much beyond that point. That would be risking contact with either the Carthaginians or the Romans, maybe even both."

They came to a river and Curtis pointed out the picket emplacements where the Rangers had set up their perimeter watch. "We've already been through and back," he said. "The confluence is located directly in front of you, approximately fifteen feet away from the riverbank. We've staked it out." He pointed to the marking stakes planted in the ground. "Crude, but effective. Five feet beyond those stakes takes you through into ancient Greece in the congruent universe. You'll be crossing over into a heavily forested area approximately three miles from the foot of Mount Pelion."

He gave them a hand-drawn map. "I'm not the world's best cartographer, but this should serve you. It'll get you to the Anaurus River and from there to Iolchos. According to the centaur's debriefing, your arrival in Iolchos should coincide roughly with the arrival of Jason, allowing for the time it would take a man traveling on foot from Mount Pelion. The centaur couldn't provide further information, since obviously it could only tell us what it knew up to the time Jason departed from Mount Pelion. The centaur's been returned to its own timestream, so the situation has been normalized at that end. That's if you can call any situation involving a centaur normal." Curtis grimaced. "I don't envy you this trip. It's bound to be peculiar."

"That's putting it mildly, Major," said Delaney.

Curtis nodded. "I guess it is, at that. Okay, synchronize coordinates. Mission clock in effect as of now. Remember, if you don't come through by tomorrow night, P.R.T., we're gone."

"And so are we," said Steiger.

"Right. I'm logging crossover. Good luck."

They stripped out of their coveralls and removed their boots to strap on their sandals. Then they picked up their ordnance, which consisted of spears, shields, short swords and bows and arrows. They shook hands with Major Curtis, then set off single file toward the confluence point. As Curtis watched, they went between the marking stakes and disappeared from view, into another universe.

2 _____

There was no physical sensation associated with the crossover, no tangible evidence of the confluence point itself other than a complete change of scenery from one step to the next. From the verdant valley at the foot of the Italian Alps, they stepped through a rupture in timespace and came out in ancient Greece, centuries displaced from their last footsteps and a universe away.

It was suddenly much warmer. They could feel the balmy breezes coming in off the Aegean Sea. They were in a wooded area several miles from the base of Mount Pelion. The scene was beautiful, peaceful and bucolic, every color seemed painted in its most vivid shade. The sky overhead was an almost cloudless, turquoise blue and the green hues of the forest were sharp and bright. Even the earth tones seemed to have a greater depth to them, a warmer substance. There was no question but that they were *elsewhere*.

The first thing they did was orient themselves by taking their bearings and checking their position with the map. It was imperative to program the new timespace coordinates so they could clock back to the exact same time and place. It was necessary for them to have selected a precise "window of opportunity" for crossover, because no one knew yet how temporal paradox might affect a confluence point. Temporal paradox was to be avoided in any case, but especially in an area of timestream instability. It wouldn't do for them to run into Major Curtis and his Rangers while they had been conducting their scouting expedition. Careful timing was essential, especially in such a narrow chronological band.

They double-checked their transition coordinates and double-checked again the synchronization of their warp discs, then quickly left the confluence area, heading in a westerly direction. They made their way toward the Anaurus River, following the exact route laid out for them by Major Curtis, one designed to make certain they did not encounter the Ranger scouting party while it had been conducting its crossover reconnaissance.

"According to this map," said Andre, "we're about three miles from the river at this point. Curtis marked out the ford, but we'll probably have to do some walking up and down the bank to find it. It's not exactly the best map in the world."

"He didn't exactly have a hell of a lot of time," said Steiger. He glanced up at the sky. "I figure we've probably got about three or four hours of daylight left."

It had been morning when they left, about half an hour ago.

"I suggest we make straight for the river, get across it before dark and then make camp," Steiger said. "I'd like to put as much distance between us and the confluence point as possible."

Delaney nodded. "You're thinking about the possibility of hostile Observers?"

"It's something we can't afford to overlook," said Steiger. "So far as we know, they haven't discovered this confluence yet and chances are they may not find it at all, but I'd feel a lot safer a good distance from the site."

"I'd feel a lot safer if we knew how they can track our warp discs," Andre said.

During their last mission in the 19th century, on the northwest frontier of the British Raj, they had been captured by soldiers from the congruent universe. They discovered their counterparts in the other timeline possessed the ability to scan for warp discs, most likely tracing them through their energy fields. It was a technology the Temporal Corps scientists had not yet been able to defeat or duplicate.

"Well, there's not much we can do about that," said Delaney. "We can't get around carrying the discs. There's no way back without them. At least the odds are in our favor. For the hostiles to track our discs, they'd have to be in the area and they'd have to be scanning. Remember when they traced us in Afghanistan that time, they couldn't do it right away. They knew we were operating in the area, but it still took some time for them to find us."

"If they had an Observer outpost back here, they'd probably have known about us by now," said Steiger. "Still, I think we should refrain from using the discs unless it's absolutely necessary. No point in giving them a stronger signal to lock onto. If we start teleporting to decrease our travel time, we just might register on somebody's scanner and then they'll be out here in force, sweeping the area."

"I agree," Delaney said.

"There is one other thing we never got around to discussing," Andre said. She looked at Steiger. "You're the ranking officer. Are you taking command of this operation?"

Steiger thought a moment. "I will if you want me to, but I'm not used to working that way. I don't really think a team of three needs a chain of command. Besides, I may have more experience with covert temporal operations, but you two have more experience adjusting temporal disruptions."

"Only none of us has any experience with *creating* temporal disruptions," Andre said.

"I guess that makes us even," Steiger said. "If it's all the same with you, I'm not going to start off our partnership by leaning on my rank. I couldn't care less about chain of command. You two have worked together before and I'm a Johnny-come-lately. Better I should work on fitting in with your methods of operation than take charge and mess up something that works. How did you function with Priest?"

"Lucas was technically in command," said Finn, "but we never played it strictly by the book. We worked best by improvising, even if it meant bending a few rules."

Steiger nodded. "Sounds good to me. Rules sometimes get in the way. Besides, I was never very good at taking orders, so I'm not too fond of giving them myself. I've always been an undercover man. I still haven't gotten used to people saluting me, much less addressing me as Colonel."

Delaney grinned. "I think we'll get along."

"I was wondering about our symbiotracers," Andre said. She looked at Steiger. "You think Dr. Darkness will be able to find us here?"

"I haven't got the faintest idea how the damn things work," said Steiger, "but then neither does anybody else. Darkness is light-years ahead of the scientists in R & D. They can't even figure out how he managed to make particle level chronocircuitry. The fact that it's molecular bonding drives them nuts. If they could figure out *how* to do it, they'd do it with warp discs."

"If they could make that work, it wouldn't be a bad idea," said Delaney.

Steiger smiled. "No, it wouldn't. I didn't have the heart to tell them Darkness was already working on it. We know warp discs function in either timestream, because soldiers from the congruent universe had no trouble getting around in ours. It's my understanding the symbiotracers work on similar principles, which means they might work here. Just the same, I wouldn't count on any help from Dr. Darkness. He told me he's not going to attempt crossing over until he has more information about the congruent universe. He has no way of telling how his subatomic structure would react to a convergence."

"Why should it react any differently from ours?" said Andre.

"How much do you know about tachyons?" said Steiger.

"Not much," she said.

"Well, he won't admit it," Steiger said, "but Darkness probably doesn't know much more about them than you do. How do you study something that's faster than light? Especially when it's yourself. He has no way of knowing what will happen to his tachyonized state if he crosses over through a confluence. He might very well wind up departing in all different directions at six hundred times the speed of light."

"Instant discorporation," Andre said. "I can see why he might be concerned. He's a strange man. You know, you never told us how you met him."

"That's because I'm not exactly sure myself," said Steiger. "He just materialized out of thin air one day and started giving me instructions, as if we'd been working together for years. He's quite a character. Sort of a human *deus ex machina*. He has agents of his own scattered throughout all of time, mostly people in the Underground. He knew all about me, so he obviously has access to all sorts of top secret information. Then again, how hard would it be for him to find out anything he wanted to know? How do you stop someone who's faster than light? He's living proof that there are more things to heaven and earth than are dreamt of in our philosophy, as the old saying goes."

"Shakespeare," Delaney said, identifying the quotation. "Prince Hamlet to Horatio."

Steiger smiled, "No, actually it was Mooney Dravott."

"Who?"

"Mooney Dravott," Steiger said. "He was a fine old Elizabethan drunk. Shakespeare used him as the model for Falstaff. Mooney would get ripped and say the most amazing things. Bill wrote them down and used them in his plays."

"Bill?" said Delaney. "You *knew* Shakespeare?"

"Oh, yeah," said Steiger. "Nice fella. I met him while I was gathering intelligence on the Temporal Underground in the late 16th century. He would have been amused to know how well his work came to be regarded and how long it has survived. He didn't take it all that seriously himself. To him, it was just a living, something he did for enjoyment and to make money. He used to say, 'It beats acting.' He did a lot of his writing in pubs, soliciting reactions and taking suggestions from just about anybody. He wrote for the people, so he had a high regard for their opinion. Much of what he wrote was taken from history, but he was more interested in the story for its own sake than in historical accuracy, which is one of the reasons I always suspect history as handed down to us by storytellers."

"Such as Apollonius of Rhodes, you mean," said Andre.

"Exactly."

"I keep thinking about the mission programming," said Delaney. "I've seen a lot of strange things, but if it wasn't for the centaur, I wouldn't have bought any of it."

"I'm not sure that's not the right approach," said Steiger. "Just because we caught a centaur who—or is it which?—corroborated some of the details of an ancient fable doesn't necessarily mean it's all true. If Apollonius really was picking up on psychic impressions of this place, how much of what he wrote can be considered reliable information and how much the result of a primitive mind attempting to make sense of science and technology beyond its grasp?''

Delaney frowned. "What are you saying?"

"Well, I've been trying to think of rational explanations for what seem to be irrational or supernatural elements in the story," said Steiger. "Maybe their technological development here is completely at variance with what we would expect at the same period in our timeline. But that's only one possible explanation. We're at war with the congruent universe. Intelligence is important to each side. It would be in their best interests to supply us with disinformation. Maybe we're actually dealing with a universe in which certain physical laws are different from those in our own timeline. On the other hand, suppose the centaur was actually created by genetic engineers in the future of this universe. This whole thing could be a setup.''

"Interesting idea," said Andre, "but it doesn't seem very likely.''

"Why not?"

"All right, let's assume that was what happened," Andre said. "They created a centaur in their genetic labs, programmed it with disinformation about this timeline and sent it through the confluence to draw us here. For one thing, if that were the case, they could have taken us by now. And for another, it would require genetic engineering capabilities far in advance of our own.''

"And that's not impossible," said Steiger. "There's also the possibility that they could have taken us, only taking us this early in the game didn't fit in with their plans.''

"Okay, I'll grant you that," Andre said. "But then it still doesn't add up, because if the centaur had been programmed, it would have shown up in the psych team's debriefing session.''

"Maybe not," said Steiger. "What if they're better at psychological conditioning than we are? Can *we* make a centaur? There's still another possibility to consider. If this is some sort of setup and they really planned the operation carefully, they could have had people on the inside, on our interrogation team.''

Delaney whistled. "Boy, that's really getting paranoid!"

"Sound too incredible to you?" said Steiger. "Don't forget, they managed to infiltrate Archives Section before and alter some of our records. There's every reason to suspect they could have managed to infiltrate us elsewhere. It sounds a lot more believable to me than the idea of gods and monsters being real.''

"Is that any less believable than my having been born in the 12th century?" said Andre, playing devil's advocate. "The first time I saw a suit of armor made from nysteel, I thought it was magic. The first time I saw someone make a temporal transition, I thought he was a sorcerer appearing out of thin air. Well, wasn't he, in a sense? Where does technology stop and magic begin? Isn't it just a matter of perspective?''

"I suppose it all depends on whether an immortal is actually a god or someone who's achieved the ultimate in life extension," Steiger said.

"But what exactly *is* a god?" said Andre. "Whose definition are we using?''

Steiger smiled, "Why don't we wait until we meet one? Then we can go right to the source.''

They reached the river shortly before dark without encountering anyone, mortal or immortal. The crossing did not prove difficult to find; it was almost exactly where Major Curtis had indicated it on his hastily drawn map. The river flowed swiftly and the water came up to their thighs, so it was necessary for them to move slowly and carry their weapons high as they waded across. They made camp not far from the riverbank. The night was warm and they decided to sleep under the stars, taking turns standing watch. It felt strange hearing the familiar sounds of crickets and nightbirds, seeing familiar constellations and knowing they were in another universe.

As their fire died down, Steiger reached into it and removed a glowing branch. He used it to light a cigarette.

"That's very non-regulation, you know," Delaney said. "You're not supposed to bring things like that through to Minus Time.''

Steiger grinned. "You want a drag?''

"Sure.''

Steiger passed him the cigarette.

They took turns standing watch and the night passed uneventfully. At dawn, they rose and washed up in the river, then checked the baited hooks they had left in the water overnight. Each of them had caught a fish. They were trained in survival techniques, but so far their journey was less a mission than a pleasant hike. Living off the land would pose no problem. As they were finishing their breakfast of cooked fish, someone hailed their campsite from the riverbank.

Exchanging glances, they made sure their weapons were within easy reach before replying to the call. A moment later, a slender, strikingly handsome young man came through the trees and stopped a short distance away from them. Like them, he was dressed in a knee-length chiton and a short mantle draped over one shoulder. He carried a small leather pouch and a bronze spear. A knife was tucked into his girdle. He had dark, curly hair that was in need of cutting. His cheeks were youthfully smooth. His features were well defined, with prominent cheekbones, a high forehead, a sharp nose and a slightly squared chin. His eyes were dark and his mouth had a proud, stubborn look about it.

"I did not wish to come into your camp and take you unaware," said the young man, "so I gave warning of my presence. As you see, I am alone and mean no harm."

"Come forward, then," said Delaney. "If you are hungry, we still have some food left."

The young man stepped forward and they could not help but notice that he wore only one sandal.

"The price of doing someone a good turn," he explained, noticing their gaze and glancing down at his unshod foot. "I was carrying a poor old woman across the river on my back. She would have been drowned for certain on her own; the current is swift and she was too frail to have stood against it. My foot became caught between two stones halfway across. While I struggled to free it, the strap upon my sandal broke. With the old woman on my back, I could not have tried to catch it before it was swept away. Faced with a choice between the loss of an old woman or a sandal, I chose to lose the sandal. The proper choice to make, I think, if not the most convenient one."

He dropped his spear on the ground and sat down beside them. "I will trade you figs for fish," he said, opening his leather pouch and passing them several fruits. "I am Jason, son of Aeson, rightful king of Iolchos. I am on my journey home to claim my birthright." He said this as casually as if he had been remarking upon the weather.

"I am called Fabius," said Delaney. "And these are my

friends and traveling companions, Creon and Atalanta. We travel to Iolchos, also."

"Excellent," said Jason. "We shall all go together, then." It did not seem to occur to him they might not want to all go together. He simply accepted it as a matter of course.

"I heard Pelias is king in Iolchos," Andre said, to see how Jason would react.

"The throne does not belong to him," said Jason, his mouth full of fish. He spat out several bones, "He took it from my father and now I will come and take it back from him."

"All by yourself?" said Steiger.

"It is mine by right," said Jason, simply.

"Pelias might not see it that way," Steiger said.

"It matters not how Pelias might see it," Jason said, masticating furiously. "The kingdom is mine to claim and claim it I shall."

"But what if Pelias disputes your claim?" said Andre.

"Then I will have to challenge him. I do not wish to do this, so I intend to ask him to step down of his own free will. He will have to see that right is on my side and so I must prevail."

Delaney rolled his eyes.

"You would not, by any chance, have any spare sandals with you?" Jason said. "No? Worse luck. It means I shall have to enter Iolchos looking like a beggar who cannot even afford two sandals. Not a very good beginning for a king. Still, perhaps it is an omen. One can never tell about such things. The whims of the gods are strange."

"Have you ever met a god? asked Steiger, smiling at Andre.

"Not knowingly," said Jason. "It is said gods often take human form to mingle with us mortals. If I have ever encountered any, I do not know of it. Of course, there is Hercules, who is said to be the son of Zeus, or so claims his mother, Alcmene." He shrugged. "One never truly knows about such things. Hercules does have strength greater than that of mortal men, so perhaps he is a demigod, indeed. I do not give much thought to such matters." He finished eating and wiped his hands on his bare legs. "Time to travel on," he said, putting himself in charge of their expedition as if it were the natural order of things. "Soon, we shall enter Iolchos and I shall meet my destiny."

He set off in the vanguard of their small troop, walking

quickly and purposefully with his shoulders squared and his head held high, as if he were a general leading a victorious army into a vanquished city.

"What do you make of this boy?" Steiger asked Delaney quietly, so that Jason would not hear.

Delaney shrugged. "He's either a fool or the most complete innocent I've ever met. If that's what comes of Chiron's teaching, I'd hate to see his other pupils."

"Well, if there's any truth to the legend," Andre said, "we'll be meeting a lot more of them before too long. So far, things seem to be happening according to the story."

"Except for us," said Delaney.

"I'm not sure he even knows we're here," said Steiger, indicating Jason up ahead.

Jason marched ahead of them without a backward glance, supremely confident in his ability to lead. He was in excellent condition and he set a good pace, devoting his energies to walking and sparing no effort for idle conversation as they went. He seemed a remarkably self-contained young man. His bearing reflected his assumption that he was destined for greatness.

They arrived in Iolchos late in the afternoon and Jason made his way directly to the palace. At least, he must have assumed it was the palace because it was the largest building in the city, which was small in spite of the grandeur of its architecture. In fact, it turned out to be the Temple of Poseidon, but it served just as well because King Pelias was there, preparing to sacrifice a bull to the sea god. A crowd had gathered at the foot of the temple steps.

Jason ploughed through the crowd as if he were an icebreaker crashing through a frozen sea, shouting, "Make way for the true king!"

People stared in amazement at the presumptuous youth who dared to shout such words in the hearing of King Pelias, who turned frowning from the carcass of the bull, a bloody knife held in his hand. Soldiers immediately started down the steps to intercept Jason, but at that moment, the king's high priest saw he was wearing only one sandal and he held the soldiers back.

"Wait!"

"It's the man with one sandal!" said the captain of the

guard. "The one the prophecy spoke of. Why not just kill him and have done with it?"

"No," the high priest said in a low voice. "How do we know that killing him will not somehow fulfill the prophecy? If, in killing him, we set in motion events which would lead to Pelias losing the throne, then he would indeed lose his kingdom to this stranger, though he be dead. The gods can be capricious in their whims. The conditions of the prophecy must be fulfilled without risking the throne."

"But how?" the captain asked. "It does not seem possible!"

"To a clever man, everything is possible," said the high priest. He turned to Jason. "Who dares profane the sacrifice?" he demanded as Jason started up the steps. "Who are you?"

"I am Jason, son of Aeson, rightful king of Iolchos. I have come to claim what is mine by birthright."

"Oh, brother," said Delaney. Beside him, standing at the foot of the stone steps leading up to the temple, a soldier groaned miserably.

"Oh, cruel gods," the soldier said, "that I should lose all for want of having stopped a foolish boy!"

"Lose all?" said Andre.

"Like as not my life as well," the soldier said, morosely. "Pelias heard a prophecy from the Oracle of Delphi that he would lose his kingdom to a man who came to him wearing but one sandal. I was charged to keep a supply of sandals ready to hand out at the palace entrance and to make certain no such man came into the presence of the king. *Months* spent with my eyes cast down, inspecting the feet of all who came to the palace seeking an audience with the king and now this wanton youth beards him at the temple! The gods must hate me!"

Pelias was staring intently at Jason, who returned his gaze confidently, as if daring him to deny his claim. "My brother, Aeson, is dead," said Pelias, "and his son with him."

"His son stands before you, very much alive," said Jason. "Look well on my face and tell me that you do not see my father."

Pelias seemed to consider. "Yes," he said at last, "there is a similarity, but that alone proves nothing. I could as easily find a dozen boys of the right age in this city who could make the same claim based upon a chance resemblance."

He smiled and gazed out at the crowd, the compassionate and understanding king taking great pains to be patient with a mad boy. When he spoke, his tone was condescending and more that a little ironic.

"You understand, surely, that as king I have great responsibilities. I must consider the welfare of the people. I cannot simply hand over my throne to the first man who comes along, claiming to be my poor dead brother's son. This is a delicate matter which requires some deliberation." He turned to speak with the high priest.

"I await your answer, Pelias!" Jason shouted after a moment, growing impatient.

"He will get his answer in a spear between his ribs," the soldier in charge of inspecting feet said. "And then, doubtless, I shall make the long journey to Hades with him."

"Perhaps," said Delaney, "you would be best served by making another long journey before the king has time to think about your fate."

"You offer sound advice, stranger," said the soldier. "My thanks. The wandering urge is suddenly upon me. I think I will depart at once."

As the soldier hastily pushed his way through the crowd, Pelias turned to Jason while the people waited expectantly to see how their king would deal with the impetuous youth.

"I have consulted with my high priest about the best way to deal with this matter," he said, speaking loudly enough for all to hear. "If, as you claim, you are truly my brother Aeson's son, then you are indeed the rightful king of Iolchos. But, on the other hand, if you are *not* my brother's son and I were to step down in your favor, then not only would I have acted foolishly, putting the fate of the people of Iolchos into the hands of an imposter, I will have angered the gods, as well. As king, I must do what is right and just, both for the sake of the people of Iolchos and to appease the gods."

"If you do what is right and just," said Jason, "you have no need to fear the gods."

"But we are mortals and not gods," said Pelias, smiling. "We cannot always see the truth of things as the Immortals can. If we could, then we would be as gods ourselves. Surely

you would not utter blasphemy by suggesting it were otherwise?''

Jason frowned, giving the matter careful thought—something which did not seem to come easily to him. "I would
never blaspheme against the gods," he said, uncertainly.

Pelias smiled. "Very well, then. Since we are but mortals
who cannot always see the truth of things, would it not be best
to let the gods guide us in our decision? I will abide by the
wishes of the gods. Will you do the same?''

Jason could not very well answer that he would not.

"You claim to be my brother's son," said Pelias. "So be it.
You appear to be an honorable young man. For the sake of
my departed brother, I will put my trust in you. I will act in
good faith and accept your word. Let all gathered here be
witness that I step down from the throne of Iolchos in favor of
my brother Aeson's son, King Jason.''

The crowd gasped with disbelief.

"However," Pelias continued, "since I have acted in good
faith, you must do likewise. You have made the claim, so it is
you who must provide the opportunity for the gods to reveal
their decision to us, as we have agreed. For the sake of the
people of Iolchos, there must be a test. I can think of no more
fitting test than for you to bring back the golden fleece from
Colchis. It will be an arduous journey, but if the gods mean
for you to rule in Iolchos, you cannot fail. In the meantime, I
will keep your throne safe. When you return, then all will
know that we have acted in accordance with the wishes of the
gods.''

"It looks like Pelias just found a loophole in the prophecy," Delaney said.

"And our boy Jason fell right through it," Steiger said.
"Things are proceeding right on schedule.''

"That's what worries me," said Andre. "Is this what you
call being at the right place in the wrong time?''

Jason's first three recruits accompanied him to the shrine at
Delphi. Jason had not been surprised when they offered to go
with him on his journey. Rather, he was surprised that there
had not been more volunteers. With the exception of the three
temporal agents, no one had stepped forward when he an-
nounced from the temple steps that he required a crew for the

voyage to bring back the golden fleece from Colchis. Apparently, the citizens of Iolchos preferred to wait for the decision of the gods.

It was dusk when they arrived at Delphi and started up the hillside trail which led to the shrine. The journey had been made at the suggestion of the high priest of Iolchos.

"If you are indeed the son of Aeson," the high priest had said, "you would do well to go to the Oracle of Delphi and ask the gods for guidance. The journey to Colchis will be hard, even for one who has the favor of the gods."

"Though you may mock me, priest," said Jason, "I shall do as you advise. I know why Pelias sends me on this quest. He thinks that I shall not return. But I shall return, for my cause is just. I will bring back the golden fleece. Then Pelias will have no choice but to step down, for he has sworn to do so before a throng of witnesses. If he denies me then, none shall dispute my right to challenge him."

The shrine of the Oracle of Delphi was a small marble altar set before an ancient oak tree that grew at the summit of a hill. A semicircular wall of white brick was built around the giant oak, closing it off at the back and sides, so that its base and trunk were visible only from the front, where the altar had been placed.

"The Speaking Oak," said Jason, reverently. "I have heard tell of it from my teacher, Chiron. We must place an offering of food upon the altar and see if the Oracle will speak."

"You mean the offering itself is not a guarantee?" said Steiger, smiling.

"It is said that the Oracle speaks only to those who are deemed worthy," Jason replied. "My cause is just and so I must be worthy. She will speak to us."

Jason placed an offering of fruits and sweetmeats on the altar, then kneeled before it with his head bowed and his arms held out in supplication. "Oh, wise, all-knowing Oracle!" he said reverently. "Jason, son of Aeson, King of Iolchos, humbly comes seeking guidance from the gods. I am commanded to seek the golden fleece to prove my worthiness to rule in Iolchos. How may I best fulfill my task?"

For a moment, nothing happened, then flames suddenly blazed up from the altar. In the glow of the firelight, a shape seemed to come out of the oak, a figure draped in dark robes with a hood covering its head and hiding its face.

"Your petition has been heard, Jason of Iolchos," said the Oracle. She spoke with a strong and resonant voice. "The gods have deemed you worthy of the task now set before you. Hear now their words. Seek out Argus, the shipwright, and bid him build a galley with fifty oars. Look not among the people of Iolchos for your crew, for they are plain folk and not suited to the undertaking. Send out a call throughout the land for heroes to go with you on your quest. When you have done so, cut down the stoutest branch of the Speaking Oak and bid Argus carve it into a figurehead for your ship, which you shall call the *Argo*. When you have gathered your crew of Argonauts, set sail across the Aegean Sea. Follow a course through the Hellespont to the Sea of Marmora. Pass through the Bosporous to the Euxine Sea and set course along the coastline of Mysia, Bithynia and Pontus for the land of Colchis. You will find that which you seek in the Sacred Grove of Ares in the kingdom of Aietes."

The flames abruptly disappeared and in the moment it took their eyes to become reaccustomed to the darkness, the figure behind the altar vanished. Delaney ran to the altar and looked around, but there was no sign of the woman. With the wall surrounding the Speaking Oak on all sides except the front, there was no way she could have gone except past them and there was no break in the wall. Steiger examined the altar and found nothing to indicate where the flames had come from. The heat must have been intense. The offering was completely crisped.

"The gods have spoken through the Oracle," said Jason. "My course is clear."

Delaney frowned. "I wish to hell ours was," he mumbled.

Andre examined the tree, but it seemed solid, with no hollow space where the woman could have hidden. She glanced at Steiger. "Technology?" she said softly. "Or magic?"

3 _____

Jason was faced with the same problem following the Oracle's advice as he had with coming to Iolchos and confronting Pelias in the first place, namely, lack of forethought. It apparently had not occurred to him that Pelias might have had grave reservations about giving up the throne and could easily have ordered him killed. In the same manner, it did not occur to him that he did not possess the means to spread the word throughout the countryside that there was a need for heroes to complete his crew, just as it did not occur to him that Argus, the shipwright, might expect to be compensated for his efforts in constructing a galley. Argus took the position that asking for payment for such an ambitious undertaking was not an unreasonable request. The only problem was that Jason had no money.

The brawny, graying, barrel-chested shipwright stood with folded arms, regarding Jason with amused tolerance as the youth protested that the ship *had* to be built. He promised Argus that he would be compensated for his labors after they returned with the golden fleece and he was on the throne. When the shipwright seemed unmoved by such promises,

Jason invoked the gods, saying it was their will that Argus build the galley that would bear his name. This appeal to vanity did not avail, either.

"I must secure the materials with which to build your ship and I must pay the laborers who will do the work," said Argus. "Among them are faithless men who are not moved by the wishes of Immortals or the promises of kings. They are moved by more practical considerations, such as wages. I will gladly build your ship and carve your figurehead. I will even whittle you a flute if you like, but first I must be paid. If it is the will of the gods that I should build this ship, then doubtless the gods will provide you with the means to pay for it."

There was an inescapable logic to this that not even Jason could dispute, but he remained undaunted. What Argus said made perfect sense to him. If it was the will of the gods that the ship be built, then the gods would obviously provide the means for him to pay for its construction. That it was their will was clear, so it was equally clear that the funds would be forthcoming. In the meantime, he sold his knife to buy another pair of sandals and made camp on the outskirts of the city in a crude lean-to constructed by the first three members of his crew.

"A somewhat shabby palace for a king," Delaney said of their lean-to as they huddled in its shelter during a rainstorm.

"Nevertheless, Fabius, it is a good beginning," Jason said, with no sign of discouragement. "Because of this, when I am in the palace, none will be able to claim that the king is ignorant of how his subjects live, for he has lived even as the poorest of them."

Steiger glanced at Andre. "He does tend to look on the bright side, doesn't he?"

"Somehow I had the feeling this would all be a great deal more dramatic," Andre said, then swore and shifted position as a stream of water broke through the thatch roof and cascaded down her back.

"The gods work in their own way and in their own time," said Jason, staring off into the distance. "If they mean for us to wait, then wait we must. It is my fate to rule in Iolchos, come what may. Pelias will learn that once I have set my mind upon a task, I always see it through. Never fear, my friends. When I am king, I shall remember that you were the first to join me in my quest and I shall not be ungrateful."

"In other words," Delaney mumbled softly, "don't hold your breath 'til payday."

It rained hard until shortly before midnight and then the storm moved on, leaving them in a dripping shelter crawling with bugs and earthworms. They did their best to rearrange the straw they had piled in the lean-to, putting the bottom layers on top so their beds would not be so damp. Just as they were settling down for the night, they heard the sounds of approaching footsteps squelching in the mud outside.

Jason grabbed his spear. "Take care, my friends," he said in a low voice. "It may be that Pelias means treachery, setting his soldiers upon us while we sleep. If so, then he shall not find us taken easily."

Someone came out of the darkness and paused just at the edge of the clearing where they had erected their shelter. In the moonlight, they could see no more than a tall, dark figure in a hooded cloak.

"Jason!" a muffled voice cried out.

"Who calls?" Jason yelled back.

"A friend."

"Then come closer so we may see you, friend," said Jason.

"Better that I not be seen," the dark figure said, without moving any closer. "Better also that I do not remain here long. Pelias has spies everywhere. Know that there are those in Iolchos who remember good King Aeson and bear Pelias no love. Word of your trouble has reached us. Among us, we have collected the necessary funds to pay Argus the shipwright for the building of your galley. We have also sent word abroad that a crew of heroes is needed to embark upon a dangerous adventure with a kingdom at stake. We have done our part, Jason, son of Aeson. Go now and do yours."

"Wait!" cried Jason. "Who are you, that I might know whom to thank for—" but the dark figure had already melted away into the darkness.

Steiger quickly moved off after the stranger.

"Fabius, where is Creon going?" Jason said.

"I think he's going to follow our benefactor," said Delaney. "You know what they say, beware of Greeks bearing gifts."

Jason frowned. "Who says that?"

Delaney shrugged. "Creon's people say it. They're not a very trusting lot."

"They would do well to trust the wisdom of the gods," said Jason. "You see? It all comes to pass. The gods have willed it and now we shall have the funds to build the *Argo* and the means to assemble its crew. It is a good omen, Fabius. Our fate now lies before us."

"Perhaps," said Delaney. "I would still prefer to know who's helping fate along."

Steiger had no difficulty closing the distance between himself and the stranger who had come calling at their camp. The man was far from an experienced woodsman. In the darkness, he crashed through the underbrush and stumbled in the mud, making more than enough noise to cover any sounds Steiger might have made in his pursuit. Steiger kept thinking about the man's voice. It sounded muffled, as if he had been speaking through a piece of cloth. Why bother to disguise his voice? They knew no one in Iolchos. And why had he been afraid to show himself?

There was something very suspicious about the recent progression of events, thought Steiger. Andre Cross seemed inclined to keep an open mind about possible differences in physical laws in this new universe, but perhaps that was because she had come from a superstitious time. When she had first seen 27th century technology, it would indeed have seemed like magic to her. Finn Delaney had not yet indicated where he stood on that question, but as for himself, Steiger preferred to look for rational explanations. Perhaps, in this universe, magic in the supernatural sense was possible, but he would reverse his judgment until he saw something that could not be explained away as anything *but* supernatural phenomena. He had yet to see anything like that.

The centaur had been real, there was no doubt about that, but was it supernatural, a being created by immortal gods? Steiger did not believe it for a moment. In his younger days, when he had been an interstellar mercenary, he had seen much stranger creatures that had been the result of natural evolution in their own respective environments—and this was a different universe, after all. He had also seen bizarre genetic manipulations and surgical creations. On one colony world, a youth fad had resulted in a subculture known as Cyberpunks, where young people voluntarily submitted to outrageous surgical and cybernetic procedures which turned them into creatures far

more exotic and surreal-looking than the centaur had been—
boys with snakeskin and forked tongues, girls with cat's eyes
and downy fur. And these were human children. No, he
wasn't ready to buy the concept of a "real" mythology just
yet.

The flames on the altar of the Oracle could easily have been
produced in a number of ways that were perfectly mundane.
The flames themselves would have provided enough cover for
the Oracle to have "appeared" and "disappeared." The fact
that they had not found a hidden doorway in the wall around
the Speaking Oak did not mean that there wasn't one.

The Oracle's "prophecy" could be even more easily explained. It was, after all, at the suggestion of the high priest
that they had traveled to the shrine at Delphi. The high priest
could easily have arrived there before them and set the whole
thing up. The question was, why? Was it merely the result of
Pelias wanting to be rid of Jason? If such were the case, why
hadn't he had Jason killed? It would have been the simplest
solution, unless he had a specific reason for not doing so. Or
was there something more to it? Could it be that the reason the
stranger's voice was muffled was because they might have
recognized it as the voice of the high priest? That was something Steiger was determined to find out before the night was
over.

The stranger was not far ahead of him, blundering through
the woods on a roundabout way back to Iolchos. The way he
was moving, Steiger would almost have to try to lose him. As
they approached the city, Steiger smiled. Something told him
he was going to follow the stranger right back to the Temple of
Poseidon.

Suddenly, instincts born of years of fighting sounded an
alarm inside his head and he knew he had done something
drastically wrong. He started to spin around, but he never saw
the blow coming. The next moment, he was on his back, unconscious, stretched out in the mud and the wet leaves.

"You're lucky you have a hard head," said Delaney.

Steiger opened his eyes to daylight and quickly shut them
once again, wincing. Delaney slowly helped him to a sitting
position.

"Take it easy, Creed. You've had a nasty crack."

"I've had worse," said Steiger. He groaned. "That doesn't

make me feel any better about this one, though."

"What happened?"

"I was following our friend and thinking how easy it was, trailing a tenderfoot like that through the woods, when somebody came up behind me and bashed my head in. No wonder it was so easy. They expected to be followed and planned an ambush. And like an idiot, I walked right into it. Where's Andre?"

"Back at the camp with Jason. We got worried when you didn't come back, so I thought I'd trail you and see if anything went wrong. Obviously, something did."

"Yes, with me," said Steiger. "I deserve having my skull fractured for letting them come up on me like that. The sponsors of this voyage seem determined not to have their identities revealed. There's something funny going on. Someone's hatching plots, but against whom? Pelias or Jason?"

"I've been thinking about that, too," Delaney said. "The story told by Apollonius didn't have a great deal of internal consistency. But then it was only a story. It didn't happen in our timeline."

"We don't know that for sure," Steiger said. "For all we know, an event similar to this could actually have occurred sometime in ancient Greece in our own timeline. Perhaps, over the years, embellishments were added to it until it became mythologized. There's no way of reliably dating a myth. Without knowing exactly at what point in time it was supposed to have taken place, there's no way to check it out. And this universe has already proven to have a different chronological timeline."

Delaney nodded. "True. Just because it's happening here doesn't mean it happened in our universe or that the dates even correspond. Or the events, for that matter. Too bad we can't clock ahead in time and check."

"How would we know which temporal coordinates to clock to?" Steiger said.

"There is that," said Delaney. "The way I see it, we've got two separate problems here. One is the possibility that the opposition might become alerted to our presence by means of tracking us through our warp discs. There's not much that can be done about that if it happens. All we can do is minimize the risk by not making any temporal transitions unless it's unavoidable. But then there's the second problem, which is that

we don't know for certain just what the historical scenario *is*
here. All we're working from is a bunch of theories and assumptions. I'm not sure I buy the theory that our mythology,
or certain aspects of it, might have been the result of some sort
of psychic feedback across the congruency, people in our
timeline somehow tuning in on events in this universe."

Steiger grunted. "That does sound pretty wild, but if it's
true, it could account for a lot of things, such as various unex-
plained psychic phenomena in our own universe. But suppose
there isn't anything like psychic feedback taking place across
the timelines. Then we're confronting an entirely different
situation. In that case, we can't depend on any information
from our own timeline, such as *The Argonautica* of Apollonius, because what we're faced with then is an alternate
universe in which events *appear* to be a mirror image of events
in our own universe, but they're not the *same* events. They're
only similar."

"Which raises the possibility that in this universe, Jason
might *not* have succeeded in his quest," said Delaney.

"Exactly. So far, we're acting on the assumption that the
events concerning Jason will more or less follow the progression of our myth. They have so far, but we can't afford to
follow through on that assumption without more information."

Delaney shook his head. "No, we can't. There's far too
much at stake. The problem is there's no way to check it out
without clocking ahead. And without proper coordinates,
we'd be clocking ahead blind. We'd have no idea what sort of
an environment we might be clocking into or even where to go.
If we luck out and experience no problems with transition,
we'd risk alerting the opposition by using our warp discs. If
they didn't get a direct fix on us and hit us with everything
they've got, they'd still know we were conducting a hostile
mission in this time period and they'd initiate a search for the
confluence point. We can't afford to let them find it. It's our
only way back home."

"I'm thinking that we have a more immediate problem,"
said Steiger.

"I know," said Delaney. "If what our friend from last
night said is true and Pelias does have spies everywhere, then it
would explain why he and his friends in Iolchos are anxious to
keep their identities a secret. On the other hand, what if the

man you followed was sent by Pelias and you were knocked out to prevent you from discovering that? That high priest seemed unusually solicitous, don't you think?''

"For someone who thinks T.I.A. agents are paranoid, you've got a very suspicious nature," Steiger said.

"Being careful isn't quite the same thing as being paranoid," Delaney said. "I won't argue the point, though. I'm more concerned about what it might indicate if the high priest *wasn't* involved."

"Meaning?"

"What about what happened at the Shrine of Delphi?"

"What about it?" Steiger said. "You didn't buy that cheap display, did you? Or do you really think supernatural events are natural here?"

"I don't know," Delaney said. "If they are, then we've bought into a lot more trouble than we bargained for. How do you fight magic? And if the high priest didn't arrange that little demonstration, then who did?"

Whoever had arranged for Argus to be paid did so in a clandestine manner. The payment was made in the middle of the night, by a man wrapped in a dark hooded cloak, and the instructions were given to the sleepy shipwright in a muffled voice. Not that Argus seemed to care much, one way or the other. He had been given a commission and the payment had been made in full, that was all that mattered to him. The next day, he hired laborers and began work on the galley.

Exhibiting a rare pragmatic streak, Jason signed himself and his first three Argonauts on as boat builders. In this manner, they were paid the same wages as the other workers out of the funds collected by their mysterious sponsors. This enabled them to secure more comfortable quarters on the waterfront. The lean-to was abandoned without regret.

The galley was the most ambitious project Argus had ever undertaken and he regarded it as a challenge. He was especially pleased that Jason did not get underfoot when it came to the design work, for no craftsman likes to take up a commission and then suffer the instructions of the client when the client clearly doesn't know the first thing about the craft.

The design Argus came up with for the galley was based upon that of a flat-bottomed Egyptian trader's boat he had once seen, only he modified it with a deep keel and a larger

mast, as well as increased dimensions. The galley would be
constructed out of pegged cedarwood, caulked and lapstraked
so that the boards overlapped each other, giving the hull
greater rigidity and strength. It would be sixty-five feet long
and twelve feet in the beam, with one mast for a large lateen
sail set slightly forward of amidships and a small wooden
deckhouse aft, atop which would be the steersman's station at
the massive oaken tiller. It was to be a ship meant for speed
and sea-kindliness, not creature comforts. Its design was
somewhat similiar to that of later Viking boats.

As the keel was laid, volunteers for Jason's voyage started
to arrive. The twin brothers, Castor and Pollux, were among
the first to sign on for the adventure. Then came Telamon and
Oileus, the fathers of the two Ajaxes who fought upon the
plains of Troy. Tiphys, who had made many sea voyages,
would be the steersman, and after him came Butes, said by
many to be the fairest of all men. Andre shrugged and said
she found him perhaps a bit *too* fair. Ancaios, who could read
the stars, would be their navigator and Meleager, slayer of the
Caledonian Boar, came in search of greater challenges. There
were Mopsus the astrologer and Idmon the soothsayer; Cae-
neus the fighter; Theseus, who killed the Minotaur; and Orpheus the harpist and singer who, the others said, had actually
been to Hades and returned to tell the tale—or sing the song,
depending on the preferences of the audience.

Last, but far from least, came Hercules and his young
squire, Hylas, a slight blond boy who strained under the
weight of his master's weapons while Hercules himself
marched unencumbered, dressed in a lion's skin and leather
sandals with silver greaves. He walked with huge strides,
swinging his massive twenty-four-inch arms, moving like a
juggernaut. His hair was black and curly and his beard was
thick and full. His eyes had the look of a man who would not
back down from anyone or anything. His voice was deep, but
he was soft-spoken, when he spoke at all, which was seldom
because he had a frightful stutter. He let Hylas do most of his
talking for him, since he could not even get his own name out
without a great deal of effort. The man who was said to be
half a god and invincible in battle was easily defeated by hard
consonants.

The shipwright, seeing the flamboyant adventurers who had
assembled for the voyage, became infected by their spirit and

let it be known that though he might be the oldest among them, he would not be denied a place among the crew, especially since the ship would bear his name. As the *Argo* neared completion, Argus set about carving the figurehead, a helmeted blonde woman with a shield on her left arm. Her right arm was extended and pointing outward. Argus proclaimed it to be the likeness of Hera, Queen of the Immortals. Her face was beautiful, yet grave and she looked as if she were about to speak. With the help of the Argonauts, the galley was completed, then painted a bright red. Following a sacrifice to Poseidon, they raised the mast and pushed the galley over log rollers into the bay. From a promontory over Iolchos, King Pelias watched with his high priest as the *Argo* embarked upon her voyage.

"I never dreamed that Jason would gather such a crew of heroes to his side," said Pelias. "It worries me. Men such as Meleager, Theseus and Hercules, with such as these, how can he fail in his quest?"

"Never fear," said the high priest. "The quest will fail, Pelias. Not all aboard the *Argo* wish for Jason to succeed."

4

The *Argo* sailed out of the bay of Iolchos on a course heading toward the Isle of Sciathos, passing the Cape of Sepius and then turning north toward Mount Pelion. They followed the coastline, keeping the open sea on their right. With Tiphys at the helm, the ship moved smoothly through the water under the power of the Argonauts, rowing to the drumbeat cadence set by Argus. The sea was dead calm and there was little wind.

Rowing was hard work and Orpheus led them in a song to the rhythm of the cadence, so the task would seem a little easier. It wasn't long before the Argonauts were glistening with sweat from their exertions. All had stripped off their chitons and they rowed dressed only in their loincloths. Andre was unclothed from the waist up, as well. Her naked breasts were no cause for excitement, since it was not unusual in this time for women to have one or both breasts bared. The only comments resulting from her nakedness were those having to do with the degree of her muscularity.

The cult of the body was a passion with the ancient Greeks, among whom sport took on spiritual overtones. All of the Argonauts were in excellent physical condition. The temporal agents, however, were a product of a time when physical training was far more developed and augmented scientifically. Among the Argonauts, only Hercules boasted a more impressive physique. He shared his oar with Hylas, but this soon proved to be an impractical arrangement. Hylas could not reach forward far enough to make the complete rowing motion and he kept being dragged off his seat by his powerful master's strokes. It was decided to spare Hylas from the task, as Hercules proved quite capable of handling the oar all by himself, and thereafter the youth performed the duties of a cabin boy, fetching water or preparing food, tasks for which he seemed much more suited.

They stopped at Mount Pelion so Chiron's old pupils could visit with him before they continued on their voyage. Dropping anchor just offshore, they waded in with Hercules carrying the slight Hylas on his shoulders, for the water was over the boy's head and he could not swim. The centaur, having seen the *Argo* from the heights, came down to greet them and escort them to his cave on Pelion. The delighted Hylas was treated to a ride upon the centaur's back as they made the climb.

At the centaur's cave, which was large and appointed comfortably with crude wooden furniture Chiron had built himself, they made a fire and sat down to a feast of venison, pork, fruits and vegetables and wine. Orpheus told the story of his descent down into Hell, which apparently many of the Argonauts had heard before, but they all listened attentively just the same.

He stood and walked into the center of the chamber, standing in the exact spot where his mellifluent tenor voice would echo best off the rock walls of Chiron's cavern. He stared down at the ground for a long moment and waited until absolute silence was achieved, then he jerked his head up abruptly, tossing his long dark curls, and his eyes seemed to glaze as he stared off into the infinite distance.

"Her name was Eurydice," he said, pronouncing the name as if it were a holy word, "and I loved her with all the mad young passion of a boy first struck by Cupid's arrow. One day, while she was running along a riverbank, a snake reared up and bit her. Her death was more than I could bear. All Thrace mourned her passing, but none mourned more than I. I alone could not accept her death. I refused to believe that she was lost to me forever. I thought a love so great as mine could reach out even into Hades and somehow bring her back to me. Night and day, I prayed to all the gods and sacrificed in all the temples until, at last, Cyrene, the goddess of the sea, heard my lament and took pity on me.

"She ordered the waters to be parted and I walked between them, descending down through the roiling waves to her where she ruled in the depths. There, surrounded by her nymphs, with sea anemones and creatures of the deep all around her, she told me to seek out Proteus, the Old Man of the Sea. 'For Proteus knows all,' she said. 'He knows all that is, all that has been, and all that is yet to be. Seize him, Orpheus,' she said to me, 'Seize him and hold him fast. Only fear will make him tell you what you wish to know. He will resist you and play upon your own fears to escape from you. He will assume the guise of beasts and monsters, yet you must not be afraid. If you relax your grip, he will swiftly leap into the sea and swim away and you shall never catch him. Hold fast to him,' Cyrene said, 'and the more he changes shape, the tighter you must hold him. Only when he reverts to his true form will you know that you have vanquished him. Then you may put your questions to him and he will be bound to answer.'

"She told me where to find the Old Man of the Sea and I journeyed far and wide until, at last, I found Proteus sleeping on a beach, his sleek form stretched out upon the sands. I crept up slowly and with the greatest of care, for Cyrene warned me that his hearing was acute, and then I leaped upon him, seizing him and holding on with all my strength! He gave a frightened start, then on the instant I perceived that I held not an old man with seaweed in his hair and a drowned look in his eyes, but a fearsome shark that writhed and thrashed and twisted, straining to fasten its terrible gaping jaws upon me!

"I screamed with terror, yet somehow I held on in desperation, and suddenly the shark was gone and in its place I held a scaled sea serpent which coiled its length about me, seeking to squeeze the very breath out of my chest! Yet even as I felt its coils tightening around me and it seemed as though my bones would burst, I held on tighter, squeezing back with every bit of strength I had! The serpent gave way to a fearsome dragon which beat its wings about my head and seared me with its breath. I made my grip still tighter, squeezing the creature's throat with all my might. The dragon disappeared and in its place I held a kraken, then a griffin, then a hideous mollusk that stung me with its slimy tendrils. Proteus changed into every terrifying creature known to man and still I would not release him until, at long last, succumbing to my choking hold, he returned, spent, to his true shape and I knew that I had won.

" 'I know what it is you wish to know of me,' Proteus said, and he told me how to find the Secret Gates of Taenarus and pass through them to the Underworld. He told me all that I must do and I followed his instructions, willing to brave any danger so that Eurydice could be restored to me. I descended into Hades and there, in the cold darkness, I found Charon the dreaded ferryman, who knew my purpose and conveyed me across the River Styx to the gates of Death's dominion. I encountered Cerebrus, the slathering three-headed hound that guards the gates, and as it howled and snapped at me, I lulled it with a song until the fearsome beast was curled beneath my feet and sleeping. I played my lyre and sang to the lost souls and eased their torment and their anguish. The Furies, yes, even Death himself, were spellbound by the profound lament I sang, spellbound because I sang with all my heart, my grief pouring out from the very bottom of my soul. And yes, I found her, on the very brink of the Inferno, my Eurydice, and I called out to her and I saw her shade approach.

"Proteus had warned me that I must not gaze upon her, for men must always avert their eyes from those of ghosts or gods, so remembering his words, I turned from her and went back the way I came, bidding her to follow me. Yet as I crossed the River Styx in Charon's ferry, a fear came over me that she may not have boarded with me, that she had been left behind, and powerless to fight the impulse, I turned around. For the briefest instant, I beheld her standing there and as our eyes met, I knew that all was lost.

"Three times did thunder crash and my love cried out, 'You have doomed me!' and faded from my sight like smoke dispersing on the winds. I cried out, pleading with the ferryman to turn around, but he would not take me back across. He drew up to the bank and pointed with his bony hand, showing me the way back to the light of day. I had no choice but to go, for my time had not yet come. Gladly would I have remained in Hades with my love, but the Fates had not decreed it should be so. There were other challenges before me, other voyages to make before the final voyage that would reunite me with my love.

"So that is why I am here with you tonight, my friends, as we embark upon this perilous quest. That is why I have no fear of whatever lies ahead, for each man must make his own voyage in his own time. Who knows what lies ahead of us? Come what may, be it glorious success or fatal failure, I know that in the end, I will make the journey down to Hades once again and this time, I will remain forever in the Underworld where spirits dwell, united with my Eurydice. I have learned that no man should fear his destiny and that no parting should bring sorrow, for all shall come together in the end."

He stood silently, looking down at the ground, then slowly returned to his seat as the Argonauts nodded and murmured their approval of the tale.

"It grows better each time he tells it," Euphemus said to Andre.

"Do you think any of it is true?" she said.

"What is truth?" said Idmon, the soothsayer. "If it were a dream, would it then be false? Who is to say what challenges the gods may put before us, even in our dreams? Who is to say that our wakeful state is not itself a dream dreamed by the Immortals? Life is a tale and therein lies its magic. The oftener the tale is told, the truer it becomes. When men stop telling tales, then life itself becomes a lie."

"What is the sound of one hand clapping?" said Delaney wryly.

Idmon turned to him and smiled. "Is it not the sound that is made when one hand claps?"

"You have me there," said Delaney, smiling. "I am neither soothsayer nor a wise man. Merely a seeker who asks foolish questions."

"Indeed," said Idmon, "yet who is the wiser? The one wise enough to know the answer or the one wise enough to ask the question?"

"Enough of this philosophy," said Menoetius. "Such musings are fit only for old men. We need tales of great deeds, not weighty thoughts."

"We shall hear a tale of a great deed then," Castor said. "Tell us, Theseus, of how you slew the Minotaur."

Theseus spat out a piece of pork fat and belched. "I was younger then," he said, patting his muscular stomach contentedly. "Young and full of fire to prove myself. Full also of anger at the unjust policy which each nine years sent seven young Athenian boys and maidens to the labyrinth of Crete, there to wander terror stricken through the maze until they were found and eaten by the Minotaur."

"Why was this done?" asked Hylas, eyes wide with wonder. "And what sort of creature was this Minotaur?"

"It was a manner of tribute paid by the Athenians to Crete," said Theseus, "and it was meant to appease the Minotaur. You may have heard that this creature was the offspring of an accursed, bestial love born of a mad and savage passion. It was said that Pasiphae, the depraved wife of King Minos of Crete, fell in love with a white bull which had a black spot between its horns, an animal held sacred by the people of Crete. In her mad obsession, Pasiphae had congress with this beast and from this union came a fearsome creature, cursed by the gods to be born in a shape that was half man, half animal. Its torso was that of a man, yet its head and hindquarters were those of a bull. Aghast at this horrible perversion, Minos wanted to remove it forever from his sight, yet he could not kill it, for it was the offspring of a sacred animal.

"He sought out the famed craftsman, Daedalus, and directed him to build a labyrinth to house the monster. Daedalus constructed this labyrinth deep within a cavern, with many passages which turned and twisted, forming a maze so intricate that once one entered it, the way out could not be found again. It was to the depths of this labyrinthine maze that Minos consigned the Minotaur and each nine years thereafter, youths and maidens were sent into this maze so that their blood would appease the creature. Over the years, this Minotaur grew large and powerful and terrifying, so that Minos greatly feared it.

"My father, King Aegeus, was the unhappy man to whom the task fell of selecting the seven sacrificial victims when the boat with the black sail departed each nine years for Crete. He was hated by the people for this, especially so since he was the one man whose own children were exempt from the deadly lottery. Anxious to prove myself in battle and test my courage, and to silence those who accused my unhappy father of being unjust, I volunteered to go, thereby sparing at least one family the agony of seeing a child depart on the ship with the black sail never to return."

"Yet you believed that you would return," said Jason. "You knew that right was on your side and therefore you would prevail."

"Well, that may be so," Theseus said, "but I have always put my faith in the strength of my own sword arm than in the power of right. I believed that since the Minotaur was a creature born of flesh, then it could be killed as any other creature born of flesh. And I believed also, as I continue to believe, that life without a challenge is a kind of death. I told my father that I would do my utmost to destroy this Minotaur, for if the Minotaur were killed, then the tribute would be ended. And I told my father that the same ship on which I sailed for Crete would return with a white sail hoisted to tell of my victory, or the black sail to tell of my failure and my death.

"Now King Minos had no love for the fearsome creature in his labyrinth. He could not order it killed himself, but if a stranger to whom the bull was not a sacred animal were to kill it, neither Minos nor any of his subjects would have profaned against their faith. For this reason, Minos allowed the young men who went into the maze to carry whatever weapons they desired. Still, he was confident that no one would succeed, for none who entered the labyrinth ever came out again into the light of day.

"King Minos had a beautiful daughter whose name was Ariadne and when she saw me, Ariadne fell in love with me." Theseus tipped back a wine skin and squeezed out a purple stream which struck his chin before it found its way into his mouth. He wiped his chin with the back of his hand, smacked his lips and broke wind profoundly.

"As a youth," he said, "I was not uncomely. Shortly before I was to go into the labyrinth, Ariadne came to me with a spool of thread. She told me to unwind the thread from the spool as I went through the maze, so that when I had killed the Minotaur, I could return the way I came by following the thread. It seemed such a simple thing, I was amazed that no one had thought of it before. Yet I had not thought of it myself, so perhaps it was not so simple.

"When the morning came, the seven of us went into the labyrinth. There was much wailing and weeping among my fellow sacrificial victims, but I told them to keep behind me and to avoid stepping on the thread, lest it should break and doom us all to be forever lost. We wandered for a long time through the maze, going from one passage to another, all the while descending ever deeper until I began to think that Hades itself lay not far ahead. It was cold within the labyrinth and damp. Our torches showed us bats in great numbers hanging from the ceiling. As we passed, they swept down upon us screaming and the maidens screamed as well, as did some of the youths.

"Rats were all around us like a furry carpet, undulating and chittering, crawling up our legs and dropping on our bodies so that we had to beat them off us with every step we took. As we went deeper, we began to pass the bones of those unfortunates who had gone before us and had been devoured by the Minotaur. I saw that many of these bones were splintered, as if struck some powerful blow, and that they had all been gnawed upon by fearsome teeth."

Theseus picked up a pork rib and gnawed at it savagely, then wiped the grease off on his legs.

"Among the bones also lay weapons, swords and spears and shields that had done their bearers not one bit of good. The shields, I saw, were buckled, hammered by strong blows. The swords were blunted and the spears were broken. And before long, in the depths ahead of us, we heard the echoing bellows of the creature, which smelled our scent and roared its hunger.

"My thread had run out to the end and now naught but the spool itself remained. I bid the others wait and went on ahead alone, trying to mark the way so that I could find them once again when—and if—I started to return. With my shield on my arm, I held the torch aloft and proceeded slowly, cautiously, not wishing the creature to surprise me, but by now its cries had ceased and there was deathly silence in the maze, broken only by the sounds of water dripping down from overhead."

Theseus stood and stepped forward slowly, acting out the last part of his tale. He had picked up his shield and he now held it close to his body. His hand rested on his sword hilt and he crouched low, as if anticipating combat.

"Suddenly, the passage ended and I was in a cavern, a large central chamber lit by torches set high into the walls. Before me was a heap of bones piled higher than a man, some still with bloody meat upon them, and crouched upon that heap of bones was the most fearsome apparition I had ever seen. It was as tall as Chiron and as powerfully built as Hercules, with arms like tree trunks and a chest big as a keg of wine!

"Blood from its grisly meals was matted on its haunches and upon its shoulders; where a man's head should have been, there was the head of a ravening bull with wild red eyes and great, terrible horns, each longer than my armspan! Foul insects crawled upon it and vermin scurried among the remnants of its victims. It saw me and it stood, towering above me, and I felt its fetid breath. Its bellow was a deafening roar that echoed through the chamber and turned my blood to ice! I quickly unsheathed my sword. . . ."

As he spoke, Theseus suddenly drew his sword out of its sheath with a wide, fast sweeping motion and several of the Argonauts were saved from being decapitated only by ducking their heads at the last moment.

"It charged, bellowing as it came, and I threw my torch at it, hoping to strike its face and blind it so that I could step in and make the killing thrust, but it reached up a massive arm and batted the torch away."

Theseus made a batting motion with his sword and knocked one of the torches out of its sconce. It flew across the room and fell at the feet of Pollux, showering him with sparks. He started batting at his head, fearful that his hair would be set on fire and Castor thoughtfully emptied his wine goblet over his twin brother's head.

"It swung at me!" Theseus shouted, his voice ringing in the cave. "I ducked beneath the blow, slashing at its midsection with my sword—"

A bowl of fruit was struck a devastating blow and it went clanging against the wall, spilling apples, pears and figs in all directions. Delaney caught an apple one-handed and bit into it. As the battle progressed, the roast pig was skewered; a quick cut and thrust separated a loin which Argus grabbed and bit into with gusto. The venison was hacked; a table was overturned.

"Its bellows filled the cavernous chamber as we met, exchanging blows and punishing each other! My shield was battered and dented, my sword blunted on its horns! It bled from a dozen wounds and still it came at me! I raised my sword high over my head—"

And as he raised his sword high over his head, Hercules caught Theseus by the wrist, forestalling further destruction. "And then you k-k-k-k—"

"And then you killed it!" Hylas finished for his master.

"No, I—" Theseus paused as Hercules frowned down at him. "Uh, yes, then I killed it," he said quickly and Hercules released him.

"After that, it was a simple matter of following the thread back to the entrance of the labyrinth and finding a warm welcome in the arms of Ariadne. We boarded the ship which had brought us all to Crete and set sail for home, full of festive spirit. Unfortunately, our spirits were so high that I forgot what I had told my father and I neglected to put up the white sail. Aegeus saw our black sail on the horizon and, thinking I had perished, became so grief-stricken that he threw himself into the sea. Thus, I vanquished the Minotaur and became a king."

"Handy little lapse of memory he had there," Delaney said to Andre.

Idmon shook his head. "Do us all a service, Castor, and do not ask Theseus to tell any more stories of his exploits. We are all guests here and his tales are hard upon the housekeeping."

The Argonauts all laughed and Theseus scowled at first, then joined in the laughter.

"I, too, have a tale to tell," said Chiron and they all fell silent as their old teacher spoke. "I dreamt that I was taken by the gods and transported to Olympus, where the Immortals all surrounded me. I stood within a chamber full of light while they asked me many questions and the magical creations of Hephaestus, creatures of living metal, gamboled at my feet. They wished to know of the affairs of mortals. They asked me about you, Jason, and you, Theseus, and you, Hercules. They asked if mortals still believed in gods and I was saddened that they feared our loss of faith. They spoke about a quest of which I knew nothing and they spoke about a crew of heroes who called themselves the Argonauts. Then they returned me to my home here on Mount Pelion without any word of explanation and it was here that I awoke, thinking it was all a dream of portent."

The massive centaur looked down at them from where he stood at the head of the long table, while his youngest pupil, a child named Achilles, ran a comb through the hairs of his long tail.

"There is truth in what Idmon has told us," the centaur said. "The gods pose challenges to us in dreams. Who is to say that this is not a dream in which the gods are speaking to us, moving us about like game pieces on a board for their own purposes? What mortal can discern the thoughts of an Immortal? You are the Argonauts and you are upon a quest, just as the gods spoke of in my dream.

"When your father brought you to me, Jason, he asked me to prepare you for the day when you would meet your destiny. And now all of you, many of you my old pupils, have united in this quest to bring back the golden fleece to Iolchos. It shall complete a tale that began with a mad king who believed that murdering his children would appease the anger of the gods. You sail upon the sea where Helle drowned and you journey to the land where Phrixus died. Your fates are intertwined with theirs.

"Your tale, Jason, is their tale also. It is a tale of children driven from their homes and denied their birthright. It is a tale of mortals invoking the desires of gods to justify their own and of gods who walk with mortals to redress those wrongs. How it all will end, no mere mortal can say, but in every dream, there is a lesson to be learned. Question all dreams to discern their lessons and question all mortals to discern their purposes, for the gods will question you in turn. It is as Idmon said, the wiser man is not he who believes he knows the answers, but he who knows to ask the questions.

"And now, it grows late and you must leave upon the morning tide. The time has come to sleep and dream and see what lessons we may learn."

The Argonauts slept deeply, all save "Fabius," who merely feigned sleep while he took his turn on watch. Andre had taken the first shift, pretending also to be asleep while she remained on watch. Her shift passed uneventfully and she then woke Steiger, who took his turn for several hours. Delaney had the last shift and Steiger woke him quietly to report that all was well. Steiger then stretched out and was asleep almost immediately while Delaney remained awake, thinking. Chiron's tale had sounded uncomfortably familiar.

Delaney had the feeling they were caught in a time when myth and reality were indistinguishable. These people were primitives, yet they were sophisticated in the way they created their own myths, then lived them. Idmon had said it best. The

oftener a tale is told, the truer it becomes. He wondered what
they'd find when they arrived at Colchis. Would there be some
enchanted golden fleece hanging on a tree branch in the Sacred
Grove of Ares or would it turn out to be a rotting sheepskin
painted gold, a moth-eaten symbol of an old tale upon which a
kingdom had been built?

Would this be just a long, dull sea voyage which, on their
return, would become the subject of embellished tales such as
the fable Orpheus had told? A part of him hoped that would
be the case, for the alternative, the one suggested by the existence of a creature such as Chiron and the strange phenomenon
at Delphi, was a frightening one, one which threatened to
shake the foundations of all that he believed and disbelieved.
Yet, at the same time, a small part of him hoped it would be
true. It was the part of him that remembered all the stories of
his childhood and experienced crushing disappointment upon
becoming an adult.

It was almost dawn when he heard the soft footfalls of
hooves and looked up to see Chiron quietly moving toward the
entrance to the cavern. Moving silently, Delaney followed
him. Chiron went outside and in the soft gray light, Delaney
could see the centaur heading down a path that led into the
woods. Keeping his distance, Delaney pursued him, curious to
see where the centaur was going at such an unlikely hour.
After a short while, Chiron came to a small clearing in the
forest in the center of which a small stone altar had been built.
He entered the clearing and stopped before the altar with his
head bowed.

For a while, the centaur simply stood there, saying and
doing nothing, as if praying, but then Delaney heard a deep,
masculine voice say, "I am here."

Standing behind the altar, in the early morning shadows,
was a figure that had not been there a moment earlier. He was
wearing a hooded cloak which hid his features.

"They have come, just as you said they would," the centaur
said. "They will be sailing on the morning tide. What would
you have me do?"

"Nothing more," the hooded figure said, "only tell me,
among the Argonauts, who are the ones you do not know, the
ones who were not among your pupils?"

"There are several," said Chiron. "Argus the shipwright is

one, as well as Idmon the soothsayer, and Mopsus the astrologer. There are Menoetius and Pirithous, and Hylas, the boy who serves Hercules . . .''

Delaney heard Chiron mention several other names, among them their own aliases, Fabius, Creon and Atalanta. The hooded figure questioned Chiron about each of them.

"Good," the strangely familiar voice said, finally. "You have done well. Go now. It is almost dawn. Tell no one about our meeting."

"I would ask only one question," Chiron said. "Many of these youths are near and dear to me. The quest they have embarked upon will hold great dangers for them. Tell me, will they succeed?"

"No man should know his fate," the hooded figure said, "nor that of another. Some will die and some will live. What becomes of them is the province of the gods. Go now. Wish them well upon their journey."

Chiron bowed from the waist, then turned and came back in Delaney's direction. Delaney ducked behind some bushes to avoid being seen and waited until the centaur had passed. When he looked up again, the hooded figure was no longer in the clearing. He ran to the stone altar and looked around in all directions, but there was no sign of a trail or even of anyone having been there in the first place. The ground around the altar and the stone platform it stood upon was damp with early morning drizzle, but the only tracks visible in the gray dawn were Chiron's hoofprints.

5 _____

"The Isle of Lemnos," Tiphys said, steering toward the green island lying ahead of them. "We had best anchor tonight in the protection of its bay, Jason. The sun is getting low and unfamiliar waters can be treacherous at night. Besides, we shall need to go ashore in search of fresh water to replenish our supply."

"And m-m-meat," said Hercules, whacking himself on the belly with a sound like wood splitting.

"Very well," said Jason. "We anchor for the night at Lemnos. Argus, Mopsus, Idmon, Telamon and Oileus, you shall remain with the ship while the rest of us go ashore in search of water and provisions."

"Lemnos," Steiger said, "according to the myth, an island of beautiful Amazon women." He glanced at Delaney and grinned. "Think that's what we'll find?"

"I'm more worried about having a ringer on this voyage," said Delaney.

Steiger nodded, suddenly serious. "If he's among the Argonauts, it would explain the hooded cloak. He wouldn't want to be recognized. But if the centaur's in on some sort of plot with him, why would he want to disguise himself for a private meeting?"

"Maybe the centaur never knew what he really looked like and he wanted to keep it that way. And that raises more questions."

"You said you thought you recognized the voice. None of the Argonauts' voices ring any bells with you?"

Delaney shook his head. "Several of them have deep voices. And whoever it was could have been altering his normal voice."

"Too bad you didn't notice if anyone was missing when you trailed Chiron."

"If anyone had left during the night, one of us should have spotted him," Delaney said. "And if someone left after I did, he should have spotted me."

"If one of these characters was equipped with a warp disc," Steiger said, "he could have clocked out of the cave and to that clearing without anyone noticing."

Delaney glanced at him sharply. "I think we'd better talk about this. Let's see if we can split away from the main group once we're ashore."

They spoke in low voices, but the *Argo* was not the best place to hold a surreptitious conversation. No space had been wasted in the construction of the galley and they were all in fairly close contact all the time. All three temporal agents had been on ocean voyages before, but no matter what the time period or what type of vessel, one thing about life on the sea remained constant. Time passed very slowly.

The *Argo* was an uncomplicated vessel. There was no need to climb the rigging to take in or let out sails, because there was only the one simple, triangular lateen sail which could be hoisted or taken down easily and quickly. There was no need to perform maintenance on armaments, because there were none. There was no need to maintain engines or generators, pumps or electrical equipment or any of the other items found on more modern ships. The *Argo* was as primitive as a ship could be short of the reed vessels of the Polynesians. Shipboard duties were simple. There was not much else to do save row or watch for leaks and bail if the need arose. When they were close to shore, one of the men would go into the bow and let down a weighted rope so that soundings could be taken. Theirs was not an ambitious ocean-crossing voyage so much as an extended offshore cruise. On their course in the Aegean Sea, they were never very far from land and much of their voyage would be spent following the coastline, sailing between the islands and the mainland. With the proper crew and under the right conditions, the *Argo* might have been capable of crossing an ocean, but even expert sailors would have found it quite a hardship.

The Vikings, sailing roughly similar vessels in the North Sea, braved far more of the dangers of the deep than did the Argonauts, and most of the Argonauts were not experienced sailors. The majority of them were landlubbers to whom the voyage took on epic proportions. When the sea was calm, they rowed, which was backbreaking work. When the winds were fair, they made slow headway under sail with the oars shipped. At such times, there was not a great deal to do on board.

The sun had burned every one of them. They had rigged an awning to provide some very much needed shade, but skin was nevertheless tender and muscles were still sore. Hylas was kept busy applying olive oil to sunburned skin and some of the crew felt seasick, even in the relatively calm seas they had experienced. Delaney, who had once endured a squall in the crow's nest of a British man o'war, wondered uneasily how this crew would fare in the event of a storm.

While they were under sail, a listless lethargy was the prevalent atmosphere on board and even Orpheus, a seemingly inexhaustible source of songs and tales, fell to sitting idly on deck and staring out to sea, lost in his own thoughts. After a day's sail, the Argonauts looked forward to spending time ashore.

They anchored in the small protected bay and waded in, pleased at the prospect of getting in some hunting. They split up into small groups and went off in different directions to explore the island. It gave the temporal agents a chance to go off by themselves.

"You're going to call me a paranoid again," said Steiger, "but hear me out first. I've been thinking about this ever since we left Mount Pelion. Something's wrong here. Someone else is conducting some sort of covert operation on this voyage. Our friend with the hooded cloak really seems to get around. He could be someone in the pay of King Pelias, someone who's infiltrated the Argonauts as we have, but there's another possibility that worries me even more. Our hooded friend might not be working for Pelias at all.''

"I'm not calling you a paranoid yet," said Finn, "but I'm reserving judgment.''

"All right. Consider this. The centaur shows up in our time-line, coming through conveniently at a point where we just happen to have Observers stationed. The fact of the centaur's existence predisposes us to consider the possibility that physical laws might be significantly different in this universe. The debriefing of the centaur seems to corroborate the events described in one of our most ancient myths, in which supernatural forces figure prominently. We witness at least one event so far, at Delphi, which appears to be supernatural. We've got some mysterious hooded figure cropping up both at Iolchos and at Pelion. Now maybe supernatural events *are* natural here, but consider that any one of us could have duplicated the seemingly magical appearance and disappearance of the Oracle . . . by using a warp disc. Our friend in the hooded cloak might be getting around the same way.''

"Wait," said Andre, "let's go back to the beginning for a moment. What do you mean by saying that the centaur appeared 'conveniently' at a point in time where we happened to have Observers on the scene? Assuming it was all planned somehow, how could the opposition have arranged to have a confluence occur at such a convenient point?''

"They didn't have to arrange it," said Steiger. "Suppose they discovered the confluence first. They could have conducted a scouting expedition just as Curtis did. They have the ability to scan for warp discs somehow. Wouldn't it make sense that it would be the first thing they'd do? They could have discovered we had Observers in the area and decided to take advantage of that fact.''

"So they created a centaur in their genetic engineering labs, programmed it, and sent it through the confluence to provide us with disinformation meant to send us on some sort of wild goose chase?'' said Delaney. "Maybe. It's a long shot, but it's possible, I suppose. But if this whole thing is a setup of some sort, then they'd have to be aware of us. Even if they hadn't spotted us at the very beginning, they'd know about you from the night you tried to follow the hooded man back to Iolchos. They would have had plenty of time to discover your warp disc while you were unconscious. And if they identified you, they'd have to know about us as well, which means that our cover has been blown. So why didn't they relieve you of your warp disc?

Why haven't they made any moves?''

"I don't know," said Steiger. "I could be wrong about all this, but my gut tells me we're being waltzed through some kind of scenario by somebody who wants us to accept things just as they appear. I have the feeling we're walking into something."

The ground suddenly seemed to leap up beneath them and seconds later, they were suspended about six feet off the ground in a large rope net. Delaney found himself staring down into the face of a lovely young woman who held a sort of leather bellows in her hands.

"What—" he began, but before he could get the next word out, she squeezed the bellows and blew a suffocating mist into his face. It blinded him and he started coughing violently. Everything started spinning and then all feeling left him.

Delaney awoke in a large room with stone walls. Light was coming into the cell from barred windows high overhead. The floor was cold and damp, made of mortared stone, and lying on it had given him a backache. His head throbbed, his eyes stung and his lungs felt as if he had breathed in acid fumes. He made an effort to sit up and discovered that both his hands and feet were manacled.

The Argonauts were lying all around him in various positions of unconsciousness, similarly shackled. He made a quick head count and saw that they had captured everyone who came ashore. Those who had remained on board the *Argo* were absent, as was Andre. Steiger rolled slightly and moaned, starting to come around.

"What was that you were saying about walking into something?" said Delaney.

Steiger sat up slowly. "God, my head feels like it's about to burst. What happened?"

"We were netted in some sort of animal trap, then neatly gassed," said Delaney. "We must have been the first ones they caught. The others are still out of it."

Steiger held up his hands and shook the chains. "Slave traders?" he said, grimacing.

"Back in our timeline, they did a pretty brisk slave trade in these days," said Delaney. "But if the one who gassed us was a slave trader, she sure didn't look the part."

"She?"

"You didn't see her?"

"Hell, I turned my head and the next thing I knew, it was like breathing tear gas. I didn't see a thing. What did she look like?"

"Diana."

"Who?"

"The goddess of the hunt. Young, beautiful, cute little figure in a miniskirt, long legs, bow, quiverful of arrows, lovely golden hair, eyes you could die for . . ."

"Right, I get the picture. You think we found our Amazons?"

"More like they found us."

"Where's Andre?"

"I don't know."

"Anyone else missing?"

"Only the men back on the boat."

Steiger looked around at the cell. "Lovely accommodations."

"According to the story, they murdered all their men for bringing back concubines from Thrace," said Delaney.

"Is there a point to this or are you just being bright and cheery?"

"Also according to the story, they made the Argonauts quite welcome, if you'll recall."

"That's right," said Steiger, "I'm still not thinking too clearly. They stayed here for a while and enjoyed the company of a lot of horny women and they would have stayed longer if Hercules hadn't kicked their butts back aboard the ship. This part wasn't in the script."

The other Argonauts started to come around. It turned out that several of the hunting parties had been caught in nets as well, others had fallen into pits, the rest were approached by lovely young women and gassed when they allowed them to get close.

"I do not understand this," Jason said. "Were all of us captured by women?"

"Why have we been chained?" roared Hercules, furiously. Suddenly, there was no trace of a stutter. The deep voice rumbled forth smoothly in ringing, stentorian tones. *"Who dares chain the son of Zeus?"*

He stood and held his arms out before him, pulling the chains taut. The muscles in his shoulders and chest bunched, standing out in sharp relief, and a moment later, the chains snapped cleanly.

Steiger stared, eyes wide. "Jesus, did you *see* that?" he whispered.

Delaney tried his own chains. "I saw it, but I don't believe it. These links are almost an inch thick!"

Hercules reached down and snapped the chains holding his feet together, then turned his attention to the chains holding Hylas. One by one, he freed each of the Argonauts and when he was done, he wasn't even breathing hard.

"I must be dreaming," Steiger said softly to Delaney. "*Nobody* could be that strong!"

"Not even Hercules?" Delaney said.

His fury building, Hercules attacked the door, throwing himself against it repeatedly like a charging rhinocerous, until the heavy wood splintered and the hinges broke, sending both Hercules and the door crashing outward into the corridor beyond.

They ran out after Hercules as he stormed down the corridor, roaring at the top of his lungs. He came to a door at the end of the corridor and launched himself against it without breaking stride, smashing through it and into the room beyond.

It was a large central chamber, brightly lit with torches. There were rich tapestries hanging on the walls and thick carpets on the stone floor. There were long, low tables and couches placed around the perimeter of the room and there was a large group of about thirty young women facing them. They were all dressed in short chitons and sandals laced up to their knees. Their hair was worn long and pulled back, fastened by clasps at the nape of the neck. Each of them held a bow drawn back with an arrow nocked and ready to fly. Confronted with this sight, even Hercules was brought up short.

"Is this how you greet all your visitors?" demanded Jason, slowly coming forward with his hands held at his sides. "What have we done to be so rudely treated? Who are you? Why have our weapons been taken? And where are all your men?"

"Our men are gone," said a young woman, coming out from behind the others. She alone carried no weapons. "I am Hypsipyle, Queen of Lemnos. Our men have all gone off to war and women left alone are vulnerable. We feared an attack by our enemies or by pirates, so we made preparations to protect ourselves. We did not know of your intentions. Which of you is Jason?"

"I am Jason, King of Iolchos."

"I ask you to forgive us, Jason," said Queen Hypsipyle. "It appears we acted hastily and misjudged you and your friends." She turned to the other women. "Put down your bows and make these strangers welcome."

"Where is Atalanta?" Delaney said.

"It is she who has convinced me that you came in peace," said Hypsipyle. "If you will follow me, I will take you to her."

She led Steiger and Delaney down one of several corridors branching off from the main chamber. They passed a number of women heading the other way, carrying trays of food. All were young and beautiful and very fit. She stopped before a door and beckoned them inside. It was a bath chamber, filled with steam and fragrant smells from the scented water and the burning braziers. The tiled sunken bath filled most of the room and Andre sat within it, being bathed by two beautiful young women.

"Do you believe this?" Delaney asked, speaking in English. "We get chained and thrown into a cold cell while Cleopatra here gets the red carpet treatment."

"Apparently there are some advantages to being a woman around here," Andre said. "Come on in and get your backs scrubbed."

"You don't have to ask me twice," said Delaney, shucking his chiton and sandals. He got in and one of the women smilingly moved over and began to scrub him gently with a soft-cloth.

Steiger sat down cross-legged on the floor. "Would it be too much trouble to ask just what in hell is happening here?"

Delaney reclined into the woman's arms and sighed. "Right this minute, I'm in no particular hurry to find out."

A woman bent down over Steiger and smiled, gesturing toward the bath, but he shook his head.

"I could force myself to stay here for a while," Delaney said, grinning.

Steiger frowned. "What did you tell Queen What's-her-name?"

"Hypsipyle," Andre said. "She thought I was being kept by the crew against my will, sort of a ship's concubine. I told her I was part of the crew, voluntarily, and we were on a voyage to Colchis to bring back the golden fleece. She thought the Argonauts were pirates. She seems to have a tendency to think the worst of men."

"Have you seen any men here at all?" said Steiger.

"Not a one. No old people or children, either."

"How did Hypsipyle account for that?"

"She said the men were away at war and the children were being kept with the old people on another part of the island, for their protection."

"And none of the men stayed behind to provide this protection?"

"The women seem quite capable of looking after themselves," said Andre, "which makes me wonder why none of them went to war with the men. I spent more time answering questions that asking them. Hypsipyle said you were all being kept in another part of the palace until she could determine whether or not you were a threat. I wasn't sure of my ground, so I didn't want to press her. Apparently, she's decided we're welcome to stay, so long as our stay is brief. Her story is obviously thin, but it matches the events of the myth."

"I know and I don't buy it."

"You sure you don't want a scrub?" Delaney asked.

"Delaney, doesn't any of this seem a little *unusual* to you?"

"Sure. But that doesn't mean I can't enjoy myself while I think about it. I do my best thinking when I'm relaxed." He looked up at the woman in whose arms he reclined and smiled. "And this sure is relaxing."

Steiger spoke to her in Greek. "Where are all the old people? Where are the children?"

She smiled at him vacuously and shook her head, as if she didn't understand. She beckoned him into the tub.

"No thanks. I'm old enough to wash myself." He got to his feet and switched back to English. "We're obviously not going to get anything out of them. I'm going to take a look around. Something about this mission has to start making sense, sooner or later."

"I thought he said he didn't get tense," said Delaney, after Steiger had left.

"He's right, you know," said Andre. "There's something very peculiar about these women. With the exception of Hypsipyle, they all seem stunted in their development. Childlike. It's as if they were all stamped out of the same mold. They're all young and beautiful, yet somehow asexual."

Delaney reached out and touched the naked breast of the woman bathing him. She made no response. "You think maybe they're just not interested in men?" he said.

"No one's made a pass at me," said Andre. "I've tried communicating with them, but you see what they're like. They don't really seem interested in us at all. We're speaking in a foreign language that they've never heard before and they're not in the least bit curious. I've spoken with Hypsipyle, but nothing I say gets more than a smile out of any of the others. I haven't even heard any of them converse among themselves."

"Interesting," said Delaney, looking thoughtful. "No men, no children and apparently no one over the age of twenty-five. They're all young, all beautiful, and they all act somehow retarded, except in direct response to Hypsipyle. And they only seem capable of limited reactions."

As if in play, Delaney threw his arms around one of the women, then suddenly bit down hard on the flesh of her upper arm.

"Finn!" Andre shouted, shocked by his action.

The woman merely looked puzzled.

"That should have made her scream," said Andre.

Delaney pushed the woman away and got out of the bath. "It should have, only androids don't feel pain."

"Androids!"

"Come on. We'd better go find Creed."

Steiger pressed himself against the wall and waited until the women passed by, then turned the corner. He heard the sounds of music and male laughter from the direction of the main chamber. The women had been carrying trays of food. The Argonauts were being royally entertained. He ran quickly down the length of the corridor until he came to a flight of steps leading down. He listened for a moment, then slowly started down the stairs.

The stone steps led down to a landing, then turned at a right angle and continued down to a floor below ground level. He went down and paused at the end of the stairs. To his left was a large wooden door before which stood two women armed with spears. One of them saw him and immediately came forward, spear held crosswise in front of her.

"I'm sorry," Steiger said in Greek, "I seem to have become lost. I saw my friends coming in this direction and I was trying to find them."

The woman made no other response save pointing in the direction from which he had come, her face expressionless.

The other woman remained near the door, watching them.

"You don't seem to understand," said Steiger. "They came this way, I'm sure of it. They were with the queen."

The woman pointed again, more emphatically.

"What's behind that door?"

She came closer, as if to push him back with her body, still pointing back toward the stairs.

"I get the message," Steiger said. He turned around as if to obey, then spun around again quickly and plucked the spear out of her hands. "All right, now we're going to—"

He ducked quickly and the spear thrown by the other woman passed inches over his head and fell clattering on the stairs behind him. The woman whose spear he had taken grabbed at it, attempting to wrestle it away from him. Steiger twisted to one side and used her strength and momentum to throw her off her feet. The other woman came at him quickly and Steiger held the spear toward her, point first, but she didn't even slow down. Only by jerking the spear away at the last moment did Steiger prevent her from impaling herself on its point.

"Are you crazy? What—"

She was on him and he had to toss the spear behind him to grapple with her. Then her companion joined the fray and Steiger quickly found his hands full. He used a judo throw to flip the first one away from him, then grasped the arm of the second and pivoted, turning her around in front of him and forcing her hand up behind her back in an armlock. She continued struggling and Steiger increased the pressure. It seemed to have no effect. He kept up the pressure, turning her to keep her body between himself and the second woman, who had recovered from his throw and was trying to get at him. Neither of them made a sound as they fought.

Steiger suddenly heard a snapping sound and felt a looseness in the woman's arm. He had broken it and she did not even cry out. He pushed her away and they both came back at him. One of them held a dagger. He had no choice but to stop holding back. He executed a spinning wheel kick and sent the knife flying out of her grasp. She went after it and her companion, now also armed with a blade, came at him. He trapped her wrist, spun backwards into her body and delivered a hard elbow strike into her solar plexus. It should have taken all the fight out of her, but she merely sagged, struggling for breath, while the other woman launched herself at him.

He blocked the knife thrust and delivered a punishing hammer-first blow to the bridge of her nose, breaking it. Blood spurted, but again there was no outcry and the woman kept at him. He smashed a blow into her midsection, knocking the wind out of her, but as she bent over, fighting for breath, her companion was already regaining hers and preparing to rush at him again.

"All right, ladies," Steiger said, breathing hard himself. "From here on in, it's hardball."

As the woman launched herself at him, Steiger's foot arced up in a powerful sidekick and caught her in the throat, smashing the trachea. Blood gushed from her mouth, but she still came at him for several steps before she fell, gargling hideously. Behind them, the heavy wooden door opened and a hooded figure came out. The moment he saw what was happening, he bolted back inside and slammed the door shut. Almost fatally distracted, Steiger twisted at the last moment and his breath hissed out in pain as the dagger slashed along his side. He smashed his elbow into the woman's temple, then drove a hard right into her stomach, doubling her over, and brought the edge of his hand down hard upon the back of her neck, breaking it. She fell to the floor, motionless.

Steiger was at the door in an instant, tugging on it, but it was bolted from inside. He quickly turned and picked up one of the long daggers, jamming it into the narrow gap between the door and the wall, working the blade in and up against the crossbar on the other side. He felt it lift and he pulled back on the door, opening it wide.

Behind the door was a small, rectangular room with stone walls and a stone floor. Illumination was provided by two torches set into the walls. There was no sign of the hooded figure. Pushed against the walls were several crudely made, low wooden tables upon which the nude bodies of beautiful young women were stacked like cordwood.

They were all clearly lifeless, but there were no signs of decomposition nor was there any evidence of the smells associated with death. He approached the tables and examined one of the bodies intently. With the exception of the fact that all signs of life were absent, the woman looked merely asleep. The body was perfectly formed, as were all the others, and on the inside of the back of the left thigh, Steiger found a tiny tattoo. A serial number. A quick examination showed that other bodies had the same tattoo, all the numbers different, but varying by no more than several digits.

"*Androids,*" Steiger said in a low voice.

He hurried into the outer chamber and quickly stripped the clothing off the two guards, then dragged them into the storage cell. He wiped off the blood—it had to be synthetic, he thought—with one of the chitons the androids had been wearing and then wadded up the clothing and tucked it beneath the stacked bodies. Then he lifted up each one and added it to the stacks, arranging the bodies carefully. He ran back up the stairs, checked to make sure the corridor was clear and encountered Finn and Andre coming the other way.

"Creed," said Andre, "we found out something about these women. They're all—"

"Androids," said Steiger.

Delaney stared at him. "How did you know?"

"I just had a nasty tussle with a couple of them in the cellar. They're dead, if that's the proper term. There's a whole roomful of inactive androids down there, stacked up in piles. Run numbers tattooed on the backs of their inner thighs, where you wouldn't notice them unless you were a lot closer than you should be. And our hooded friend was down there, as well. He got a good look at me while I was fighting with the android guards stationed in front of that storage room. He ducked back into the room and by the time I got in there, he was gone. The only way he could have gotten out without my seeing him was through a secret passage or by clocking out."

"You were right," said Delaney. "This changes everything. They're onto us for sure."

"It still doesn't explain the centaur, though," said Andre. "There's no way an android could have gotten by that examination, no matter how sophisticated it was."

"There's no time to think about that now," said Delaney. "We've got to get out of here and fast."

"Good luck convincing the Argonauts to leave," said Andre. "They're having a high old time, enjoying the feast and watching the dancing girls. We've got a problem."

"Let's not panic," Steiger said. "They may not find the bodies right away. I stripped them down and piled them on top of the others. And unless our hooded friend gets to Hypsipyle, she's going to be busy with the entertainment for a while. My guess is that she's probably human. If we can get her alone, maybe we can get some answers. Let's go back to

the feast before she sends someone to the bath looking for
us."

"What happens if our hooded friend clocks back with rein-
forcements?" asked Delaney.

"We'll burn that bridge when we get to it. We've probably
been blown right from the beginning. I'd like to know why
nobody's come after us yet."

"It does look as if we're following a script," said Andre.
"Only what *is* the script?"

"Nothing to do but follow it and see," said Steiger.
"Maybe if we improvise some changes, we'll force their
hand."

"What bothers me is *why,*" said Delaney. "It just doesn't
make any sense. It almost looks as if they're trying to create
some sort of a disruption in their own timeline!"

"Or maybe it's the other way around," Steiger said.

"What do you mean?" asked Andre.

"Maybe the convergence effect has caused a disruption in
their history that they're attempting to adjust," said Steiger.
"We've apparently become involved in some sort of complex
plot and I find it hard to believe that all this was staged ex-
pressly for our benefit. I can't think of a reason for it. What if
we've accidentally stumbled into one of their temporal adjustments?"

"It would explain a lot," said Delaney. "If that's the case,
then it increases our chances of creating a significant disruption in their timeline. All we have to do is sabotage their adjustment."

"It also increases the risk," said Andre.

"We'd have to know what their plan was before we could
interfere," said Steiger. "Otherwise, we just might wind up
accomplishing their mission for them. Besides, we could be
wrong. We simply don't have enough information. The hooded
man seems to be the key. He keeps turning up at all the right
places. If we could only get our hands on him . . ."

"So what's our next move?" said Andre. "Do we try to in-
terrogate Hypsipyle?"

"If we get the chance," said Steiger, "but it would be very
risky. This whole thing is liable to blow up on us at any time,
the moment those two androids I put down are discovered.
No, unless we get a clear shot, I don't think we should chance
it. They're going through this charade with the Argonauts for
a reason. I say we change the game plan on them. We've got to

get the Argonauts to leave. At least it will buy us time."

"Only how do we break up the party?" asked Andre.

Delaney snapped his fingers. "Hercules!"

"What?"

"Why not use the myth to our advantage?" Delaney said. "According to the story, Hercules became outraged that the Argonauts were carrying on with women when they had a mission to accomplish. You saw what he was like when his temper was aroused."

"Yeah, I saw," said Steiger. "And it makes me wonder. That kind of strength is more than a little inhuman, wouldn't you say?"

Andre shut her eyes. "I don't want to know about it," she said, wearily. "Hercules an android, too? This is insane."

"Before our paranoia completely runs away with us," Delaney said, "remember there have been lots of documented cases of strongmen capable of breaking chains and bending iron. Hercules may be unbelievably strong, but he seems human enough to me. Besides, I've never heard of an android that stutters. And he loses his stutter when he's angry, like some people who stutter lose it when they're singing or otherwise preoccupied. That's a purely human characteristic."

"All right, you've got a point," said Steiger, "but I'm not taking anything at face value anymore. Whichever way it goes, we can always scrub the mission and clock out. But I want to get to the bottom of this somehow."

"I think we're all agreed on that," said Andre.

"Okay, then. Let's see what we can do to get the Argonauts moving before all hell breaks loose."

"Too late," said Delaney.

Hypsipyle was walking swiftly down the corridor in the vanguard of about twenty android Amazons. On seeing them, she pointed and shouted, "There they are! Seize them!"

As the androids started forward, Delaney charged unexpectedly. He ploughed into them, moving fast and low. In the narrow corridor, there was no room for them to spread out and he bowled several over, pushing past the others to grab at Hypsipyle and spin her around in front of him, his arm across her throat applying pressure.

"Call them off or I'll break your neck," he said.

"Stay where you are!" said Hypsipyle, her voice cracking slightly. The androids froze where they stood, looking at her expressionlessly.

"All right," said Delaney, "now you tell them to head back to the main chamber and we'll follow. If any of them makes a move against us, I'll start breaking things in this lovely body."

She did as she was told and the androids filed past Delaney. They all went into the main chamber, where the party had almost completely broken up. The music had stopped and there was no more revelry and dancing. About half the Argonauts were passed out on the floor, the others were slumping in a stupor, on the verge of unconsciousness. Steiger ran over to Hercules, who sat with his back against a wall, shaking his head slowly and trying to focus his gaze.

"Hercules! Hercules, come on, wake up!" He slapped the strongman several times, then checked his eyes. "They've all been drugged!"

The androids in the room all stared at Hypsipyle, as if awaiting instructions. None of them spoke.

"What have you done to them?" said Delaney, squeezing her throat.

She coughed and gasped for breath. "If you harm me, none of you will leave here alive."

"Perhaps," said Delaney. "And perhaps with you dead, none of them will know what to do. It's not as if they're living, reasoning beings, is it?"

"I—I do not understand."

"I think you do. Now answer my question."

"There—there was a potent sleeping draught mixed into their wine," she said.

"Why?"

She did not answer and he squeezed harder, blocking off the flow of blood to her brain just long enough to bring her to the brink of unconsciousness.

"Why?"

She gasped and coughed. "I do not know. I swear it! I merely did as I was told."

"Told? By whom?"

"By—by Hermes."

"Hermes?" said Steiger.

"The messenger of the gods. He who hides his face so that mortals may not look upon it."

"Sound familiar?" Andre said.

"Tell them to bring all our weapons here," said Delaney. "Do precisely as I say and we'll let you go unharmed. Otherwise—"

"I—I will tell them."

She directed the androids to return the weapons of the Argonauts and they silently moved to follow her orders.

"You think maybe she really doesn't know?" said Andre.

"I don't know," said Delaney. "It's possible. The truth now," he said to Hypsipyle. "There *are* no men here, are there?"

She shook her head.

"And no children? No old people?"

She shook her head again.

"Of course," said Delaney. "No one grows old here, do they?"

Hypsipyle burst into tears. "I was promised! I was promised that I, too, would never age! I was promised that if I took care of them I would be their queen and live forever!"

"She may be a terrific actress, Finn," said Andre, "but I believe her. Look at her. She's terrified."

Steiger looked at her closely and nodded. "She's coming down with the cold sweats, all right."

"What are you saying? I do not understand you!"

Delaney switched back to Greek. "What happened to the women in the cellar?"

"They broke faith with the gods and their immortality was taken from them. They suffered for their lack of faith, as you too shall suffer!"

"Perhaps we shall," said Delaney. "Now listen carefully, your life depends upon it. I want you to tell them to pick up our weapons, and the Argonauts, and carry them all back to our ship. We'll be watching closely, so don't try any tricks. Tell them."

It was a strange procession through the woods to the shore of Lemnos, androids carrying weapons followed by others carrying the limp bodies of the Argonauts, with the temporal agents and Queen Hypsipyle bringing up the rear, Creed and Andre supporting a groggy, semi-conscious Hercules between them. They came out of the woods and saw the *Argo* riding gracefully at anchor just offshore. Delaney hailed the ship.

"Telamon! Argus!"

There was no response.

He called again. "Oileus! Idmon! Mopsus!"

Silence.

"What happened to them?" Delaney said, tightening his arm around Hypsipyle's throat. "Where are they?"

"Still aboard your ship," she said, weakly. Delaney could feel her trembling. "No doubt asleep by now. Wine was brought to them with a message from Jason, saying that you were all being feasted generously and promising to send men back to take their place so that they could come ashore and partake as well. Meanwhile, here was wine for them."

"Very clever. I hope you're telling the truth. Andre, go out to the ship and make ready to sail. And you, Your Highness, tell your subjects to take the weapons and the men and put them aboard our ship. Remember, at the first sign of trickery, I'll wring your neck."

Delaney and Steiger watched carefully as the androids carried the weapons and the unconscious Argonauts out to the ship and Andre helped lift them aboard.

"All right, Creed, go on out."

Steiger nodded. "I'll signal when we're ready to cast off. Watch yourself."

"You will die for this," said Hypsipyle. "You cannot defy the gods! You cannot escape their vengeance!"

"Shut up, Your Majesty."

She gasped for breath and coughed again as Delaney applied pressure to her throat and then released it. Steiger soon gave his signal from the ship and when the last android had waded back ashore, Delaney ordered Hypsipyle to send them back to the palace. After the last one was out of sight, he shoved her forward hard and she fell sprawling on the beach.

"Go back to your subjects," he said and turned to wade out to the ship.

Hypsipyle scrambled to her feet and started running toward the woods. *"Come back!"* she screamed at the top of her lungs. *"Come back! Kill them! Kill them all!"*

"Goddamn you—" Delaney started splashing out toward the ship as fast as the water would allow him. He was about halfway out when they came running out of the woods, sprinting down the beach.

"Cast off!" he shouted. *"Cast off!"*

He saw the anchor being hauled up and the sail being raised and he dived forward into the shallow water and started swimming furiously. The large sail luffed and then filled as Steiger turned the *Argo* into the wind. The ship began to move. Andre shouted at him to hurry and threw a rope over the side. He pulled himself aboard and glanced back. The androids were halfway out to the ship. On deck, the Argonauts all lay sprawled, unconscious. Hercules was snoring.

"It might get a bit sticky," Steiger called to them from the tiller.

Finn and Andre both grabbed swords from the pile of weapons. The wind was not strong and the ship moved slowly in the bay. With a spray of water, one of the androids leaped up out of the bay like a porpoise and grasped the side. Andre hit it in the face with the flat of her sword and the android fell back. Two more climbed up over the side and Delaney kicked one off and ran the other through. The ship was moving more quickly now, leaving the shallow water. Some of the androids were being left behind, but that still left others who had been in the forefront swimming beside the ship and trying to climb on board. Delaney grabbed one of the oars and swept several of them off deck while Andre was kept busy knocking them off with her sword. And then they were all falling behind as the ship outdistanced them, picking up speed and heading out to sea. From the shore, they could barely hear Hypsipyle screaming after them.

Delaney dropped the oar to the deck and took a deep breath. "Well, that was certainly stimulating."

"What, you tired?" Steiger shouted, from the steersman's post. "Who's going to trim the sail?"

Delaney shot him an obscene gesture.

"What do we tell these sleeping beauties when they wake up?" asked Andre, looking down at the senseless Greeks.

"Why don't we tell them what a great time we all had?" said Delaney.

Andre grimaced. "They're liable not to remember it."

"So? You think that'll be a problem?"

"Won't it?"

Delaney shook his head. "I doubt it. I've yet to meet a Greek who would admit he couldn't hold his liquor."

6 _____

When the Argonauts awoke, aided by buckets of seawater poured over them, they were surprised to find that they were back aboard the ship. As their hangovers subsided, their departure hastened by the brisk sea air, the Argonauts spoke of the beautiful women of Lemnos and the wonderful adventure they had, each of them embellishing upon imaginary amorous exploits. Not one of them would admit to any lapse of memory, although a few of them did confess that drink had dulled their senses slightly.

They even "remembered" how they had staggered back to the ship and set sail, setting course for Thrace. That they had been able to accomplish this while drunk convinced them of their natural ability as sailors. Finn Delaney chose not to disabuse them of this notion. Ahead of them still lay the Sea of Marmora and the Euxine Sea, which would one day be known as the Black Sea. He felt they'd learn the true extent of their sailing abilities soon enough.

The winds were fair and Tiphys took the tiller while Orpheus led the Argonauts in an improvised song about themselves, the chorus of which was the refrain, "The Argonauts are we; men of the open sea."

"Pray for fair weather," Delaney said to Steiger.

"Storms are among the least of my worries," Steiger said as the Argonauts bellowed the chorus of their self-glorifying song. "I just wish Hypsipyle had given us some answers."

"I really don't think she could have," said Delaney. "Her terror seemed genuine. I don't believe she knew those women weren't human beings."

"It doesn't make any sense," said Steiger. "If the people from the future of this timeline wanted the Argonauts to fail in their quest, why not simply clock back a small submarine and sink the ship? There are any number of ways they could accomplish it with far less trouble. We all could have been killed while we were unconscious in that cell. Damn it, Finn, none of this adds up!"

"It has to add up somehow," said Delaney. "On one hand, the events—or the orchestration of events—are following those of our myth very closely. On the other hand, they seem to be aiming for a totally different result. And they're taking a lot of risks to do it. I can't understand it, either. How do we know what to do? Ot what *not* to do?"

"I don't know," said Steiger. "They have to know about us, yet they haven't made any serious effort to knock us out of the picture. It's as if they *want* us with the Argonauts."

"If your theory is right that we've stumbled into one of their temporal adjustments, then there has to be a key moment in the scenario that's crucial. Maybe that's what they're saving us for."

Steiger nodded. "Maybe. But we're still only guessing."

"I keep thinking about those androids," said Delaney. "By the standards of our artificial intelligence technology, they were relatively unsophisticated. That doesn't fit in with the centaur. If the centaur was an android too, then it's so advanced that none of our tests revealed it for what it was. And if it was genetically engineered, then that indicates a level of technology that should have enabled them to build better androids. If they were capable of such sophisticated technology, why didn't they follow through with it on Lemnos?"

Steiger swore through clenched teeth. "There has to be something we're overlooking. I've never been in a temporal scenario that was so damned inconsistent."

"You've never been in another universe, either," said Delaney.

"So what are you saying, that this universe isn't logical? I don't buy that. There has to be a logical framework to all of this. It's got to be there. We're just not seeing it."

The wind picked up and the Argonauts shipped their oars as the lateen sail filled and the *Argo* began making good headway in the blow. They sailed past Samothrace through the Hellespont and into the Sea of Marmora, the spray soaking them all thoroughly as the bow of the ship rose and fell crashing into the waves. Not a few of the "men of the open sea" wound up hanging over the side, contributing to the volume of the water. By the end of the day, the winds died down and they were rowing along the Mysian coast.

They had failed to properly provision the ship at Lemnos and stores were running dangerously low. As they dropped anchor and waded ashore, a large group of people came running down to greet them. It was a friendly reception by the Dalions, ruled by King Cyzicus, and the Argonauts were invited to the palace by emissaries of the king. When they arrived, they found a feast being prepared in their honor. King Cyzicus greeted them warmly, offering to provision their ship with food, water and wine as well as clothing to replace their worn and soiled garments.

It was clear that the Dalions were not a wealthy people, but they spared nothing in making the Argonauts feel welcome. During the feast, musicians played and a wrestling exhibition was staged. Young women came out to dance for them and children brought them garlands of flowers.

"We are grateful for this kind reception," Jason told the king. "When we return, we shall sing the praises of Dalion hospitality and of the goodness of King Cyzicus. Would that we could somehow repay your kindness."

Cyzicus suddenly looked tired. "In truth, I had hoped you would respond in such a manner, as I could see from the beginning that all of you were warriors. We have but few soldiers of our own and my people are sorely beset by a fearsome enemy who plunders us at will."

"Fear not, Cyzicus," said Theseus. "If you have enemies who prey upon you, you have but to name them and they are vanquished."

"This is one enemy that will not be vanquished easily," said

Cyzicus, "if, indeed, they can be vanquished at all."

"What manner of men are these fearsome foes?" asked Jason.

"These are not men, but giants," Cyzicus said. "Each of them possesses not two arms, but six. And in the hand of each arm is held a heavy wooden club that with one blow can crush a skull or break all of a man's ribs. They descend upon us from the hills and seize our harvests and our livestock. There is nothing we can do to stop them. Our bravest men have fallen to them and our fairest women have been carried off."

"Be they men with two arms or giants with six," said Jason, "I was not taught to refuse help to those in need of it, nor is it in my blood to flee from danger. You have welcomed us and treated us as honored guests. You have acted honorably and we can do no less. What say you men? Shall we give these six-armed titans a foe worthy of doing battle with them?"

"Just how big are these giants, anyway?" Delaney said, but his question was lost in the cheer given by the others.

The Argonauts gathered up their weapons and followed Cyzicus outside, where they were joined by a group of soldiers who led them to the stables. Within a short time, they were mounted and riding toward the hills. The three temporal agents hung back at the rear so they could talk without being overheard.

"Six-armed giants?" Andre said.

"I know what you're thinking," said Delaney. "I'm thinking the same thing."

"First Amazons, now six-armed giants?" Steiger said. "What in God's name is going on here? What are these people doing, clocking androids back here by the dozens?"

"Why would androids carry off their women?" said Delaney.

"It almost seems as if they studied the events and creatures of our Greek mythology and are trying to duplicate them," Andre said.

Steiger stared at her. "That's a hell of an idea," he said.

"Let's run with it for a minute," said Delaney. "*The Argonautica* of Apollonius is supposedly based on actual historical events which became mythologized over the years. The situation here seems similar. Let's assume we're confronted with an attempt to recreate those mythical events and *make* them real. Why?"

"Is it possible they could be trying to redirect the flow of
their own history for some specific purpose?" Andre said.

"That would amount to creating a split in their own timeline," said Delaney. "Why would they want to jeopardize
their own temporal stability?"

"We keep coming back to square one," said Steiger. "No
matter what kind of explanation we come up with, nothing
about this scenario seems to fit together. We're not getting
anywhere."

"We're getting closer to Colchis," Andre said. "If events
continue to progress according to the myth, then that has to be
the focal point of this scenario."

"Then why use androids to try to stop the Argonauts at
Lemnos?" asked Delaney.

"It leads nowhere again," said Steiger. "Every hypothetical
scenario we put together falls apart from inconsistencies."

"Maybe that's where we're going wrong," said Andre.
"We keep trying to come up with rational explanations."

"Meaning there's an irrational one?" said Steiger. "We're
back to the supernatural again? It's going to take a lot of convincing to get me to buy that."

"If the answer keeps coming out incorrect, something has
to be wrong with the equation," Andre said.

"So let's take another look at the equation," said Delaney.
"Let's go back to the beginning and take it one step at a time.
A number of factors seem to indicate that the people from the
future of this timeline are attempting to construct a temporal
scenario based upon the voyage of the Argonauts. We have
the centaur and the incident at Delphi, plus the hooded man
who keeps turning up everywhere. He may be with us on the
voyage, posing as one of the Argonauts or there may be other
explanations for his sudden appearances and disappearances,
as well as for the centaur and what we saw at Delphi, but the
androids at Lemnos can't be explained away. We're assuming
our cover has been blown. We can't get rid of our warp discs.
Our only alternative is to abort the mission and run if they
close in. Only they haven't closed in. Why? Because they've
made that choice or because they haven't had an opportunity?"

"They've had plenty of opportunities," said Steiger.

"'Have they? I'm not so sure. Maybe we're making some
incorrect assumptions. Let's take the centaur first. What are

the odds of a creature like that having evolved naturally?''

"I should think it would require a radically different evolutionary process in this universe," said Steiger, "involving significantly different life forms. Nothing we've seen so far supports that. If the centaur didn't evolve naturally, then that leaves us with either magic or some sort of genetic engineering, including the possibility of android technology advanced beyond our level. The think-tank boys in Archives Section considered the possibility of magic based on prior intelligence that certain physical laws in this universe may be different from ours. But we've seen no real evidence of that. Until we do, I'm going to look for *rational* explanations. So the only rational explanation possible is that the centaur is an artificially created being. The hooded man is linked with both the centaur and the androids, which supports that theory. The centaur is considerably more sophisticated than the android women, so it's either a more advanced model or a genetically engineered creature."

"But that still leaves us with several elements that don't seem to fit together," said Andre. "If the centaur was sent through the confluence to draw us in, then for what purpose? So they could capture us and wring us dry? They could have done that before we ever got to Iolchos or at any time during the construction of the *Argo*. Did they intend to use us as part of their scenario? Again, why? Why not use their own people? Why risk our disrupting their timeline? And if they wanted us alive to use us, why did Hypsipyle order the androids to kill us? And why would they be careless enough to let us discover that the Lemnos women were androids in the first place?"

"I think our original assumption was correct," Delaney said. "The centaur came through the confluence by accident. As a result, we crossed over and stumbled into a temporal adjustment scenario of some sort. If we assume the opposition never detected us, then there was no reason for them to expect anyone from our timeline on the scene because they didn't know about the confluence."

He looked at Steiger. "Remember when you followed the hooded man in Iolchos and someone jumped you? If there was no reason for anyone to suspect we were anything but what we appeared to be, the logical assumption for them to make was that you were following the hooded man to find out who Jason's secret benefactors were. It never occurred to them that you might be a temporal agent from another timeline, so it never occurred to them to check you for a warp disc. If we work from that assumption, then that means our cover was still safe at that point. It would explain why they never moved against us while we were unconscious in the cell at Lemnos. They didn't know who we really were. The only other time when our cover might have been blown occurred when the hooded man saw you fight those two androids. I'm sure that even in this universe, ancient Greeks never used combat karate. But could that have tipped him off? You said he pulled a fast disappearing act. Could he have put it all together so quickly? He saw you using modern fighting techniques, but it's still a long jump to make from realizing that to concluding you were from another timeline.''

Steiger nodded. "He could have checked with someone and reported what he saw, asked if anyone knew what the hell was going on. They may have problems of their own we know nothing about.''

"And meanwhile,'' said Delaney, "we were getting the hell out of there and in the process, I didn't exactly treat Hypsipyle in a very queenly manner. If she wasn't part of their adjustment team, but just a local they were using, then she obviously wouldn't have been fully briefed. So she lost her temper and ordered the androids to kill us on her own. It's possible they never meant to kill the Argonauts.''

Steiger expelled a heavy breath. "So that means I'm the one who blew our cover. Great. Some pro I turned out to be.''

"You couldn't have known the hooded man would be there,'' said Delaney. "What's more, you weren't exactly in a position to make lots of choices.''

"There's still a chance we haven't been found out,'' Andre said. "At least, not all the way. If the hooded man is one of the Argonauts, he knows the three of us are together, but he may not have had enough time to make his report.''

"It's possible,'' said Steiger, "but he could have clocked ahead, made his report, then clocked back.''

"Maybe not,'' said Andre. "You said he got out of there in one hell of a hurry. He would have had to make several rather tricky temporal transitions. He had to cut it pretty close. All the Argonauts were accounted for when we got back to the main room of the palace.''

"It could explain why no one's made a move against us up

'til now," Delaney said. "But we're still left with some big problems. Until we know what their scenario is, we can't work against it effectively. The scope of it means they have to have a sizable team running this operation and we have no way of knowing who *they* are."

"Well, at least we managed to come up with a rational explanation that accounts for all the inconsistencies," said Steiger. "I think we can put the Archives boys and their cockamamie theories about magic right where they belong. We've finally got a logical sequence of events to work with."

"Now all we have to do is figure out what they mean," said Andre. "Why are they recreating the myth of Jason and the Argonauts down to the last detail?"

"Maybe it's a dress rehearsal," said Delaney.

"What?" said Steiger.

"What if all this is just . . . some sort of war game? What if they're on maneuvers?"

"Maneuvers?" Steiger said. "What are you talking about?"

"Andre just gave me a really wild idea—recreating the story of Jason and the Argonauts down to the last detail. Why would they want to take a myth based on a historical incident and run an operation that would turn the historical incident into the myth itself?"

"Whoa," said Steiger. "You've lost me." His horse came to a halt. "Not *you,*" said Steiger, giving the horse a kick. "All right, now run this by me again?"

"Considering what our situation is," Delaney said, "we have to examine every possibility, no matter how off-the-wall it may sound. I admit this one sounds pretty farfetched, but think about it. Maybe it won't seem quite so crazy. Remember what happened on our last mission in the Khyber. They discovered a confluence point and crossed over with a mission team to set up an operation. They mobilized the Pathan tribes and took advantage of an uprising to bring troops in. They had a good plan, but much of it depended on a great deal of improvisation in a timeline they were unfamiliar with. Remember how they controlled the Pathans?"

"They played on their superstitions," Andre replied. "They posed as gods."

"And the hooded man seems to be doing the same thing," Steiger said.

"Exactly," said Delaney. "You said if they wanted to sabotage the voyage of the Argonauts, there were easier ways to do it. But suppose that *isn't* what they want? Suppose what they're actually doing is making sure their temporal continuity isn't disturbed while they conduct what is essentially a trial operation, maybe even two operations—a practice temporal adjustment under controlled conditions and a dress rehearsal for massive temporal disruption in our timeline?"

"You're right," said Steiger. "It does sound crazy. It would mean risking temporal disruptions in their own timeline."

"True," said Andre, "but would the interference be significant enough to endanger their temporal continuity? They've dropped the androids on a relatively remote island, where they remain. The Dalions, too, are isolated in a tiny kingdom, surrounded by high country. The centaur is on Mount Pelion, living in a cave—all relatively isolated locations in which they can control the variable factors. If they wanted to test their temporal adjustment capabilities under controlled conditions, they couldn't have made better choices. In our timeline, there's hardly any documentation of this period at all. Travel was severely limited and what communication there was took place on the most primitive levels. It would be a very simple matter for them to keep one step ahead of the Argonauts and clean up any problems after they've moved on. How great could the potential risks be?"

"There would still be risks," Delaney said, "but if they're not as experienced with temporal adjustments as we are, it would be worthwhile taking them. We're at war and they need to develop strategy and train the troops."

"And by using androids," Steiger said, "they'd be minimizing the danger to their personnel. They could also be testing out the feasibility of using androids in offensive operations directed against our timeline. Finn, maybe your idea's not so crazy, after all. Androids make great cannon fodder. They don't retreat and they fight 'til they drop. They could be experimenting with different types of androids—the women on Lemnos, the giants here, if that's what they are—"

With a scream, a body landed upon Steiger, knocking him from his horse. It was a body twice as big as he was, with an unusually long torso from which sprouted six muscular arms. The creature was matted with hair so that it almost seemed covered with fur. It looked like a human spider with four of its arms wrapped around Steiger, pinning him to the ground, while the two remaining arms pummeled him with blows. Andre unsheathed her sword and brought it down hard upon the creature's neck, decapitating it with one stroke. Warm blood spurted from its neck and splattered Steiger.

The things were leaping down upon the Argonauts from the rocks above, screaming as they fell, knocking the riders from their horses. Andre wheeled her horse and avoided one, then managed to shake loose another that had landed on her horse behind her. Delaney was brought down, but he broke the creature's grip and slashed his sword across its face. It did not even cry out. A second blow with the sword split its skull and it fell.

Several of the king's soldiers died in the initial assault, but none of the Argonauts had fallen. While they were at best barely adequate as sailors, in hand to hand combat, each was in his element. The few who were not warriors, such as Mopsus, Idmon and young Hylas, had stayed behind at the palace. Jason and Theseus stood back to back, laying about them with their swords. Hercules caught one of the giants on the fly, then dropped the creature on his knee, breaking its back. He unslung his bow, which no one but he could pull, and started to let loose his long war arrows. Each one found a mark.

Only a killing blow would stop the giants. They didn't seem to feel lesser wounds at all. If one arm was cut off, the others would continue fighting. The battle raged as the sky darkened and visibility grew poorer. Hercules ran out of arrows and drew his sword, striking such powerful strokes that his opponents were cut cleanly in half. A club struck Andre's sword arm and it went numb from her hand up to her shoulder. As the giant struck again, she rolled, avoiding the blow, and came up with her sword held in her left hand, but a sword point ripped through the giant's chest as Orpheus ran it through from behind and the creature fell.

The battle seemed to last for hours, but at the end, the Argonauts emerged victorious. When it was over, the ground was littered with the bodies of dead giants, as well as those of soldiers and several of the Argonauts. They had lost Euphemus, as well as Admetus, Pirithous, Menoetius, Zetes and Calais. Most of the surviving Argonauts were covered with blood, if not their own, then that of the giants. Tiphys had sustained the most severe injuries. Meleager had been knocked unconscious and King Cyzicus was dead, transfixed by an arrow shot by Hercules. It had struck its target with such force that it passed completely through the giant and penetrated the ruler of the Dalions.

"Some maneuvers," Steiger said to Delaney as they stared down at the dead king. "If these are war games, friend, they're playing them for keeps."

"I checked one of the bodies to see if the giants had any run numbers tattooed on them, like the Lemnos women did," said Andre.

"And?"

"I couldn't find any."

"That doesn't prove they weren't androids," Steiger said.

"True," said Andre. "But it also doesn't prove they were."

7

They accompanied a party of Dalions into the hills the next day and returned to the scene of the battle. The Dalions surmised that the surviving giants had carried off their dead, because there were no corpses to be found. Shortly before nightfall, they found the caves where the giants had been living. There was no sign of the six-armed creatures, but there was evidence that the caves had been abandoned in a hurry. They did not discover any of the women whom the giants had carried off, but they discovered clothing that had belonged to them. They also discovered an item of clothing that seemed too large for a woman and too small for a giant.

Steiger held up the hooded cloak. "You suppose it's just a coincidence?" he said, not sounding as if he believed it.

"It could have belonged to anyone," Delaney said.

"And it could also have been left behind on purpose," Andre said.

"Somebody's playing cat and mouse with us," said Steiger grimly, "and I'm not in the mood for games."

They returned to the town and attended the funeral for King Cyzicus, the soldiers who had died with him and their fellow

Argonauts who fell in battle. In honor of the dead, the Dalions held games in which all their finest athletes participated. The day after the ceremonies, the Dalions provisioned the *Argo*, as Cyzicus had promised, and the Argonauts set sail once again. With Tiphys badly injured and feverish, Argus took the tiller as they rowed along the Mysian shore, past the mouth of the Rhindacus to the Bay of Arganthus. They sailed on through the Bosporous and as the day neared its end, they were approaching the Euxine Sea.

Jason directed Argus to steer in toward a sheltered cove because a storm was brewing. On the heights above, they could see a structure with tall marble columns that looked like a temple. When they came ashore, they found a pathway leading up to it running alongside the cliff. The sky grew dark as they approached the structure and it began to thunder. Jagged lightning flashes lit up the sky. The rain came pelting down and they ran inside the temple to find shelter. It was dark inside the ruined edifice and it appeared to be deserted.

"We will rest here for the night and wait out the storm," said Jason. "We cannot be far from the Euxine Sea. Once we leave the Bosporous, we can follow the coastline and it should bring us to Colchis."

"I have an intuition that our journey shall not be an easy one," said Idmon, frowning. "And I also feel that we must leave this place at once."

"Why?" said Theseus. "There is nothing here."

From somewhere within the temple echoed a screeching sound.

"What was that?" said Theseus.

"It must have been the wind," said Argus. "This place is deserted."

"Not quite deserted," Hylas said, pointing.

A very old man in filthy robes was slowly coming toward them with a shambling gait, holding his arms out before him. His hair was long and gray, hanging to his shoulders. He looked emaciated.

"Who is there?" he shouted. "Is someone there? I was certain I heard voices! *Is anyone there?"*

"I am Jason, King of Iolchos and captain of the Argonauts. We did not mean to intrude upon your home, old man. We only came seeking shelter from the storm."

The old man stopped and his arms fell to his sides. "There *is* someone," he said, with obvious relief. "Thank the gods. I thought surely I was going mad. Who spoke? Where are you?"

"We stand before you, old man," Theseus said. "Can you not see?"

"No, I cannot," he said in a quivering voice. "I am blind. I am poor, blind, cursed Phineus, once king of Bithynia, now no more than a half-mad penitent who lives in this cold, dreary abandoned place."

"My apologies, King Phineus, for coming unbidden to your home," said Jason. "But why, if this place is so wretched, do you remain?"

"Because I may not leave," said Phineus. "They will not let me."

"Who will not let you?" Jason asked. "Who keeps you here?"

"It is my penance to remain here and suffer for my sins," said the old man, as if he hadn't heard. "You will not remain. I know it. They will drive you from this place. It has been years since I have heard another human voice. How I have longed for it!"

"He is mad," said Theseus.

"He is starving," said Idmon. "Look at him. He is nothing but skin and bone. Reduced to such a state, what man would not go mad?"

"Come closer, King Phineus," said Jason. "Come, we shall not harm you. Come and share our food."

The old man licked his lips and took one step forward, then moved back again. "No! No, I dare not! They will not allow it! Perhaps, if I stay here, at a distance, they will not disturb you. Perhaps they will allow you to remain awhile, until the storm has cleared, and I can at least take pleasure in the sound of human voices. Perhaps, for just one night, for just one hour, they may give me peace."

"Whom do you speak of?" Jason said. "Who is it that torments you so?"

"Creatures of his poor, deluded mind, no doubt," said Argus.

"Creatures!" cried Phineus. "Yes, they are creatures, my tormentors, but not creatures of my mind! Would that they were! Listen! Listen! Did you not hear the flapping of their wings?"

Jason approached him. "There is no one, Phineus. Come, rest with us. You are hungry. We have enough to share."

"No! Stay away!"

Jason took his arm and the touch seemed to terrify the old blind king. He shrank from it, but Jason gently led him back to join the others, where they all sat upon the floor.

"Come and sit with us," said Jason soothingly. "There is no need to be afraid. None will harm you here. We have wine and food that we shall gladly share with you."

As Orpheus passed him a leather sack which contained some of their provisions, a piercing, inhuman shriek echoed throughout the temple. Something swooped down upon them with such speed they never even saw it clearly, feeling only the wind of its passage. The sack was plucked away from Orpheus and he fell back as whatever it was came out of its impossibly fast glide and flew above them. They heard the beating of great wings, like the sounds made by a sail luffing in the wind.

Phineus let out a wail and covered his head with his hands as the Argonauts jumped to their feet.

"By the gods!" swore Theseus. "What *was* that?"

Hercules strung his bow and nocked an arrow. He stared into the gloom above, seeking a target. All was silent in the temple once again, save for the whimpering noises made by the old man.

"Will they never cease?" he cried. "How long can a man live without food? They will not let me eat, nor sleep, nor leave this cursed place! They will see me starve to death in my wretched exile, an old blind king whose people had no further use for him!"

"What manner of birds are these, Phineus?" asked Jason. "I have never heard tell of birds who tormented men in such a manner!"

"Not birds, but harpies," Phineus said. "They are demons! They are the very Furies, themselves, sent by the gods to plague me for my sins!"

"Hercules, behind you!" shouted Argus.

They saw a huge, birdlike shape plummeting down out of the darkness. Even as Hercules spun around, it struck, clipping him with its wings and tearing the bow out of his grasp. They caught a quick glimpse of a large, avian body, about the size of a man's torso, with huge talons and a leathery wingspread of at least twenty or thirty feet.

They heard another feral cry and felt the rush of wind as huge wings passed overhead. Hercules cursed at the loss of his bow. Delaney brought up his own bow and let fly an arrow, but he missed and they heard it strike the ceiling.

"Fast as hell for something that big," he said.

"How many of them are there?" asked Jason.

"I count at least three," said Theseus.

They stood with weapons drawn, waiting for the next attack. It came quickly. They heard the whoosh of something moving with incredible speed and Andre cried out as talons sank into her shoulders, lifting her off the ground. She twisted in the creature's grasp as it bore her up and struck at it repeatedly with her sword. It screeched, a sound somewhere between a woman's scream and an eagle's cry and a moment later, a tangled shape fell out of the air and struck the floor of the temple with an audible impact. They rushed over and found Andre lying on top of the creature. Its body had cushioned her fall, but there were large bloody wounds in her shoulders where the hooked talons had pierced the skin and she was stunned from the shock of the impact.

"Stay by me, boy," said Idmon, putting a protective arm around Hylas and glancing up fearfully.

"By Zeus, look at that!" said Theseus. "Have you ever seen such a creature? The old man spoke the truth. They are demons, indeed!"

The harpy had the body of a giant hawk, with disproportionately large talons and huge, batlike, jointed wings. Its face was that of a woman, but a woman only superficially. The eyes were vulture's eyes, dull yellow and filmed, with a ridge of feathers where the eyebrows should have been. The jaw was outsized, hinged like a snake's, and two sharp, curving fangs protruded from the dead monster's open mouth.

"Are you all right?" said Steiger.

Andre gasped for breath and nodded her head. "I will be as soon as my heart stops fibrillating." She touched her shoulder and winced with pain.

"Well, demons or not, we have downed one of them," said Theseus. "And I, for one, shall not rest until we have accounted for the others! Who attacks one of us attacks us all!"

"Come on then!" Jason cried, his voice echoing off the temple walls. "Show yourselves! Let us see what you can do with men who are not old and blind and weak!"

Steiger bent down over the body of the harpy, examining it carefully. It was bloody where Andre had hacked it with her sword. Steiger dipped his fingers in the blood and sniffed them.

"Creon! Beware!" Hylas shouted.

It came down like a dive bombing eagle, talons outstretched, swooping down on Steiger's exposed back. Hercules moved with amazing speed for such a large man and tackled it. His brawny arms wrapped themselves around the creature's torso and he would have brought it down but for the beating of its wings. It attempted to take flight, but Hercules sagged down, becoming dead weight and the creature was unable to lift his heavy bulk. It shrieked at him, its face darting forward to snap at him, its fangs striking for his throat. He reached out quickly and clamped his fingers around the harpy's throat, just below the jaw. With one hand, he kept the deadly fangs at bay, with the other, he held the creature fast as its wings beat at him and its talons raked his chest.

"Hold it fast, Hercules!" cried Jason, running up with his sword held poised to strike.

"Stay back!" shouted Hercules. "This beast is mine to deal with!"

He forced the creature down, bending it back slowly over his knee and it struggled in vain against his awesome strength, keening wildly. Then they heard the crunch of its spine snapping and it went limp in his grasp. He dropped it and it fell to the floor with a soft thump. When he turned around, they saw his chest was scored with deep talon marks, as if someone had taken a sharp rake to him, yet he showed no sign that he was even aware of what had to be unbelievably painful wounds.

"T-t-two dead," he said, in a perfectly conversational voice. "B-b-b—"

"Bring on the third!" shouted Hylas.

He laid a huge hand on the boy's head, grinned and tousled his hair.

"Spread out," said Theseus. "Give it a chance to strike."

They moved apart, crouching, holding their weapons ready. For several moments, nothing happened. They all stared up into the shadows, looking for any signs of movement. It came from an unexpected direction. The third harpy came in low, its wings tucked back, gliding only inches from the floor. It struck Orpheus and tumbled him to the ground, then Jason spun and hurled his dagger. It buried itself to the hilt in the creature's throat. The harpy skidded to the floor and died in convulsions at their feet with a grotesque, rasping gargle.

"Well thrown," said Orpheus, picking himself up shakily.

Jason bent down and retrieved his dagger. "Foul beast," he said. "They will trouble you no more, Phineus. We—" he stopped, frowning. "Where has he gone?"

There was no sign of the old king.

"The old man must have fled while we fought the harpies," said Orpheus.

"Not very grateful of him, was it?" Theseus said.

"Perhaps, but who can blame him?" said Jason. "A blind old man faced with monsters such as these, is it any wonder he took flight at his first chance? It is not as if he had deserted us. A blind man could not have helped us. He shall have troubles enough making his way in the world. Let us not think ill of him."

"You are wounded, master," Hylas said to Hercules. "And you, my lady." He examined Andre's shoulder. "Does it pain you greatly?"

"Chiron taught us how to heal wounds," said Jason. "Let us return to the ship. The rain has stopped and we would all doubtless sleep safer back aboard the *Argo*. There may be other such creatures about."

"Did you see the old man leave?" Delaney said softly to Steiger.

Steiger shook his head.

"How could someone so frail and blind move so quickly?" said Delaney. "One minute he was there, weeping and wailing, the next he was gone and nobody saw him leave."

"You want to stay behind and search the temple?" asked Steiger.

"The others are already leaving," Delaney said, "and we should see to Andre's wounds. Besides, I'm willing to bet we wouldn't find a thing. Remember how there was no trace of the giants to be found after the battle?"

"But in the legend, the harpies didn't die," said Steiger. "The Argonauts drove them away. If someone's recreating the events of our myth, they're not following the script exactly."

"What did you make of that harpy you were looking at?" Delaney asked. "Another android?"

98   *Simon Hawke*

"It had to be," said Steiger. "I can't bring myself to believe
it was anything else. I can't accept that it could have evolved
naturally and think what it would mean to create a life form
like that in a bioscience lab. One creature, like the centaur, I
might accept, but the giants and now these? Think of the cost,
to say nothing of the time it would take for them to reach
maturity. They *had* to be androids. But it was an incredible
job. I wish to hell we could clock one back to the labs so the
pathologists could have a look at it."

"I wish to hell I knew what we've stumbled into," said
Delaney.

"Sooner or later, we'll find out," Steiger said, "and I have
a feeling when we do, we're not going to like it one damn bit."

"It will be interesting to see if the next event in the story
takes place on schedule," said Delaney.

"The Symplegades," Steiger said. "The Clashing Rocks at
the north end of the Bosporous. The special effects might be a
little hard to manage."

"Just the same, I'll feel better when we've passed them,"
said Delaney.

That night, Tiphys lost consciousness and never recovered,
dying of the injuries he had sustained in their battle with the
giants. They buried him ashore at dawn. Jason treated
Andre's wounds and those of Hercules, who seemed to think it
was all highly unnecessary and would have been content to
continue disregarding them had Jason not insisted. To be on
the safe side, Delaney gave Andre some antibiotics from their
medikit hidden in his pouch. The talons of the harpy had not
done any irreparable damage, but she would be in severe pain
for a while, so she was excused from rowing. Hercules merely
waved Jason away when it was suggested he should also ab-
stain from rowing and give his wounds some time to heal.
Jason seemed undecided about whether or not he should try
ordering Hercules not to row, but Hylas settled the matter by
pulling him aside gently and explaining in an apologetic manner.

"He is always like this," Hylas said. "As if it were not
enough that he is stronger than any mortal man, he must also
disregard any sickness or injury, to prove he is above such
things. He allows me to tend to him as if to humor me. His
wounds must pain him, but he would not admit it. At such

times, he can be difficult. I have always found it best to let him have his way."

"Well, you know him best, Hylas," Jason said. He smiled and rested a hand on the boy's shoulder. "I will leave the welfare of the son of Zeus in your capable hands."

As the ship set sail up the Bosporous, Hylas appointed himself nurse to Andre, as well. He rubbed some balm into her wounds that he said always worked wonders on his master and he changed her bandages, made from some of the spare clothing the Dalions had given them. He brought food to her and fresh water to drink.

"How old are you, Hylas?" Andre asked.

"Sixteen, my lady."

"Indeed? You seem younger."

"It is because I am so small. I am as nothing next to Hercules. I am not as small and weak as I once was, though. I have grown stronger from carrying my master's weapons and from trying to work with them. Hercules teaches me so that I might be an armorer one day. It seems it is not my fate to be a hero, like my master and the others."

She smiled. "You admire Hercules very much, don't you?"

"He is the greatest man alive!"

"How long have you known him?"

"Many years, my lady. Since I was but a child."

"How did you meet?"

"My parents were killed by bandits," Hylas said. "Hercules came and rescued me from them. With my parents dead, I had no one left. At first, Hercules told me I could stay with him until we found someone to take me in, but who would want another's child, one so small and frail that anyone could see he would be of little use, only another mouth to feed. When he saw that no one wanted me, Hercules said I could remain with him. He understood my feelings. It is because . . ." Hylas lowered his voice, ". . . he sometimes has trouble speaking. Not all the time. Whenever there is hero's work to be done, his voice flows forth as befits the son of Zeus. But at other times, his voice often stumbles and fails him."

Hylas leaned closer to her. "I think it is because he is so big," he said softly, almost whispering. "He is a giant among men and the world was made for men, not giants. No matter where he goes, people cannot help but stare at him. Often, he must bend down and walk sideways to enter through a doorway. I have seen him sit down in a chair, only to have the chair break beneath his weight and send him crashing to the floor. Then he must pick himself up and as he does so, no one looks and no one laughs, for who would dare to laugh at Hercules? Still, I have seen his face burning with shame because he knows that they have seen. He knows that they will doubtless laugh after we have gone. You have heard his voice when he is roused to anger, how it rings out like thunder? Yet, at other times, his voice is soft and low and he falters in his speech. I think it is because he is afraid to loose that godlike voice. I think that he does not wish to seem too proud.''

"And so you become his voice," said Andre.

"It is because I have been with him so long, I know what he would say even as he thinks it. I know what is in his heart. You see, we are somewhat alike, but not in any way that you might notice. He is only half a god who must live in a world of lesser men and I am only half a boy who must live in a world where only little children can look up to me. Each of us, in his own way, does not belong with others, so we belong to one another.''

Andre reached out and touched his cheek. "You may be small, Hylas, but in some ways you stand above most men."

He stared at her, puzzled. "In what ways, my lady?"

"You see things more clearly than most men do and you understand them better. It is the rarest of all gifts. Perhaps that is why the gods have made you small. So you would not be envied.''

"I had never thought of that," said Hylas. "Can it be true?''

"The greatest gifts are those that are not easily discerned," said Andre. "Those who have them are often not aware of them and if they are, they do not hold them up for all to see.''

"You must be very wise, my lady."

Andre shook her head. "No, Hylas, I am not wise. But I have been to many places and I have witnessed many things. And I once had a little brother who was very much like you.''

"What became of him?"

Andre sat silent for a moment. "He was killed."

"I am very sorry."

She nodded. "So am I, Hylas. You would have liked him. And he would have liked you.''

"If I remind you of him, I am glad," said Hylas.

"Thank you," Andre said. "I think I will rest now and have some sleep. Wake me if I am needed."

"I will, my lady. If you need me, you have but to call. I wish you pleasant dreams."

They rowed slowly as they approached the end of the Bosporous. Between them and the Euxine Sea, rocks protruded from the water like jagged teeth, some small, some large enough to form small islands. They had taken down the sail and Mopsus stood in the prow, taking soundings with a weighted rope and watching for rocks that were submerged. Even the smallest of them could easily tear the bottom out of the ship and the larger ones had jagged edges extending out just below the water.

"Slowly," Argus cautioned the rowers from his position at the tiller. "Slowly, now."

Mopsus kept calling out the depths, so that Argus could steer away from unseen hazards. The ship slid between the rocks as if cautiously picking its way through an obstacle course. They could hear waves crashing against the two giant rock formations at the far end of the stone forest, two towering spires between which they would have to pass.

"We are almost through," Mopsus shouted from the prow. "Once we pass between those two mountains of rock, we shall be clear and in the open sea once more."

"Remain alert!" Argus shouted from the aft end of the ship. "They may be wider at the base, below the surface. We must not scrape against them!"

"Or be crushed between them, either," Steiger said, wryly.

"Don't even joke about it," said Delaney as they rowed together. "Let's not tempt the gods, okay?"

"A storm is coming," Jason called out.

"But the sky is clear," said Orpheus.

"I heard thunder."

"You heard the waves crashing on the rocks," said Theseus.

"No, something else. Thunder, from far away."

"I heard it, too," said Idmon. "And I feel that it is very close."

The ship started to pass slowly between the giant rocks. No one could help staring up at the walls towering above them.

"There!" said Jason. *"Listen!"*

This time, there was no mistaking the sound, a deep, far off rumbling which grew in volume as the *Argo* slid between the rocks. Small stones started to rain down on the ship from above, then, ahead of them, larger pieces of rock fell into the water, some quite close to the ship, sending up sprays which soaked them all.

"They're moving!" Mopsus shouted hoarsely.

Unmistakably, the walls of rock to either side of them were shifting, moving inwards, closer to the ship.

"We'll be crushed!" Idmon shouted.

"Damn it, you *had* to say it, didn't you?" Delaney said, giving Steiger a venemous look.

"Row!" shouted Argus, leaning on the tiller. *"Put your backs into it! Row for your lives!"*

He shouted out a fast cadence as the Argonauts pulled for all they were worth. Rock debris fell all around them, some pieces striking the ship and holing the deck in places. One large piece fell directly in their path, striking the figurehead and jarring it loose, sending a shudder through the entire ship. The figurehead fell into the water and another rock fell near it, the water displaced by its mass pushing the figurehead toward the shuddering, moving wall of rock. The outstretched arm of the figurehead struck against the rock.

The rock suddenly started to move the other way, settling deeper in the water, sliding back away from the ship.

"Look!" shouted Jason. "The goddess pushes back the rock!"

"Pull! screamed Argus. *"Pull 'til your backs break*! *Pull*! *Pull*!"

The ship shot forward, clearing the rocks and entering the open water of the Euxine Sea. Behind them, the thundering, grinding noises stopped and the rocks settled in the water, lower than before, no longer moving. For a few moments, smaller pieces continued to drop into the channel between them, then all was still again.

"The goddess saved us," Jason said. "Did you see? She pushed back the rock so we could pass through unharmed!"

"An earthquake," Steiger told Delaney. "An earthquake, that's all it was."

"Sure," Delaney said. "Probably volcanic action. The bottom shifted, the rock crumbled at the base and it was just a coincidence that it settled backwards just as the figurehead drifted against it."

"Yeah, that's what it was," said Steiger.

"Right, that's what must have happened."

They looked at each other.

"Don't even think it," Steiger said.

"Think what?"

"Nothing. Never mind. Shut up and row."

8

On their third day of sailing on the Euxine Sea, the winds began to strengthen and, noting the appearance of the sky, Delaney feared the worst. Jason wouldn't hear of going in toward shore and seeking a protected bay when strong winds were prevailing. All he could think of was Colchis lying ahead of them and he was determined to take advantage of the blow. He insisted that there would be plenty of time to head toward shore if the weather took a turn for the worse. Nothing Delaney or Steiger could say would dissuade him. Argus lent his weight to their argument, but Jason wouldn't listen.

"If we ran for shore each time the sky grew a little gray," he said, "we would never reach our destination. We have fought fierce battles and emerged victorious. We have survived the Clashing Rocks. The gods watch over us. Are we to shake with fear at the merest threat of rain?"

"What's coming is a great deal more than just a little rain," Delaney said. "You've never seen a real storm at sea."

"If one comes, then I shall see it," Jason said, impatiently. "I grow weary of this journey. The gods have sent us wind to

104

speed us on our way. I shall not fail to take advantage of their gift.''

"You'll be calling it a curse before too long," Delaney said. I've been at sea before, Jason, and I'm telling you—''

"Enough!" said Jason. "Who is captain here? If you had not the nerve to make this voyage, you should not have come.''

He turned away angrily and walked up forward to stand in the bow, looking out to sea intently, as if he could see Colchis just over the horizon.

"I ought to turn that kid over my knee and give him a good spanking," said Delaney.

"Well, if he wants to see a storm, he's about to get an eyeful," Steiger said.

"Get some rope," Delaney shouted. "Bring all we have. If it gets as rough as I think it's going to get, we're going to need it.''

The winds continued to gather strength and the sky grew dark. The sea went from choppy to roiling and the swells grew larger, then the squall struck. The rain came down in stinging sheets and the waves crashed down upon the *Argo*. Jason quickly experienced a change of heart and ordered Argus to turn in toward shore. Delaney immediately contermanded his order. Jason turned on him furiously.

"You must be mad!" he shouted. "At the first sign of a little wind, you plead to go ashore and now you wish to head out for the open sea? You would take us from safety to disaster! What do you wish to do, drown us all? To shore, Argus!''

"You fool," Delaney said. "It's too late now. We won't even reach the shore in these conditions, whether the gods are watching over us or not! We'll be battered to bits by the waves or smashed upon a reef! Our only chance now is to head out to open sea and ride the storm out!''

"And if your house were to catch fire, you would run into the flames? I have never heard such nonsense! Argus, steer toward shore!''

"Jason, my lad, I'm about to show you something else that happens at sea sometimes," Delaney said. "It's called a mutiny.''

He dropped Jason with a hard right cross to the jaw. "Lash him down!" he yelled to Steiger. "The rest of you, take some rope and tie yourselves to something or you'll be swept overboard!''

He ran back to join Argus and they lashed themselves to the tiller together. The other Argonauts were in no mood for argument. The wind was screaming like a hundred banshees and the waves were crashing down upon the deck, soaking them all and knocking them off their seats. They moved quickly to secure the oars and tie themselves down.

Delaney estimated that the gale was at least Force 9. The waves were now cresting at about 30 feet and the *Argo* was being tossed about as if it were a toy. There was no point in trying to rig some sort of sea anchor, the *Argo* was too large for such a solution to be practical. The greatest danger to the ship was not the winds, but the seas shaped by those winds.

In such conditions, the *Argo* could easily be knocked down or the waves could come aboard and pound the deck to splinters. Even with the sail down, the mast might be torn away and if the distance between the waves was less from crest to crest than twice the length of the *Argo*, the ship would come over one wave and crash into the next as if it were a solid wall. The different movements of the water at the tops and bottoms of the swells created strong turning forces on the ship, inviting the danger of a broach.

Delaney was not for heaving to. It meant giving up control. An experienced sailor, his solution ran contrary to what common sense would seem to dictate. It terrified the Argonauts and even Argus thought it was insane. Both Steiger and Delaney were grateful for the fact that the crew had tied themselves down, otherwise they might have interfered.

Instead of taking down the sail, Delaney did just the opposite. With Steiger working on deck with the aid of an improvised safety line, they ran under full sail, surfing down the waves at a twenty degree angle to the crest. The idea was to keep the ship sailing as fast as possible and to avoid allowing the sea to get dead behind them, for if the ship sailed straight down a wave, the bow would almost certainly "catch" on the next wave and the ship would flip end over end.

Riding out the storm in the open sea was far less hazardous than it would have been to take the ship close in to land. There, they would have risked running into unseen capes or sandbars or crunching on a reef due to lack of visibility. The currents close in to land in heavy weather would be completely unpredictable and there was the risk of outlying rocks and tidal bores, tidal floods which ran roaring into rivers or narrow bays in a succession of large, irregularly breaking waves that could broach the ship or hurl it up onto a reef or beach.

Delaney held the ship on course for the open sea as he and Argus leaned their combined weight on the tiller. The *Argo* rose up on the swells as if it were climbing vertical walls, then shot down the faces of the waves into the troughs between them. The Argonauts soon saw the reason why they had been directed to secure themselves, as the waves swept over the ship and forced their bodies to strain against the ropes which held them. With a modern yacht, such conditions would have been arduous enough, but with a primitive vessel like the *Argo*, it was torture.

Argus quickly assimilated Delaney's technique of running full tilt before the storm and ceased to require prompting, but after several hours of such punishment, the old shipbuilder's strength started to give out and soon he was little more than dead weight on the tiller. Suddenly Hercules appeared at Delaney's side, having fought his way back to them. He untied Argus and lowered him down, then secured him once again and took the tiller with Delaney. Together, with their hair and beards matted down and the spray stinging their muscles and threatening to blind them, they strained against the tiller and controlled the ship on its roller coaster ride up and down the swells. They fought the storm all night, sailing more by feel than by sight, for it was impossible to see well in the hurricane force winds.

By dawn, the winds started to die down and soon the sea was once more choppy and covered with whitecaps. As the sun came up, the storm moved past them and the seas grew calmer. They were out of sight of land. Argus, though still weary, took over the tiller and steered south toward shore as Hercules helped Delaney down, supporting his weight with an arm around his shoulders.

"Aren't you even tired?" asked Delaney.

"You have l-labored for m-m-much l-longer than I," said Hercules. "Sleep now."

"Right," Delaney murmured. "Wake me when we get to Colchis."

He closed his eyes and fell asleep almost immediately.

"Let him sleep," said Jason, who had recovered from

Delaney's blow in plenty of time to see the worst of the storm. "He has earned his rest and my respect. We have seen Poseidon's fury unleashed and he faced it without fear. Truly, he must be in favor with the gods."

"If he were," Steiger mumbled under his breath, "he wouldn't be here."

"It is as I have always known," said Jason. "When right is on one's side, one must prevail. And we have prevailed. Titans, winged demons, clashing rocks, the fury of the sea, all have tried to stop us and we have prevailed over all. The mightiest of forces have been aligned against us and we have defeated each of them."

"Yet not without cost," said Idmon. He was staring off into the distance.

"Come, soothsayer," Theseus said, "after the fearsome foes that we have faced, what is there left to fear?"

"I cannot say," said Idmon. "My vision is not always clear. Still I perceive a danger that seems inexplicable to me. The vision seems quite strong."

"What vision, soothsayer?" Theseus said. "What danger is it that lies ahead of us?"

"One of us shall die soon," Idmon said. "I cannot see which one. Yet death seems very near. And death from a most unexpected source." He looked around at all of them, as if something in their faces would make the vision clearer. "You will think me mad," he said, "but I see that one of us shall be felled by a feather."

"We must be getting close to shore," said Jason, pointing to the south. "See? A flock of birds."

"Can you see land?" asked Theseus.

Jason shook his head. "Not yet, but it cannot be far away. It will be good to reach our destination. I am weary of the sea."

"We still have to return," said Orpheus.

"But we will not be returning empty-handed," Jason said, grinning. "We shall have the golden fleece aboard with us and a kingdom will be mine to claim when we reach home."

"What sort of birds are those, I wonder?" Argus said, looking up at the sky. "They do not look like any I have ever seen."

"It is a large flock," Mopsus said. "Perhaps they migrate."

"It is not the season," Argus said.

The birds were almost overhead now and they could see how large they were, like frigate birds, with wingspans of forty inches or more. There were at least a hundred of them, flying in a V formation like migrating geese.

"See how they shine!" cried Hylas.

Indeed, the birds did appear to shine. Sunlight glinted on their feathers as they flew so that they almost seemed to give off sparks. Orpheus suddenly cried out and grabbed his shoulder. A steel shaft protruded from between his fingers, as if he had been shot with an arrow. Theseus carefully pulled it out.

"Why, it's a feather!" he said, astonished.

Something went "phfft" and thunked into Mopsus' forehead. For a moment, he stood there openmouthed with a steel feather protruding from his skull, then he fell back onto the deck, lifeless. More feathers flew down at them, embedding themselves in the deck and sticking in the mast. Hercules swore as one stuck in his leg. Another shaft struck Jason in the arm.

"Down!" shouted Steiger. "Down on the deck! Raise your shields, everyone!"

They all crouched down on the deck, grouped together with their shields raised over their heads as the steel feathers rained down on them, beating a metallic tattoo as they struck the shields and bounced off. The birds made a circle around the ship and came back again, loosing another deadly volley, firing their feathers like steel darts. Several of them found their way through gaps between the shields and struck a number of the Argonauts in their arms and shoulders. The birds made several more passes over the ship, then headed north, flying out to sea.

They remained beneath their shields until they were certain that the birds had gone, then they slowly lowered them. The entire deck of the ship looked like a bed of nails. Delaney pulled one of the feathers out of the wood and examined it closely.

"What strange manner of metal is this?" asked Jason, examining the feather he had pulled free from the deck. "Silver?"

Argus plucked another feather from the mast. "No, not

silver," he said, puzzled. "I have never seen the like of it."

"Birds with metal feathers," Hylas said, with wonder. "How can they fly?"

"How can they shoot them as if they were arrows?" Theseus said.

As the Argonauts plucked the metal feathers free from where they had stuck in the ship, marveling at them, Delaney handed his feather to Steiger. "Take a look at this," he said in a low voice.

Andre came up beside them, also holding a feather in her hand. "It's nysteel," she said.

"Robot drones?" said Steiger, looking out in the direction the birds had taken. "Either preprogrammed or remote controlled." He looked down at the feather thoughtfully. "This could just as easily have contained an exploding warhead."

"I don't get it," said Delaney. "Why throw this kind of stuff against the Argonauts without going all the way? Why go to all this trouble to kill a few people indiscriminately?"

Steiger threw his nysteel feather overboard. "I'm fresh out of ideas. There's no rational pattern to any of this."

"Land!" shouted Orpheus, pointing to a fog enshrouded coast off the starboard bow. They could barely make out the peaks of a large mountain in the distance, looming up out of the mist.

"Caucasus," said Jason, excitedly. "The peak where Prometheus was chained. We have reached Colchis at last."

They sailed along the coast, looking for a place to anchor. As the sun went down, they discovered a small, marshy inlet. They pulled the ship in close to shore, took down the mast, lashed it to its crutch and covered the *Argo* with tall reeds that grew in profusion along the banks. Jason poured wine upon the ground, an offering to the earth and the gods of the land, then they buried Mopsus.

"Your vision proved prophetic, Idmon," Jason said. "The astrologer was indeed felled by a feather."

"I only wish I had been wrong," said Idmon, gravely. "Mine is, at times, a most unwelcome gift. I sometimes see things I wish I had not seen."

"Can you look into the future now?" asked Orpheus. "Can you see if we shall find the golden fleece in Colchis?"

Idmon closed his eyes and remained silent for a long time.

"I have the intuition that more of us will die here," he said at last. He opened his eyes. "Ask me no more. The gods are watching us, gods who kill and gods who create life and it frightens me to be so close to them."

They camped in a thick grove of birch trees so their fires would not be seen from a distance. After the Argonauts bedded down, the temporal agents took advantage of the opportunity to hold a conference during their watch. They sat around the embers of their campfire, speaking in low voices.

"We still don't have much more of a handle on this scenario than when we started," said Steiger. "We're going to have to take what we know and improvise a plan of action. The trouble is we don't know very much."

"We know there's a temporal mission being conducted here by people from the future of this timeline," Andre said. "We know events aren't following our myth exactly. Maybe their version is different. According to our version, Hercules left the voyage at Arganthus when Hylas was pulled into a lake by water nymphs and drowned, but we never stopped at Arganthus, Hylas is still alive and Hercules is still with us. There were a number of other events mentioned in the story that haven't occurred. In fact, if you eliminate everything the opposition has done to alter this scenario, what you're left with is a perfectly ordinary sea voyage. Ordinary except for the episode of the Clashing Rocks, which was undoubtedly the result of an earthquake or volcanic action, just the sort of incident that could give rise to a legend.

"We know from historical records that Theseus actually lived in our timeline. If we assume the same about the others, then we have a logical explanation for the origins of our myth. A sea voyage was made during which certain events occurred, such as the earthquake which resulted in the story of the Clashing Rocks. We saw how the story about Athena pushing the rocks out of the way so the ship could get through must have started. The figurehead broke off, struck against the rock at the same moment that it settled backwards in the water and Jason assumed that Hera moved the rock. So the name got changed. Or maybe in this universe, it was Hera who moved the rock instead of Athena. When they returned, the Argonauts told the story of the Clashing Rocks and added some other exaggerations or they were added later as the story was passed on in the oral tradition. Eventually, the myth was recorded according to that tradition. That tells us the Argonauts returned safely from their voyage, otherwise the story would not have been started in the first place. What we've experienced so far supports that. It's like Forrester said, a mirror-image universe, but the image is slightly distorted."

"That still doesn't tell us what the opposition is up to," Steiger said. "They're restaging the events according to the myth, or their version of it. The question is, what happens when you're confronted with a temporal scenario in which the actual historical details aren't known? If there's no known historical account of the voyage, you can clock back and gather intelligence so you can verify what actually happened, separating the facts from the legend. Once you have those facts, you could then stage a temporal scenario in which the mythical elements of the story are made into the historical elements, but that brings us back to the one question we can't answer. What reason would there be for doing it? It would have to affect the original historical outcome."

"Perhaps," Delaney said. "It's possible that it would only have a minimal effect, not significant enough to disrupt temporal continuity."

"How do you figure that?" asked Steiger.

"When I was studying zen physics in RCS, we worked with some hypothetical problem modules designed to break down our notions of common sense," Delaney said. "One problem module postulated an imaginary court case involving a murder. The defendant was innocent, but was mistakenly convicted on circumstantial evidence and executed. Now suppose you clocked back and restaged the temporal scenario so that the defendant was actually guilty and the evidence was incontrovertible. You've changed the facts, but you haven't changed the outcome. History remains unchanged."

"That's hardly the same situation we have here," said Steiger. "People have died on this voyage, people who wouldn't have died if the restaging elements hadn't been present. That amounts to temporal interference."

"We don't know that for a fact," said Delaney. "It's possible they might have died in some other manner during the course of this voyage. What we're part of is no longer the original scenario. It's also possible that their deaths weren't significant enough to affect temporal continuity. It wouldn't

have been difficult to assess the historical impact of the Argonauts. In some cases, it would have been fairly simple. Take
Mopsus. He was getting on in years and had no children. All
they'd have to do is evaluate his individual actions in terms of
temporal significance. And don't forget that these men are all
warriors. Some of them might have died in battle not long
after this voyage took place. There are any number of
variables that could result in a break of ancestral continuity.
It's even possible the scenario was designed to *control* which
people died. You can program robots and androids to recognize certain individuals and differentiate between them."

"So you still think they're conducting some sort of war
game in preparation for an invasion of our timeline?" Steiger
asked.

"I think it's a possibility," Delaney said. "It's the best explanation I've been able to come up with."

"There's only one thing wrong with it," said Steiger. "*Us.*
If they've gone to all that trouble to verify the original scenario and conduct a controlled disruption, then they must
have known from the beginning that we were never part of it."

"What if they didn't?" said Andre. "We've become one of
the variable elements in this scenario. If we hadn't met Jason
at the Anaurus River, he would have arrived in Iolchos alone.
We don't have a record of the entire crew for this voyage.
Even in the myth, not all of the Argonauts were named."

"That's right!" Delaney said. "We've been so concerned
with the anomalous elements of this mission, we overlooked
one of the most obvious ones. We must have displaced three
of the original crew members! The hooded man might be
among the Argonauts, but if he isn't, then he must be clocking
ahead to all the significant points along their route. If that's
the case, then they may not have realized that there were three
people on the crew who weren't supposed to be there."

"At least not at the beginning of the voyage," Andre said.

Delaney glanced at Steiger. "I think we're onto something.
It was the middle of the night when you were knocked out at
Iolchos. In the dark, you might have been taken for Jason or
one of the original crew members we displaced. During their
secret meeting on Mount Pelion, the hooded man asked Chiron about the Argonauts who weren't among his pupils, the
ones the centaur didn't know before. He asked Chiron to
name and describe them all. That must have been when they

first suspected something was out of sync with the original scenario. It was confirmed for them at Lemnos, but they had to check it out. We would have done the same. If we introduced variables into a temporal scenario and something popped up that didn't seem to fit the historical events, we'd try to make sure we knew exactly what the variable was and how it might affect the outcome."

Steiger nodded. "It makes sense. They must have scrambled to check us out against any possible historical variables. Were there any people like us around originally who might have been part of the crew? When they didn't turn up anything, they had to look for another explanation. They must have been as baffled as we've been. They couldn't learn anything from the centaur, because the centaur was one of *their* variables that they inserted into the scenario; and when the hooded man saw me at Lemnos, it must have tipped him off that I was from the future."

"Only *which* future?" Andre said. "There wasn't supposed to be anyone from their future on the scene they didn't know about."

"They had to check it out," said Steiger, nodding. "And they would have wanted another, closer look."

"The old blind king," Delaney said.

"Our hooded friend?" said Steiger.

"Or someone else on their mission team," Delaney said. "It had to be."

"I'm keeping my eye on Idmon," Steiger said. "I don't know about these 'visions' and 'intuitions' of his."

"There is a chance they're genuine," Delaney said. "He could be a sensitive."

"And he could be planted," said Steiger. "I have a 'strong intuition' myself that the opposition is up to something tricky."

"If they guessed we were from another timeline," Andre said, "they must have started searching for the confluence, but if our original theory was correct that the centaur came through by accident, they wouldn't know exactly where and when to look for it."

"And if they haven't found it by now, it explains why we're still alive," Delaney said. "They need us to tell them where it is."

"It fits," said Steiger, nodding. "It finally fits together."

"That's right," Delaney said, wryly. "We've got them right where they want us."

"Perhaps not," said Andre. "One of us can clock back to the confluence point and warn Curtis to summon the Counter-Insurgency Strike Force. Then all we have to do is give them what they want. Lead them directly to the confluence. It'll be just like the Khyber Pass. The minute they come through, they'll be hit with everything we've got."

"And what about us?" said Steiger. "You figure once we tell them where the confluence point is, they'll be nice enough to let us go?"

"I didn't say there'd be no risk," said Andre.

"No, there'd be risk all right and not only to us," said Steiger. "We were damned lucky in Afghanistan. The confluence point shifted just in time or the battle would have lasted longer. It might have interfered with the action between the British and the Pathans, to say nothing of the casualties our people would have sustained. We've got a similar situation here. Hannibal and his Carthaginians on one side, Scipio and his Roman legion on the other. Fighting a temporal battle smack dab in between would be dangerous as hell. The object of this mission was to disrupt their timeline, not invite a situation that could disrupt our own."

"Do you have an alternative?" said Andre.

"I say we carry on with our original plan," said Steiger. "Let's take our best shot. If we blow it, there's still a good chance at least one of us can get back and warn the Rangers."

"What if they take their best shot before we take ours?" asked Andre.

Steiger smiled. "I didn't say there'd be no risk."

"Touché," said Andre, wryly.

"I'm in favor of it," said Delaney. "Now that we've reached Colchis, we're in a good position to cut and run. If we stick close to the principals in this scenario, it could make it difficult for the opposition to move against us. The minute we get a reading on the situation, we interfere, create the disruption and clock out fast. They'll be watching us every minute, but we might have a chance to pull it off."

"Maybe," Steiger said, "but there's still one option we haven't considered. It's not a very pleasant one."

"What?" Delaney asked.

"We could kill Jason."

9

They broke camp at dawn and headed inland, following a spirited debate about their plan of action. As usual, Jason had not given any thought to *how* they would obtain the golden fleece once they arrived in Colchis. Planning ahead did not seem to be his forte. He had simply assumed that they would come, pick it up and leave. Now that they had arrived, it occurred to him that it might not be so simple. This realization was brought home to him when the other Argonauts asked him how they should proceed. It was not until then that Jason realized he didn't even know where the Sacred Grove of Ares was.

"How are we to find it, then?" asked Orpheus.

"We could ask directions of people we encounter on the way," said Jason, pleased that a solution had been found.

"Did we not hide the *Argo* so the Colchins would not find it?" Argus said. "If we encounter people on our way and ask directions, word will quickly reach King Aietes that a force of armed men has arrived seeking the Sacred Grove of Ares. We would have no chance to take the golden fleece by stealth."

"By stealth?" said Jason, outraged at the suggestion.

"Would you have us act as thieves come skulking in the night?"

"In what other manner did you think to obtain the fleece?" asked Theseus. "Surely, you did not suppose King Aietes would simply give it to you?"

"Was not my father Aeson, cousin to Phrixus?" Jason asked. "Is not the fleece the rightful possession of my family?"

"As I heard the story, Phrixus gave the fleece to Aietes for his daughter's hand in marriage," Orpheus said. "If that is true, then the fleece rightfully belongs to him."

Jason bit his lower lip. "I had not thought of that."

"Why am I not surprised?" said Steiger.

"It changes nothing," Jason said. "We must bring back the fleece if I am to rule in Iolchos. It is the will of the gods. I will explain it to King Aietes and ask him for the fleece."

"And what if he refuses?" Orpheus asked.

"Then we shall take it by force," said Jason. "It cannot be called stealing if we are obeying the wishes of the gods."

"Interesting logic," Steiger mumbled to Delaney.

"You don't suppose there really is a golden fleece, do you?" said Delaney.

"Be damned if I know," Steiger said. "It's probably some old sheepskin painted gold. Or maybe high suphur content in some sheep's drinking water altered the pigmentation and made the wool turn yellow. They'd probably attribute something like that to the gods. Hell of a thing to go to all this trouble for."

"I've seen knights in the Middle Ages hacking each other to pieces over a splinter alleged to be a piece of the true cross," said Andre. "The value of a sacred relic has less to do with what it is than what it's believed to be."

"The oftener a tale is told, the truer it becomes?" said Delaney.

"Something like that, I suppose."

Steiger snorted. "I can't wait to see the Old Man's face when we plop some rotten old rag down on his desk and tell him it's the golden fleece. There you are, sir, hang it right up there in your den with your collection, next to El Cid's jewel-encrusted sword and Patton's pearl-handled .45."

"I'll just settle for getting back and being able to tell him anything," Delaney said.

By the time they reached the city of Aea, they had picked up a sizable escort. Crowds followed on both sides of the road as the Argonauts marched into the city with Jason strutting proudly in the lead. Wide-eyed children ran beside them, staring at the bearded warriors with the sun-bronzed skin, and after seeing that the Argonauts seemed friendly, some of the bolder ones ventured to touch their metal shields. A few of the children picked up sticks to carry as mock spears and fell in behind the procession, comically imitating Jason's bantam rooster bearing, their heads held high, their shoulders thrown back, their free arms swinging in exaggerated motions. Hercules, Andre and Hylas attracted the most attention; Andre because she was the only woman among such an imposing looking crew, Hercules because of his physique and Hylas because he seemed the same age as the children, though he was older than most of them.

A large crowd had gathered at the palace steps to see the strangers. King Aietes' soldiers waited there as well, in a show of force. It did not escape the notice of the Argonauts that the soldiers outnumbered them considerably. The soldiers of King Aietes blocked the palace steps. They stood in ranks three deep, looking very disciplined in their feather-crested helmets with bronze cheek and nose pieces, metal-studded leather breastplates and short white chlamys fastened at their throats by metal clasps. They carried short iron swords and long javelins and each of them held a small, round iron shield with the likeness of a ram's head on it. Their commanding officer stepped forward and pointed with his sword at Jason.

"Are you the leader of these men?" he asked.

"I am," said Jason, stepping forward until the soldier's sword point touched his chest so as to show no fear. "I am King Jason of Iolchos and we have come in peace, though if we are not received in peace, we are prepared to fight, as well."

"How's that for diplomacy?" Delaney said to Andre.

She merely shook her head.

The officer lowered his sword. "You are either very brave or very foolish, Jason, King of Iolchos. Or perhaps you are only very young. Those are bold words for a stranger who arrives uninvited with armed men. I am Kovalos, captain of the palace guard. Look about you first and then choose your next words carefully. We are five times your number and those are only the soldiers that you see. What is your purpose here?"

"That I will reveal only to King Aietes," Jason said. "It is unseemly for a king to be questioned by a captain of the palace guard. Inform your ruler that a king has come from Thessaly and that he requests an audience."

Kovalos stared at Jason for a long moment, then turned to his soldiers. He beckoned to an officer. "You heard?" he asked.

"I heard."

"Repeat our visitor's words to King Aietes exactly as you heard them and then hasten back with his reply." He turned back to Jason as the officer ran into the palace. "We will soon know how you shall be received," he said, curtly.

"I am not accustomed to be kept waiting," Jason said.

Kovalos pursed his lips. "Nor am I. Nevertheless, it seems that we shall both be obliged to suffer some slight demands upon our patience. I will try to bear up under the strain."

"If I were Jason," Argus said, "I would not speak to such a man in such a manner. He is not yet crowned king and we are too few to make an army."

"This was badly done," said Orpheus, looking around. "Have you observed the archers on the rooftops? We should have sought out the Sacred Grove of Ares and made off with the golden fleece so that no one was the wiser. Our position here is most disadvantageous."

"Perhaps if you sang one of your songs, you could lull them all to sleep as you did the hound of Hades," Theseus said. "Then we could take the golden fleece and be back aboard the ship before they woke up from their peaceful slumber."

"Or perhaps you could tell them the tale of how you slew the Minotaur," Orpheus countered. "Then if any of them survived the telling of the tale, we could do battle with them on more even terms."

"Be silent, both of you!" said Argus. "We have enough troubles on our hands without arguing amongst ourselves."

"I think we are about to find out exactly what our position is," said Idmon, as the officer Kovalos had sent in to the king had returned.

"King Aietes will see you," said Kovalos.

Jason started forward and the others followed, but Kovalos stopped him with a hand upon his chest. "A moment," he said. He shouted an order and the soldiers broke formation, then reformed flanking the Argonauts, with a squad of men in front and behind as well. They moved in close, hemming the

Argonauts in tightly so as to restrict their ability to move
quickly. "Now," said Kovalos.

They were marched into the palace, into the large, marble-
columned main hall where Aietes sat upon his throne, surrounded by his courtiers and protected by a line of armed men
stationed at the foot of the steps leading to the throne. He
leaned forward in his chair as the Argonauts approached and
stared at them intently, stroking his long black beard. His appearance was a marked contrast to that of the Dalion king,
Cyzicus. Where the Dalions were a small, impoverished
people, Aietes ruled over a large and wealthy kingdom and his
palace and his dress reflected this.

Dressed in a long, gold and silver embroidered gown and
wearing a high crown of hammered gold set with rubies,
Aietes had a ring on every finger and bracelets studded with
jewels on both wrists. He looked like a debauched Talmudic
scholar with long, jet black hair that fell in heavy ringlets to
his shoulders and a coarse, black beard that obscured the entire lower half of his face. His eyes were dark and deeply set
and his face was gaunt and striking. He was sharp featured,
with a large hooked nose and a high forehead, all of which
combined to give him a brooding, menacing air. Kovalos
halted them halfway across the room.

"Which of you is Jason?" Aietes said. "Come forward."

Jason pushed his way past the soldiers standing in front of
him and approached the steps to the throne. There was an interested murmuring among the courtiers at the sight of so
young a king. "I am Jason of Iolchos."

"You have traveled far," Aietes said. "What is your purpose here?"

"I have come for the golden fleece," said Jason.

There was a stunned silence.

"The boy gets right to the point," said Steiger, softly.

Aietes stared hard at Jason for a long time. Jason stood his
ground, meeting his steady gaze unflinchingly. Finally, Aietes
broke the silence.

"The golden fleece is the most sacred relic of my kingdom,"
Aietes said. "By what right do you come seeking it?"

"By divine right," Jason said. "My father, Aeson, was
cousin to that very Phrixus who was brought here by the ram
whose fleece now hangs in the Sacred Grove of Ares. It is the
will of the gods that the golden fleece be brought back to

Iolchos, so that the spirit of my relative may at last find peace."

"If this is the will of the gods," said Aietes, "why have they not revealed it to me?"

"They have revealed it to *me,*" said Jason, "in a prophecy spoken by the Oracle of Delphi. It was the gods, speaking through the Oracle, who led me here. The golden fleece rightfully belongs in Iolchos and I have come to ask you to surrender it."

"And you come asking with armed warriors at your side," Aietes said.

"I have done the bidding of the gods," said Jason. "The journey was a long and arduous one and we have encountered many dangers on the way. Yet if it had been the will of the gods that I should come alone, that too would I have done. We did not come here as raiders or as thieves, else we would not have marched here openly in the full light of day, nor would we have allowed ourselves to be placed at such a disadvantage by your soldiers."

"Yet even as we speak, your other men could be plotting to conduct the very raid which you deny."

"I have no other men," said Jason. "You see before you all who have journeyed here with me."

"Good move, kid," Steiger mumbled. "Give our strength away, why don't you?"

"*Our* strength?" Delaney whispered. "Let me get this straight. Are we going to try to help him or were we thinking we might have to kill him?"

Steiger glanced at him with surprise. "Hell of a thing, isn't it?" he whispered back. "I'm starting to get caught up in this."

"Well, make up your mind, Colonel."

Steiger grinned in spite of himself. "Have you made up yours?"

Delaney grimaced. "I'm working at it real hard."

Aietes smiled as he stroked his beard. "You claim the golden fleece rightfully belongs in your kingdom," he said to Jason, "yet it was Phrixus who brought it here, your own kinsman on whom you base your claim. With his own hands, he gave me the golden fleece to commemorate his marriage to my daughter, Chalciope, who stands there with her sister, Medea." He swept his arm out in an exaggerated gesture, indictating two women standing together among the courtiers on his right. "Will you tell the widow of your kinsman that you would take away a sacred relic with which the gods had blessed their union? Would you take from her this one remaining token of her departed husband?"

They all looked at the two women who stood close together, the eldest clutching her younger sister's arm. Chalciope had brown hair streaked with gray and a full, soft, pretty face that she must have inherited from her mother, for it had none of the harsh angles and sharp planes of her father's features. Yet Medea had her father's coloring, hair that was raven black and fell in long, curly tresses down her back. The darkness of her hair made her face look paler than her sister's, but it was not the pallor of ill health. Her lips were red and full and her features sharp, like her father's, but on her the effect was one of striking beauty. She had not inherited her father's beaklike nose, but she had his black eyes and penetrating gaze, which she now directed pointedly at Jason, staring at him with curious intensity.

Jason swallowed hard and floundered for a moment, whether from the question Aietes asked or from Medea's gaze it was impossible to tell, but he finally found words for a suitable reply and, for once, his tone of voice lacked its usual arrogance.

"I would tell my kinsman's widow that I come not to cause her any sorrow, but to bring her husband's spirit rest, for it has been told how the shade of Phrixus appeared in dreams to many of my people, pleading with them to bring the golden fleece back to his native land. Though he married here and lived well for the remainder of his days, Colchis was not the country of his birth. In life, he was denied his birthright and in death, he was denied rest in his native soil. The spirit of Phrixus is bound up in the golden fleece. If we bring it back to Iolchos with us, he may at last find peace."

"A very pretty speech," Aietes said, "yet what proof do you offer us that it is true? We have but your word and you are unknown to us. You are not the first to come seeking the golden fleece. Its fame has spread throughout the world and the fortune of our kingdom is bound up in it. It is our most holy treasure and it makes our country fruitful. Since the time I placed it in the Sacred Grove of Ares, our harvests have become more bountiful and the earth had yielded up its wealth to us. It is well known that there is much gold to be found in Colchis and many have come before you, seeking both that gold and the sacred relic whose power draws it forth out of the earth for us to find. The golden fleece is the greatest treasure of our kingdom, yet you expect me to give it to you for the asking? It is clear to me what you have planned. You hope to play upon our sympathies and upon my daughter's grief so that you may trick us into giving up the fleece. Failing this, you have brought warriors with you so that you could seize the golden fleece by force."

Aietes rose from his throne and pointed a finger at Jason, moving and speaking like an orator whose every nuance and gesture was calculated to achieve maximum effect.

"Yet you have miscalculated, Jason of Iolchos. We are not fools to be taken in by tales such as yours! If the gods wish for the golden fleece to be removed from Colchis, why have they not revealed their designs to *us?* If the spirit of my eldest daughter's husband is tormented, why has it not appeared to *us* in dreams? If the gods meant for strangers to arrive upon our shores and bear the fleece back with them, why have they not warned us of your coming, so that we would not treat you as invaders, but welcome you and do their bidding?

"No!" Aietes shouted. "We are not fools in Colchis! Nor are we a passive, docile people to be ill-used by pirates coming to our shores! The golden fleece has brought us prosperity and we maintain a mighty army to defend it and a fleet of swift ships to pursue all those who would come to plunder us! We have dealt severely with such men before and we shall do so again with any who attempt to steal from us! It is clear to me that you have not reckoned with our strength, else you never would have dared to march here in force so brazenly. As you can see, Jason of Iolchos, we are not easily frightened."

Aietes lowered his voice to a more conversational tone and made a gesture to encompass everyone around him. "Yet we are not a barbarous people. Though you may have come here bearing arms and making arrogant demands upon us, you have not committed any hostile acts. You say your voyage has been long and arduous. We are prepared to extend our hospitality to you so that you may rest briefly before starting on your journey home. Quarters shall be set aside for your men in our soldiers' barracks. As a foreign king, you shall be made welcome in the palace and you may select a number of your people to attend you, not to exceed five. When you return, you may tell others that we make strangers welcome here and

treat them with the courtesy to which their rank entitles them,
but if they come to us bearing the sword, then they shall die by
the sword. This audience is ended. You may go."

While Aietes spoke, Jason had turned several different
shades of purple and when the king summarily dismissed him,
he would surely have exploded but for the presence of mind
displayed by Idmon, who came running up to Jason's side and
took his arm in a firm grasp.

"We are most grateful for your hospitality, King Aietes,"
Idmon said quickly and loudly, so that Jason could not inter-
rupt. "With your leave, we will go now and rest from our long
journey."

He practically dragged Jason away, a feat which would
have been more difficult if Jason weren't so furious that he
could do no more than sputter with inarticulate outrage. The
moment they had rejoined the main body of the Argonauts,
the soldiers turned about smartly and almost frog-marched the
Argonauts out of the palace. They crossed the city square and
stopped at the soldiers' barracks, a long, fortresslike stone
building with a low wall surrounding it. Not looking to pro-
voke a confrontation, Kovalos told Idmon, rather than Jason,
that he would return "with a proper escort for the king" when
rooms had been made ready for him in the palace. In the
meantime, he showed them the area designated for their temporary use—stressing the word temporary—and promised that
slaves would shortly bring food and fresh water to them.

"Never has my patience been so sorely tried," said Jason,
as soon as they were left alone. "I thank you, Idmon, for your
timely intervention. If not for you, I would surely have lost
my temper with Aietes. I came to him honorably and spoke
plainly of my intent, yet was forced to stand there in mute rage
while he accused me of the basest motives!"

"We *did* come to take the golden fleece," said Theseus, "so
for myself, I am little surprised at his response. Yet I am not
displeased at this turn of events. It would have posed no
challenge if Aietes had given up the golden fleece without a
fight."

"Without a fight?" said Argus. "Has it escaped your notice
that Aietes has at least five men for every one of us?"

"If the odds intimidate you, Argus," Theseus said non-
chalantly, "I would be pleased to take on your five as well as
mine."

"It would be difficult for us to take on anyone at this

point," Idmon said, stepping between them. "These quarters are built like a prison and you may be sure that we are watched. We would not take two steps beyond these walls before their archers dropped us in our tracks. Unless the situation changes, there is not much we can do at present except to plan a way out of this predicament. It was not for the sake of being gracious that Aietes 'invited' Jason to stay at the palace. He means to have him as a hostage for our good behavior until we can be safely sent back on our way. You may be sure that he will have soldiers searching for the *Argo* in the meantime. It was fortunate indeed that we concealed the ship and that no one saw us land."

"So what would you have us do, soothsayer?" Theseus asked. "What portents do you see to guide us in our actions?"

"I have seen no portents," Idmon said, "but I have a feeling that we shall receive help from an unexpected quarter, perhaps from within the palace itself. While we were there, I had the strongest intuition that an event of great significance would soon occur within those walls."

"Then I would be best served to take you with me to stay within the palace tonight," said Jason. "Theseus, you shall come as well and Fabius, Creon and Atalanta, since you were the first to join me. That makes up the five Aietes has so graciously allowed me. Hercules, I leave you in charge in my absence. Should anything befall us, I will leave it to you to decide what's to be done, but if I am killed, then it shall mean that I have lost the favor of the gods and there will be little to gain in pursuing that which they have chosen to deny me. In that event, I charge you to bring the Argonauts back home in safety. In the meantime, I will take council with these five and plan a way for us to get the golden fleece. When we have decided what to do, I shall contrive to send a message to you. The soldiers may try to antagonize you. Do not allow yourselves to be provoked. And beware the food and drink Aietes sends. Best to eat from the supplies we brought with us."

"The escort has arrived to take you to the palace, Jason," Hylas said from the window.

Jason picked up his weapons and his leather sack. "Be patient," he told the others, "and wait to hear from me. The golden fleece is not yet lost to us. Trust to the gods to see us through."

10 _____

The rooms set aside for them within the palace had been carefully chosen. They were in the right wing, at the end of a long and narrow corridor with no other doors or hallways leading off from it. At the end of the corridor was the largest room, the one set aside for Jason, with two smaller rooms on either side of it through connecting doors. The palace was situated on the heights over the city and the only windows in their rooms looked out over a deep ravine.

"They have us well in hand here," Theseus said. "We cannot climb down and the only other way out is down that narrow corridor, which affords no shelter and little room to move. We will not be in a good position if it comes to fighting our way out. The guards posted at the corridor's end would see us coming in enough time to give alarm and two or three archers could easily dispatch us before we had a chance to reach them."

"Perhaps not," said Jason. He walked over to a large oval table standing in the center of the room. "This would make a useful shield against archers or spearmen if we carried it before us."

126

"It would if it were not wider than the corridor," said Idmon, looking down at it.

"How could it be wider than the corridor?" asked Jason. "If it were, how could they have brought it in here?"

"Lengthwise," Idmon said, wryly, "carried by each end. It would not make much of a shield that way."

Jason frowned. "We could hack the ends off with our swords until it was of a right size to carry before us."

"And make such a racket that they would be upon us before we were half finished with the task," said Idmon. "Observe its thickness. We should give less thought to carpentry and more to planning what to do when morning comes. There is little doubt that Aietes' soldiers are even now searching for our ship. Aietes will wish to be certain that we did not leave other men outside the city. I would not expect him to take you at your word. If they find the ship and discover it to be unmanned, they will no doubt burn it to the waterline and then attend to us."

"It is fortunate that we have hidden it," said Theseus. "They will look first to see it anchored just offshore and it may escape their notice. There will not be time to make a careful search of the entire coastline in one night."

"You three have been silent," Jason said to the agents. "Have you no thoughts to add? Fabius, you acted well and quickly in the storm. Do you agree with Idmon?"

"I think Idmon is right," Delaney said. "Aietes has nothing to gain by allowing us to leave. What would prevent us from returning with more men, enough to meet his army on more equal terms? If his soldiers do not find the ship tonight, he can have us lead them to it when we are forced to leave tomorrow. Once we are well away from the city and caught with the sea at our backs, his soldiers will attack."

"Those would be sound tactics," Theseus said. "It means that we must somehow act tonight."

"Only there seems to be no course of action open to us," Jason said. He glanced at Idmon. "Where is this unexpected help your intuition told you of?"

Idmon shook his head. "I cannot say. I can only repeat that I have the certain feeling that it will arrive. As to when or what form it may take, that I cannot tell you."

"For a soothsayer, you do not reveal much," Theseus said, sourly.

"Nor do I embellish," Idmon said. "I reveal only what I know. I do not embroider upon my revelations, as do other soothsayers, who cloak their revelations with imponderables meant to reassure the gullible."

"This quarreling serves no purpose," Jason said. "We have not come all this way for nothing. Thus far, the gods have seen us through and they will see us through it to the end. Aietes cannot defy the gods. Nor can we anticipate them. When the time is right, they will show us what must be done."

"It may not be wise to depend too much upon the gods," said Theseus. "I have always found that the gods help those who help themselves. We should never have allowed ourselves to be separated from the others. With us here as his hostages, Aietes may try to force our friends to reveal the location of our ship."

"I do not think that Hercules would be an easy man to force," said Idmon. "Have faith, Theseus. And patience. Both are kingly virtues. We have not yet—" he stopped, abruptly. "Listen!"

"I hear nothing," Theseus said.

But a moment later, they all heard it, a distinct, low scraping sound like that of large stones grinding against one another. A portion of the wall began to swing out slowly, revealing a secret passageway that had been concealed by the mortared cracks between the stones.

Theseus unsheathed his sword and moved to stand concealed behind the hidden door as it opened slowly. Jason stood where he was, so that whoever was behind the door would see him clearly, but he too unsheathed his sword.

"Our benefactor has arrived," said Idmon and Medea came into the room.

Theseus quickly looked to see if anyone was coming through behind her, but she said, "I am alone. I have come to help you."

"Why would Aietes' daughter wish to help us?" Theseus said. "Take care, Jason, this is some sort of trick."

"No trick," Medea said. She came up close to Jason and placed her hands upon his chest. "Look into my eyes and say if you see trickery."

"What man has ever discerned trickery in a woman's eyes?" said Theseus, but his words did not stop Jason from gazing long and not at all hard into Medea's eyes.

"From the first moment that I saw you," Medea said, "I knew that you were not like other men. It took great courage to have come so far and to have marched so boldly to the palace and spoken so plainly to my father's face. I have never met another who would dare such things!"

"Would you have us believe," said Theseus, "that you would turn against your father merely because Jason has impressed you with his daring and his courage?"

"When you went to Crete to slay the Minotaur, did not Ariadne turn against her father because she was impressed with yours?" said Jason. "Is that not how I heard it from your own lips when you told the tale?"

"Well, perhaps that was not quite the same," said Theseus, uneasily.

"It is not the only reason," said Medea. "I do this for my poor grieving sister as much as for myself. She, too, has dreamed of Phrixus since he died and took it to be an omen that his spirit cannot rest. After you had gone, Chalciope came to me, weeping because her husband's spirit was tormented and heartbroken that brave men had to die because our father will not part with the golden fleece.

"He believes it to be the source of all the wealth and good fortune in our kingdom," she continued. "He wishes to keep it because it brings him fame. He has commissioned poets to compose works about it which increase his fame and bring many here to pay him tribute, yet these works also bring pirates and thieves to Colchis."

"You mean men such as ourselves," said Theseus.

"No," said Medea. "You are different. It was clear at once, even to my father, that you were not brigands. Jason came openly, in the full light of day, and spoke to my father as one ruler to another. We in Colchis have also heard the tale of Theseus, who killed the Minotaur and became the king of Athens. And who has not heard of Hercules? Among our soldiers are men who came from Thebes and know him. Aietes knows that such men do not join with pirates."

"Perhaps not," said Theseus, a bit less antagonistic now that his vanity had been appealed to. "Yet that still does not tell us why you would wish to help us."

"You do not know what it is like here," she said. "Since the golden fleece came into his possession, my father has become obsessed with it. To him, it is a token from the gods in recognition of his power. He has employed men such as Kovalos to protect it, but what protection is there from Kovalos? The mercenaries who make up the palace guard place Kovalos first, before my father, who will do anything to keep his favor. Kovalos does whatever pleases him and I fear that it would please him to have me for his wife. Chalciope has sent her sons away, fearing for their lives, yet in doing so has only made the way clear for Kovalos, who has convinced my father that they have gone away to raise an army so that they might come back and seize the throne. My father became frightened and gave him permission to recruit even more soldiers, mercenaries who came from some foreign land and care more for gold than for our kingdom. You can guess to whom those men will give their loyalty. There is only one more thing Kovalos needs to make his place secure and that is me. With the sons of Phrixus gone and Aietes' daughter as his wife, no one could dispute his right to rule in Colchis. My father knows I loathe Kovalos, but he fears him and has already promised me to him, thinking to gain his favor. You are my only chance. Tonight, while the soldiers are kept occupied watching your men and searching for your ship, Chalciope plans to escape and join her sons. I can help you get the golden fleece. All I ask in return is that you take me with you.''

''How would we escape the palace?'' Jason asked. ''And what of my men?''

''This passageway leads to others that will take us from the palace,'' said Medea, ''but you will need me to show the way. Chalciope can arrange to have your friends escape. There are still some soldiers in our army who remember Phrixus and will help us, but we must not waste time. I heard my father tell Kovalos to send soldiers in here through this very secret passage while you slept tonight, to put you in chains.''

Jason shook his head. ''It does not sit well with me, to sneak off in the middle of the night like someone running from a fight.''

''Yet there is no fight to run from,'' Idmon said. ''Under the pretext of hospitality, we have been taken prisoner. True, we have been allowed to keep our weapons, but that was only to strengthen the pretext. If an effort had been made to take our arms, or if we had been asked to give them up, we would have suspected trickery and had a chance to fight, but as it turned out that chance was denied us. We have acted honorably, no one would dispute that. It was Aietes who tricked us into this position, so that we are now his prisoners. And as prisoners, it is our honorable duty to attempt escape."

Jason pursed his lips and nodded, "Yes, that is true. I see that now. Escaping from imprisonment is not the same as running from a fight."

"Nicely done," Delaney whispered to Idmon.

"Yes, I thought so too," the soothsayer whispered back.

"But stealing the fleece like a common thief does not seem right," said Jason. "I would much rather win it in fair combat."

"But how could it be fair when my father's men outnumber you so greatly?" asked Medea.

"That is beside the point," said Jason. "A brave man does not reckon odds before he goes into a battle."

"Quite right, on both counts," Idmon said. "A brave man does not reckon odds, indeed, and that is beside the point. You yourself said that it would not be stealing if you were only carrying out the wishes of the gods. And it cannot be called stealing if you were to take from Aietes that which does not belong to him so that you might return it to its proper owner."

Jason frowned. "You confound me, Idmon. Explain what you mean."

Idmon raised his eyebrows and shrugged elaborately. "I should think it would be obvious," he said. "Does not the golden fleece rightfully belong in Iolchos? Did not the gods themselves reveal to you that it was so? And was not the ram itself, from which the fleece came, given to Nephele? As I recall the story, she sent the ram to carry Phrixus and Helle out of danger, but the story makes no mention of her *giving* the ram to them. For all we know, she must have told it to return to her so that she would know that Phrixus and Helle had reached safety. How was she to know the ram would die? With Nephele's own death, her possessions would have passed on to her children, but with both her children dead now, it is clear that the next of kin stand to inherit and that would have been your father, Aeson. But now, with your father gone, *you* are the next of kin, so the golden fleece rightfully belongs to you. Surely, a man cannot steal that which already belongs to him!"

Steiger stared at Idmon. "Good God," he said softly, so that only Andre and Delaney heard. "Now I know what happened to the soothsaying profession. They all became attorneys.''

Jason slapped his hand down on the table. ''Of course!'' he said. ''What could I have been thinking of? Rather than being a thief, I am the *victim* of a theft! How could a man steal what rightfully belongs to him? What nonsense! The golden fleece belongs to me by rights of inheritance! Lead on, Medea! Take us to the Sacred Grove of Ares! I must reclaim my property!''

Medea looked at Idmon with obvious relief and the agents looked at him with new respect. ''Maybe we can take him back with us,'' Delaney said to Steiger as they followed the others through the secret doorway. ''Can you imagine an attorney with precognitive abilities?''

''That's too scary even to think about,'' said Steiger.

They followed Medea down the passageway, which ran parallel to the corridor beyond the wall and then around the hall to the opposite wing of the palace.

''We must first tell Chalciope to send men to help your friends and prepare her own escape. She has had it arranged for quite some time now, but was only awaiting the opportunity. Now will be her chance to go and join her sons. Then they can indeed gather an army to march against our father and Kovalos, but by then, I will be with you in Iolchos.'' She gave Jason such a look that he almost grabbed her on the spot, but she held him off and said there would be time enough for them during the voyage back to Iolchos. ''For now, we must arrange to set your friends free so they can make your ship ready to depart the moment we come back with the golden fleece.''

''It would be best for one of us to accompany the men Chalciope will send to help our friends,'' said Idmon. ''That way, they will not think it may be a trap. Theseus, perhaps you should be the one to go. There may be fighting if anything goes wrong and you would be sorely needed. The rest of us will remain behind with Jason and Medea.''

''Yes, that would be wise,'' said Jason. ''Go, Theseus, and tell Hercules our plan. We will all meet at the ship before dawn.''

They met Chalciope and left Theseus with her and several of the soldiers who had served under Phrixus. Their plan called for disguising Theseus as one of the soldiers and then march-

ing together in a group to the barracks where the Argonauts
were being kept, with "orders from Kovalos" to release them
so that they could be escorted to their ship and sent back home
with a ransom demand for Jason and Theseus. Holding kings
for ransom was something the mercenaries would understand.
Meanwhile, Theseus would warn Hercules and the others to go
along with the ruse. Once they were free, their only danger
would be running into Kovalos and the soldiers who were out
searching for the *Argo*. Theseus was to tell them to stay hidden unless Kovalos found the *Argo*, in which case their only
choice would be to fight, though they would stand a better
chance at night, out in the open.

Medea then led the others back down the same passageway
they had come from, making many different turnings which
led downward until they were out of the bowels of the palace
and within the caverns which honeycombed the mountain.
Steiger remained close to Idmon, watching him every moment.

Medea used a torch to light their way through the damp
stone caves until they came out into the open, far below the
palace and the city. They were in the thickly wooded foothills
and the full moon hung in a cloudless sky above them. Just
below them was a trail which led into the woods.

"That path leads to the Sacred Grove of Ares," said
Medea. "The only way to reach it is through the caverns, as
we came. Only my father and the high priests and priestesses
know the way, as it is they who bring the golden fleece into the
palace for occasions of importance and then return it to the
Sacred Grove."

"Yet you knew the way," said Jason.

"Because I am the High Priestess of Hecate," said Medea.
"In bringing you here, I have profaned against the goddess. If
we are caught, it means my death."

"Are there guards posted at the Sacred Grove?" asked
Jason. "Or is it watched only by priests?"

"There are no guards and there are no priests," Medea said,
"but the golden fleece is watched over by a dragon."

"A *dragon*?" Jason said. "You did not mention this before!"

"No?" said Medea, a touch uncomfortably. "Well, perhaps I had forgotten."

"How could you forget a dragon?"

"I-I don't know. I suppose that in all my concern for your

safety and for the safety of my sister and your men, it must have simply slipped my mind.''

"By the gods," said Jason, "a dragon! This changes things!''

"It is too late for things to change," Medea said. "There can be no turning back, Jason. For better or for worse, I have cast my lot with you. The only way out is through the caverns. You would not find your way without me and I cannot return now. The only way to go is forward, down that trail. It is the *only way*. To reach your ship, you will have to take that trail to the river at the bottom of the ravine and the trail passes through the Sacred Grove of Ares.''

"I see," said Jason. "So there is no going back and there is no way to avoid the dragon. I think, Medea, you did not forget about the dragon. I think you never meant to tell us until now.''

"Very well," Medea said, looking down at the ground, "I was afraid to tell you." She looked up at him beseechingly. "I know it was wrong, but I was afraid that your courage may have failed you. Where would that have left me? I would have been forced to remain here and marry that detestable Kovalos! I have risked everything for you! The golden fleece will make you a great king in Iolchos and you shall have me in the bargain. Losing it will serve my father right for promising me to that common mercenary!''

"There is nothing to do but to go on," said Jason. "I will not return to Iolchos without the golden fleece. It is only that news of this dragon comes unexpectedly to me. I have heard tales of dragons, but I have yet to see one for myself.''

"Then you will see one soon," Medea said. "To a man such as yourself, a dragon is no obstacle! Come, we must go quickly if we are to meet your friends by dawn." She grabbed Jason by the arm and started pulling him toward the trail.

"I fear that Jason will have two dragons to contend with," Idmon said. "If he can slay the first, the second will take him for a husband.''

"Have you ever seen a dragon, Idmon?" asked Delaney.

"I confess that I have not," the soothsayer said. "Indeed, I had not thought that there really were such creatures, but we have seen so many wonders on this voyage that a dragon somehow comes as no surprise. It is a pity we have left Hercules behind." He closed his eyes and stood very still for a moment. "How large do dragons grow, I wonder?"

The agents exchanged nervous glances.

"Does your intuition tell you something, Idmon?" said Delaney.

Idmon sighed. "It is a most vexing and peculiar gift," he said, "not very dependable at all, I am afraid. Just now, I had a presentiment that this dragon may not be a large one. Yet there still remains a question to which I have no answer. What is small for a dragon?"

11 _____

"How do your priests deal with this dragon when they come to the grove?" asked Jason.

"They mix a potion into its food which puts it to sleep for a time," Medea said.

"Can we not also use this potion?" Jason asked.

"I fear not," said Medea. "Only the High Priest of Ares administers this potion and only he knows how to mix it. It is his sacred trust and I could not ask him for it without arousing his suspicion. You shall have to kill the dragon before we can get the golden fleece. You can do it, Jason. I know you can."

Jason sighed. "Yes, but does the dragon know?"

The well-worn narrow pathway took them down a rocky slope, through a dense thicket of birch trees. They had to proceed in single file until the trail widened and brought them to a large clearing. They entered the Sacred Grove by passing between two large boulders which had long ago fallen from the heights above. The rock-strewn clearing was roughly circular in shape and about thirty yards in diameter. A number of stone altars ringed its circumference, each with a small bowel-shaped sink carved into it. Each of these sinks held pitch and there were large urns on either side of each stone altar which held oil and incense. Near the entrance to the grove stood two braziers which were always kept burning.

In the center of the clearing stood a leviathan of a tree, ancient and gnarled, its thick branches spreading out all around it in twisted shapes. In the moonlight, they could discern the shape of something hanging from one of the thicker, lower branches, a dark mass that looked like heavy Spanish moss.

Medea lit a torch from one of the burning braziers and started to light the pitch bowels in the altars near them. As the crackling flames leaped up, the dark mass hanging from the lower tree limb reflected the firelight in a metallic, golden glow.

"The golden fleece," said Jason, softly.

As Medea poured scented oil on the flames to make them burn more brightly, there was a rustling at the foot of the huge tree and what looked like a mound of earth started to move. The dark shape came at them quickly, moving with an ungainly, splayfooted motion that was deceptively fast. It charged them and stopped with an abrupt jerk about twenty feet away, making hissing and snapping noises. It resembled a small prehistoric reptile, a dinosaur from the Mesozoic era. It was thirty feet long from its head to the tip of its tail. They had scattered when it charged them, but they recovered when they saw that the creature could not come any closer. It strained at them, but a long heavy chain fastened to the tree held it back.

"It really *is* a dragon!" Andre said.

"It's a monitor lizard," said Steiger, staring at the creature. "Also known as a Komodo dragon. I've seen them before in Indochina, but not as big as this."

"Is it dangerous?" asked Andre.

"Oh, yes," Steiger said. "Komodo dragons are carnivorous. They'll eat wild pigs and deer. They could kill a man. This one is certainly large enough. I don't think it does too well in this climate, though. Probably makes it sluggish."

"It doesn't seem all that sluggish to me," said Delaney, apprehensively.

Jason stood with his back against the rock, his sword held out before him, his gaze riveted to the lizard as its long tongue lashed out repeatedly.

"Kill it!" yelled Medea, crouching behind one of the stone altars. "Kill it, Jason! Quickly!"

"There is no need for haste," said Jason. "The chain holds it fast. Does it breathe fire?"

"I have never seen it do so," said Medea, uncertainly.

Steiger nocked an arrow to his bow.

"That will serve no purpose," said Medea. "It cannot be killed in such a manner. Arrows cannot pierce its hide."

"Who told you that?" said Steiger. He pulled the bow back to his ear and let the arrow fly. It struck the lizard in the throat, penetrating deeply. The lizard thrashed, making hissing, rasping noises. He fired another arrow into its eye and the creature fell. It twitched several times and then lay still.

"But my father told us all that the dragon was impervious to arrows!" cried Medea.

Steiger shrugged. "Your father lied."

Medea flew into a rage. "*Oh, how I hate him!* I can draw a bow as well as any man! Had I but known it was so simple, I could have slain the beast myself!"

"Then you would have had the golden fleece and you would not have needed Jason," said Delaney. He grinned. "Too bad. Looks like you're stuck."

"You did nothing!" said Medea, turning on Jason. "You merely stood there while your friend dispatched the beast!"

"I took you at your word when you said that arrows would not pierce its flesh," Jason said. "I was thinking how to kill the creature when Creon put an arrow in its throat."

"You were afraid!" Medea said.

"I was *not* afraid!"

He carefully walked in a wide circle around the dragon and approached the tree. He stretched his arm out to pull down the fleece, but it would not budge. He grabbed it with both hands and pulled again. It moved a little, but still remained draped over the tree limb. With a curse, he put all his weight on it and the fleece abruptly came down. Jason fell and the golden fleece came down on top of him, pinning him to the ground. He struggled to get up, but could not move.

"Fabius! Creon! Help me!"

Delaney bent down over the fleece. "Jesus Christ," he said. "It weighs a ton!" He grunted and pulled it off Jason. "I'll be damned," he said, looking at the fleece. "It really *is* gold!"

"Yes, exquisite craftsmanship, wouldn't you say?"

Steiger spun around. "Who said that?" The voice had

spoken in English and there was something about it that was unpleasantly familiar.

A tall figure in a long, hooded cloak came out from behind one of the stone altars on the far side of the clearing. A plasma pistol was held in his right hand. With his left hand, he reached up and pulled back the hood which concealed his face. His dark complected Slavic features were handsome, marred only by the long scar that ran from beneath his left eye, across his cheekbone and down to the corner of his mouth. A thick shock of curly black hair gave him a Byronic aspect and his bright green eyes stared at them mockingly.

"Drakov!" said Andre.

"Who are you?" said Medea. "Where did you come from?"

"That need not concern you," Nikolai Drakov said to her in her own language.

"It concerns me!" said Jason, moving toward Drakov with his sword raised. Drakov fired a plasma charge at the ground in front of Jason. The white hot blast burst into blue flame on the rocks. Jason leaped back with a cry.

"Think twice before you raise your sword against a god, Jason of Iolchos," Drakov told him. "That was merely a warning. I have no wish to harm you, but if you attempt to interfere, the next ball of fire will not miss you." He looked at the agents, smiled and switched to English. "The same applies to the three of you, of course."

"I should have known," Delaney said. "I should have known we'd be running into you again."

"Yes, we do meet in the oddest places, don't we, Mr. Delaney?" Drakov said. "By the way, allow me to convey my belated condolences on the death of Lt. Col. Priest. He was a worthy adversary. A pity I was cheated of my chance to kill him. However, I see his place has been taken by my old friend Martingale. Or is it Sharif Khan? Tell me, am I allowed to know your real name or will you present me with yet another alias?"

"It's Steiger. Col. Creed Steiger."

Drakov smiled. "All the time we've known each other and we're only now being properly introduced. It's fortunate I let you live when I had you at my mercy in the Khyber Pass. If I hadn't, I never would have known whom I had killed."

"A situation you're finally going to remedy, I suppose," said Steiger.

"What, kill you, you mean? Indeed, not. It would upset my plans somewhat if I were to kill you now. Besides, it wouldn't be very sporting with you three armed only with those primitive weapons and dressed in those silly skirts, although the costume looks most becoming on you, Miss Cross. No, your lives are safe enough," said Drakov. "At least for the time being."

"What's this all about, Nikolai?" said Steiger. "What the hell are you doing here?"

"Conducting a rather interesting experiment," said Drakov, "of which you three have been an integral part. When I sent the centaur through the confluence, I had an idea you three would be the ones to come. Of course, it didn't have to be you, but I'm rather pleased it was. It's made it all a great deal more amusing."

"So it was a plot to draw us here right from the start," said Delaney. "But why? What do they hope to gain that could be worth the chances they're taking?"

"By 'they,' I assume you mean your counterparts in this timeline, the Special Operations Group," said Drakov. "The S.O.G. has not been entirely responsible for what you've seen. In fact, they will think *you* were responsible, which is not surprising as I have gone to a good deal of trouble to encourage them in this belief."

"Whose side are you on?" asked Delaney.

"My own, of course. Admittedly, I was forced into collaboration with the Special Operations Group when I first stumbled into this timeline, but I have managed to improve my situation considerably since then. I intend to finish what I started, in spite of your previous interference. Only now with *two* timelines vulnerable to disruption, the odds of creating multiple timestream splits have increased exponentially."

"Now everything falls into place," said Andre. "Small wonder nothing about this scenario made any sense. There was a lunatic behind it."

"You do me an injustice, Miss Cross. From my point of view, it makes a great deal of sense. I have succeeded in playing both ends against the middle and in doing so I have managed to develop my plan sufficiently to escalate it into its next stage. My creatures have performed rather well, wouldn't you say?"

"*Your* creatures?" asked Delaney incredulously. "Whoever made those androids had to be a genius. Somehow I don't think you qualify."

Drakov pretended to look hurt. "I'm sorry you have such a low opinion of me, Mr. Delaney. However, you are quite correct, in at least one sense. My creatures are indeed works of genius. I did not create them, I merely provided the necessary inspiration and the funds. In fact, you have already met the man responsible. You will recall the old blind king? He was neither very old nor was he blind. He was most anxious to see how his harpies would respond in a field situation. But you are wrong in thinking them androids. They are the products of rather unusual genetic engineering."

"I don't believe you," Steiger said. "Those women at Lemnos were androids. I saw the series stampings on them."

"Prototypes, Mr. Steiger, or may I presume upon our previous relationship and call you Creed? I must say I like that name better than your others. It seems to fit you."

"Prototypes of what?" asked Steiger.

"An entirely new form of temporal weapon," Drakov said. "Their creator calls them hominoids. They are genetically tailored beings made from cloned human cells and gestated in artificial wombs, then surgically and cybernetically augmented at various stages of their natural development. We use time travel to allow them to mature to the various necessary stages, then bring them back at optimal growth periods so that we may progress to the next developmental stage. They are natural beings, yet I suppose you could also call them supernatural, in a sense. Cybernetic implants make them completely programmable.

"The Lemnos women were part of a very primitive, early run of prototypes created under the auspices of the Special Operations Group. It was their intention to create an army of totally expendable temporal soldiers, but they lacked imagination. They were content merely to create an unsophisticated sub-race of humans that would have been little more than cannon fodder. They were afraid to create what could become a competitive species. I, on the other hand, offered their creator a chance to let his imagination run wild and to test his talents to their limits. What scientist could resist such an opportunity? You have seen the results being tested in the field, partially by yourselves. The Lemnos women were only the first generation. The titans were the next, followed by the harpies and the centaur. Each new generation has proved more successful than the previous one. The next generation is even more impressive.''

"And I suppose the Special Operations Group is merely going to stand by idle while you disrupt their temporal continuity with your hominoids,'' said Delaney.

"No, Mr. Delaney, I don't imagine they will. However, the Special Operations Group believes that *your* people are responsible. They believe that a small commando strike force carried off a successful assault on their Project Infiltrator laboratory complex and captured its director, along with a substantial number of Infiltrator prototypes and genetic culture samples. They think the Temporal Intelligence Agency is now in possession of Project Infiltrator. I imagine they will probably launch a massive preventive strike against your timeline before you can bring Infiltrator hominoids of your own on line in a significant strike against them. And there we have the beauty of this little situation I have engineered.''

Drakov smiled. "My plan has threatened your timeline with a strategic temporal strike. The only way you can prevent this strike, or at best delay it, is by helping me complete my operation here. Because if you successfully complete your mission, you will have added your disruptive influence to mine to create a significant temporal adjustment problem in this time period. That will immediately occupy a large portion of the Special Operations Group's attention, thereby preventing them from launching their strike before you can prepare for it. So, in effect, I will be helping you in the short run. But in the long run, by helping me, you will assist me in staging disruptions in your *own* timeline.'' He chuckled. "And there is nothing you can do about it. You have absolutely no choice at all.''

"He can't be right,'' said Andre, glancing at the others.

Delaney clenched his teeth and swore softly. "I'm afraid he is. We can't exactly go to the opposition and tell them that we weren't responsible for heisting their Infiltrator Project. In the first place, they wouldn't believe us. And in the second place, even if they did, they couldn't afford to let us go. We'd be too valuable to their interrogation teams.''

"We lose out either way,'' Steiger said. "If we abort the mission, we leave ourselves open to the opposition. If we complete the mission, we'll be helping Drakov.''

"I see you grasp the situation," said Drakov. "Consider it a payback for your sanction of the Nautilus. And this time it's *my* turn to tell *you* that it's over. You have no options left."

"All right, Drakov," said Delaney. "For the moment, let's assume we let you call the shots. What do you want?"

"That somewhat weighty golden rug at your feet is the key to this entire scenario," said Drakov. "It is not the original golden fleece, but for all practical purposes, that makes no difference. The original fleece came from one of my creatures." He grinned. "Yes, there really was a flying ram and it was I who gave it to Nephele, who was no more a cloud nymph that I am a god. Aietes had the creature killed and skinned. It was the fleece of that creature, a sort of yellow-gold in color, which he first hung in this very grove. However, it soon began to rot, so he had this one made of real gold—thin gold wires fastened to several heavy layers of horsehide. The head is the actual skull of the original ram, covered with a thin coat of hammered gold. I imagine it would be almost priceless in the 27th century, even discounting its historical value.

"If Jason succeeds in bringing it back with him, it will result in the downfall of King Pelias," Drakov continued. "However, two things stand in his way. One is that Pelias has placed a spy among the Argonauts. Regrettably, I have not been able to learn who that spy is. My creatures were programmed not to kill certain key individuals in this scenario, but there is a chance that one of those they did kill was the spy. Unfortunately, there is no way to know for certain. The only one who knew the spy's identity was the High Priest of Iolchos and he died without revealing it. It seems I underestimated my ability to frighten him. The thought of being chastised by a god gave the poor man a heart attack. The second obstacle to Jason bringing back the golden fleece is you, which was why I chose this moment to enlighten you.

"You see," Drakov continued, "there never was an historical voyage of Jason and the Argonauts in this timeline. I made it all happen. The real Jason died along with his father, Aeson, murdered by cutthroats in the employ of Pelias, who now believes that his assassins bungled the job with the boy."

"The *real* Jason?" Delaney said, looking at Jason, who stood alongside Idmon and Medea, watching them with a bewildered expression on his face as they conversed in English.

"Yes, Mr. Delaney. It was necessary to create several hominoids to complete the mythical cast of this fascinating voyage. Jason is one, Hercules is the other. Neither of them realizes what he is of course. They were created in a laboratory and clocked back to this time period as children to be given into Chiron's care. And the centaur had precise instructions as to how to raise them. In that sense, the experiment has been wonderfully successful. We can create hominoids, place them in a temporal scenario, and have their development supervised by other hominoids, even in the midst of humans. All I need do is check on them from time to time, if you will pardon the pun. The others are all genuine, historical figures who would have followed slightly different paths had I not interfered. Theseus, for example, would never have made the voyage, but would have remained in Athens. Meleager would have found other challenges elsewhere. Argus would have built other vessels. I merely created a detour in their lives.''

"So the voyage itself is the disruption," said Delaney. "If we had sabotaged the quest, we would have sabotaged our own mission.''

"Which he suckered us into," Steiger added.

"On the other hand," said Drakov, "if you help Jason fulfill his quest, you will not only succeed in dethroning Pelias and altering the history of this timeline, you will contribute to the fame of all the others, many of whom will go on to become significant historical figures in this time period. Hercules is already an excellent example. Reversing the effects of this voyage will be a monumental task for the Special Operations Group, *if* they can accomplish it. And chances are excellent that they have already begun. I have taken great pains to keep this operation secret, but due to the extent of it, it is doubtful that it has escaped the attention of their temporal observers. They will realize, of course, that Hercules never actually existed in this timeline, but they won't be able to attack the ship without endangering Theseus and the others, whose deaths could be significantly disruptive. And, needless to say, they will wish to capture you alive, if possible. I'll be interested to see how they will try it.''

"So that's what you needed us for," said Andre, "to help your Jason hominoid complete the quest and make sure the Special Operations Group doesn't interfere with it.''

"Precisely," Drakov said. "Isn't it amusing, Miss Cross? For once, we have a common goal. And your presence in this scenario diverts attention from me. Who knows, perhaps there is a way I can arrange for the Special Operations Group to help me do the same in your timeline. I feel rather like the hunter who has happened upon two stags battling for supremacy. While they are busy ramming at each other, the hunter bags two kills.''

He touched the warp disc on his wrist and suddenly he wasn't there anymore.

"A god!" said Jason, in a low and reverent voice. "I have seen and spoken with a god!"

"What tongue was that you spoke?" Medea asked. "And which god was it? What did he say to you?" She swallowed hard and dropped her voice. "Have we incurred their vengeance? Am I to be punished for what I have done?"

Delaney improvised. "The god spoke to us in the language of our people. And he did not give his name. He spoke to us because you angered him, Jason, but he wishes you well upon your quest. Yet the gods are divided in their desires. Some of them wish for us to succeed and return to Iolchos with the golden fleece. Others wish for us to fail. In pleasing some, we shall anger others and there is nothing to be done."

"That is because gods are capricious," Jason said. "Chiron taught me so. The only way to please all the gods together is to prevail over whatever obstacles they may set before us, so that they will deem us worthy."

"It may not be wise to defy the gods," said Medea. "Some are more powerful than others."

"And what of my throne?" said Jason.

"One throne is as good as any other," said Medea. "You have a force of warriors behind you. We could seize some other kingdom, maybe just a small one in the beginning until we can increase our army, or perhaps we could join with my sister and march upon my father. Then we could seize the throne of Aea and—"

"No!" said Jason. "I am not some freebooter who takes that which is not his by right. I want only what is mine! Pelias will surrender the throne of Iolchos to me or I shall have his life. That is what I have sworn and that is what I shall do! I will hear no more talk of seizing kingdoms. I have told you what I shall do. Now it is for you to decide. I will go to Iolchos with the fleece. You may come and share my fate or you can stay and face your father and Kovalos. Make your choice now, but do not come to me later with regrets.''

"I will go with you,'' Medea said softly, "if you will have me.''

"Done,'' said Jason. "We have wasted enough time. It will be dawn soon. We must hurry to join the others.''

"The boy learns slowly,'' Idmon said, "but he does learn. Who knows, perhaps he may yet slay this second dragon. Yet I fear that we are not yet done with gods.''

"What do you mean?'' Delaney asked.

The soothsayer sighed. "We still have a long journey home to make and much can happen in that time.'' He nodded. "Yes, much can happen, and I have a strong feeling that much will.''

12 _____

They left the Sacred Grove of Ares by the trail leading from the opposite side of the clearing. It took them on a winding course down to the bottom of the ravine and curled around to follow the river that ran down from the mountains to the sea. It was a narrow path that necessitated their traveling single file along the riverbank, making it difficult for Jason and Delaney to carry the golden fleece. It was too heavy for one man to carry any distance by himself and between Jason, Steiger and Delaney, they spelled each other. Idmon walked ahead of them with Medea leading as they picked their way among the rocks and shrubs. The trail was old and clearly little used. In many places, it took them over flat rock surfaces slick with the water spray from the rapids. Even without the weighty burden of the golden fleece, making fast time would have been difficult. The sky was already growing gray by the time they left the trail along the riverbank and circled round roughly parallel to the coastline on a path which led down to the shore.

"From here on, you must lead," Medea said to Jason, "as I do not know where you have hidden your ship." She pointed.

"The main road to the city lies just north and to the east of here."

"Then we must go north and to the west," said Jason. "We must keep to the shelter of the trees as much as possible, in case we should encounter any of Aietes' soldiers." He looked up at the sky. "The sun will rise soon. I had hoped to be underway by now. Theseus and the others should already be at the ship, unless something has gone amiss." He glanced at Idmon. "What do you see, soothsayer? Shall we put safely out to sea?"

Idmon was frowning. "I do not know. But I have a strong sense of death nearby."

"Whose death?" Medea said, frightened.

Idmon shook his head. "I cannot tell," he said. "I only feel death's presence. Death itself, waiting in the shadows, hidden. Death armed and waiting to do battle."

They walked along the shoreline, staying out of the open and away from the beach, which slowed them down still more. The sun was rising and starting to dispel the early morning mists by the time they neared the place where they had hidden the *Argo.*

"Something has gone wrong," said Idmon, staring at the still hidden ship. "If the others had arrived, they should have uncovered the ship by now and made ready to sail."

Medea looked bewildered. "Where is it?"

"There," said Jason, pointing. "Hidden in the reeds." He gave a slight start. "I just saw something move!"

He glanced at the others. "Wait here. Guard the golden fleece."

He started to run across the open stretch toward the reed-bank where the ship was hidden. When he was not quite half-way to the ship, some of the reeds on board were thrown aside and Theseus leaped out, along with Hercules, Orpheus and several of the others. They ran toward Jason, who quickened his pace at the sight of them.

"We were beginning to think you had been killed or captured," Theseus said. "What happened to the others?"

"They are back there," Jason said, pointing, "with the golden fleece."

"You have it, then!"

"We have it!" Jason said. He turned and shouted to the others. "Come on, then! All is well! Come quickly!"

"We kept the ship hidden in case there were any patrols about," said Orpheus, "but it appears that we have foxed them." He stared hard at the approaching party. "Who is that girl? Not Aietes' daughter!"

"Yes, Medea," Jason said. "She is returning with us."

"You *have* been busy," Orpheus said with a grin. "A throne and a queen gained at one stroke!"

"Make ready to sail!" Theseus shouted back at the ship. Instantly, the camouflaging reeds were thrown aside as the Argonauts cleared the decks and started to raise the mast. "We'll be halfway back to Iolchos before Aietes is any the wiser!"

"I fear not," said Idmon softly. He pointed. "Look."

"STAND WHERE YOU ARE!" shouted Kovalos. He was seated on horseback at the head of a troop of cavalry on a crest some fifty yards away. In front of the mounted soldiers were several squads of archers, arrows nocked and bows drawn back.

"Are we in range?" asked Idmon.

"I'm afraid so," said Delaney. "And caught right out in the open."

The rest of the Argonauts quickly worked to raise the mast.

"The archers can pin us down until the cavalry rides in to finish us off," said Steiger. "We can try to make a run for it, but nobody's going to be moving very fast carrying the golden fleece. And whoever carries it will be their main target."

"Th-then we sh-shall see how g-good th-their archers are," said Hercules, bending down and picking up the golden fleece as easily as if it were a sheepskin throw rug.

"What is he doing?" asked Medea. Kovalos had dismounted and he now stood before the archers, both hands raised high over his head. His voice carried down to them as he threw his head back and shouted at the heavens.

"ARISE, WARRIORS OF ARES! ARISE AND RID COLCHIS OF THE INVADERS! ARISE AND LIVE AGAIN!"

"He's gone straight off his nut," said Steiger.

"Death comes!" whispered Idmon, harshly.

"Where?" cred Jason, looking around wildly.

"Look!" said Orpheus, pointing.

Medea screamed.

A hand was clawing up from beneath the ground about a dozen yards away. Near it, two more hands appeared like crabs scuttling out from beneath the sand, twisted fingers grasping at the air. Arms were sprouting from the ground like impossibly fast growing plants, thrashing around and pushing to pull the bodies free. A head became visible, then another, and another. Dozens of upper torsos were visible, arms pushing against the sand, straining to free legs. They crawled forward, pulling themselves out, dozens of them, to stand unsteadily on their feet like stalks of wheat swaying gently in the wind.

"They are dead men," Orpheus said with horror.

They stood as if in catatonic trance, bedraggled, life-sized marionettes held up by loose strings, rotted, decomposing flesh flapping, bones protruding, eyes encrusted or absent altogether from the vacant sockets, gums retreating from yellowed and blackened teeth, wisps of white-gray hair escaping from beneath corroded helmets. The leather armor was dry and veined with cracks like the surface of some long dry, sunbaked riverbed and the cloaks hung down in tatters from bony shoulders. The rusted noseguards of the helmets shielded nonexistent noses and the earpieces covered holes no longer graced by earlobes. Worms and maggots writhed in places where decayed flesh was exposed and pieces of once living tissue dropped down onto the sand.

Medea could not stop screaming. Her hands were up over her ears, as if to shut out the sound of her own shrieks. She stood frozen to the spot, paralyzed with terror. Hercules dropped the fleece onto the sand and stared at the living dead with disbelief.

"Corpses," said Jason, his voice cracking. "How does one fight corpses? How to kill that which is already dead?"

"If a corpse cannot be killed," said Theseus, drawing his sword, "it can still be dismembered."

"Remember what you said about people who don't panic?" Andre said to Finn. She nodded at Theseus. "There's one. You think maybe he can tell us how it's done? I just went numb all over."

"It's Drakov," Steiger said. "That bastard's brewed himself up a bunch of zombies."

"Cybernetically augmented," Delaney said. "Isn't that what he said? He found the ship, clocked back in time and buried a bunch of his hominoids out here. They died, but the cybernetics kept on working, sending impulses to circuits buried in the decomposing muscles or in the skeletal structure.''

"That lunatic has set us up," said Steiger. "The only way out is to do what Theseus said, dismember them or smash their skulls and destroy the implants. Then all we have to figure out is what to do about Kovalos with his archers and his cavalry. Piece of cake. Or we could run out into the water and try swimming back to Iolchos.''

"KILL THEM!" Kovalos screamed.

The corpses shambled toward them slowly, dead hands pulling rusted blades from rotted scabbards.

"Remember that emergency we were saving the warp discs for?" said Andre. "I think this is it, guys.''

"I think you're right," said Finn. "Creed?"

"I'm not about to be cut up by a remote controlled cadaver," Steiger said.

He glanced over his shoulder as the main body of the Argonauts came leaping over the side of the ship to join the battle while a few remained behind with Argus to push the ship off from the shore and hoist the sail. He looked back toward the crest, where Kovalos stood watching with his soldiers.

"We'd better do something about that group up there or no one's getting out of here," he said.

"Fugue sequence?" said Delaney.

"You know any other way three can take on about fifty?" Steiger said.

"All three of us fugue clocking at once?" said Andre. "The three of us could wind up being one of us if we accidentally synchronize our fugue patterns. That could get real messy.''

"Don't take this personally," said Steiger, "but I have no intention of sharing my space with you. We'll use a three/six staggered fugue sequence, zero-three-six initiation with me first, you second and Finn third. Estimate your best coordinates for about fifteen to twenty yards behind our friends up there on the crest and make every arrow count. Got it? Now *stage*, and fast!"

As the corpses tottered toward them, swords raised, Theseus gave out a yell and charged them. Hercules picked up the golden fleece with one arm and hoisted the hysterical Medea with the other and started sprinting toward the ship as the other Argonauts joined Theseus and Jason in their charge.

"Staged!" shouted Delaney, left wrist cocked in front of

him, right hand on the control studs.

"Staged!" shouted Andre, in a similar position.

Several of the corpse soldiers were getting dangerously close.

"Staged!" shouted Steiger.

One of the corpses was less than three feet from Delaney, but he could spare no time to deal with it. It swung its sword down in a swift arc toward his head.

"TIME!" yelled Steiger.

The sword came down, but it slashed through empty space. All three of them had disappeared.

Meleager ran a corpse through with his sword. It didn't even slow it down. It slashed at him as he pulled his sword free of the soggy flesh and only by falling quickly and rolling aside could he avoid the killing stroke. Jason parried a sword thrust, then quickly brought his blade up and around and severed a rotting arm from its shoulder. The arm, hand still holding the sword, fell to the ground, but the corpse kept coming at him. Jason ran it through. It lurched forward, impaling itself even further on the blade as its one remaining hand, fingers like talons, reached for Jason's throat. He batted the hand away and struck at the corpse's face with all his might. The head flew off and landed in the sand several feet away. As the body collapsed to the ground, the head continued to twitch slowly from side to side, moving with the spastic motion of a windup toy.

Theseus wasted no time in engaging any one of the corpses in single combat. He moved like a whirling dervish, slashing quickly at one and immediately twisting away and slashing at another. Holding his sword with both hands as if it were an axe, he spun through the grisly army like a buzz saw, taking advantage of their slow "reactions" to inflict as much damage as he could to as many of them as he could, aiming always for the extremities and putting all his power behind every stroke, accompanying each one with a grunt of effort, like a butcher laying about him with a maul.

Up on the crest, Kovalos watched the combat, his soldiers staring with horrified fascination at the army of the living dead their captain had raised. They had both feared and respected him before, but they had never dreamed he was a sorcerer and now they regarded their commander with a terrified awe. When the corpses had first started to claw their way free of the earth, not a few of them almost ran in abject panic from the sight, but they were rooted in their place both by the hypnotic aspect of the spectacle and their terror of what their commander might do to them if they showed fear. What chance would there be to flee from a man who could raise the dead?

Kovalos stood before them, watching as the corpses closed with the Argonauts, but when he spotted Hercules sprinting back toward the ship with Medea and the golden fleece, he pointed and shouted to his archers, "There! That one, Hercules! Shoot him down! He must not reach the ship!"

As one of the archers shifted his aim to the massive, running figure, an arrow came whistling between the ranks of cavalry behind him and thudded home into the base of his skull. He toppled forward and fell onto the rocks below. Several of the archers had time to loose their arrows, but they had failed to properly estimate the speed with which Hercules ran, not thinking that a man so large could move so quickly, so they did not lead him well when they had aimed. When their fellow archer fell over the edge, they hesitated and in that time two more arrows passing between the horses behind them claimed two more of their number.

The cavalry soldiers wheeled their horses as soon as they realized there was an enemy behind them, but instead of a force of opposing archers, they were confronted with a sight that baffled them completely. Several of the horsemen near the center of the formation caught what they thought was a glimpse of a bowman, but in the next instant, he was no longer there. Several others on the right flank caught sight of a woman archer pulling back her bow, but just as they were about to charge her, she seemed to vanish. There was a shout from the left flank of the cavalry as someone spotted yet another archer shooting at them, then confusion when the man who saw him found himself pointing to a spot where no one stood.

The mercenaries of Kovalos found themselves confronted with a phenomenon beyond any understanding. It was the most dangerous maneuver in temporal warfare, dangerous to both the attacked and the attackers—fugue clocking. With the proper skill and a great deal of luck, one man using a fugue clocking sequence could become an army. Yet one mistake could result in utter disaster, trapping the temporal soldier in

limbo forever in the dead zone of non-specific time or causing
him to clock in at the exact time-space coordinates as those occupied by another mass, either living or inanimate. Several
temporal soldiers fugue clocking at the same time, using a
hastily programmed fugue sequence, could conceivably mater-
ialize in the same place at the same time, resulting in an instant
and agonizing death. For temporal soldiers, the options regarding fugue clocking were clearly and rigidly defined. It was
a worst case scenario option, a tactic of last resort.

The three/six staggered sequence program with a zero-
three-six initiation Steiger had called for was one of the standard drills among temporal adjustment teams. They were
frightening, but necessary drills, necessary because in a situation that called for such a desperate maneuver, there could be
no time for thought. The programming had to be accomplished quickly, almost by instinct, and whoever called the sequence was immediately and automatically in charge, not to
be questioned under any circumstances. Later, if the team
concerned survived and the tactic was found to be unnecessary, they could exercise the option of beating him to death.

Three/six: Three seconds in, six seconds out. Three seconds
during which to act in real time, six seconds spent in temporal
limbo. Zero-three-six initiation: the moment all three team
members were "staged," fugue sequence programming locked
in, zero-three-six designated the initiation of the sequence for
all three of them. On the command, *"Time,"* the zero-designated team member would start the sequence with three
seconds in real time, zero initiation gap. The three-designated
team member would start the sequence with three seconds in
temporal limbo, clocking in to real time the second after the
zero-designated team member clocked out of real time for six
seconds in limbo. The six-designated team member would
begin the fugue with six seconds spent in temporal limbo,
clocking in to real time the second after the three-designated
team member clocked out, three seconds after the zero-
designated team member had clocked out with three seconds
left to spend in limbo.

The staggered fugue sequence was designed to eliminate the
possibility of any two of them materializing simultaneously in
the same location and once it was locked in for a set time cor-
responding to a given sequence order, it was irreversible for
that length of time, completely automatic. It left each team

member with three seconds in real time during which to fight, but those three seconds were a slim margin in real time combat situations, where remaining in the same place could easily prove fatal. Constant movement in real time was essential.

As Steiger began the sequence by clocking in approximately sixteen yards behind the soldiers, he aimed his bow quickly and fired, drawing another arrow and nocking it as he ran quickly to his right. He vanished into temporal limbo before taking two steps and Andre clocked in, shot her arrow, drew and nocked while moving and likewise disappeared. Delaney clocked in and followed the same procedure, clocking out as Steiger materialized already running. A quick halt, an arrow flight and the procedure was repeated.

It was an exhausting, taxing strategy, leaving no room for error and almost no time in which to aim, but the result was that the soldiers of Kovalos were confronted with three archers who appeared in lightning sequence out of thin air, shot, killed, and disappeared, only to reappear elsewhere and shoot again. Their first response was one of confusion, then came disbelief, then the realization that they were under attack by what seemed to be a phantom army of bowmen, which led quickly to blind panic. Every three seconds, a soldier fell dead, killed by what seemed to be ghosts shooting very real arrows. After what they had already witnessed on the beach below them, this was too much for the soldiers. They broke and ran, screaming with terror, posing an immediate danger for the three temporal agents.

Andre clocked in, her bow held ready, only to find a fleeing cavalry soldier bearing down upon her. She threw herself to her left and the horse missed her by inches. Delaney clocked in a fraction of a second before a galloping horse would have crossed the same time-space and only his forward momentum saved him from being trampled. The horse caught him a glancing blow and he fell spinning to the ground, vanishing from sight the instant that he fell. Steiger clocked in two inches in front of a running archer, who slammed into him at full speed. Both men fell to the ground, stunned, but only one of them remained there.

The archer was not as badly stunned as Steiger and he started to get back to his feet almost at once, looking all about him to see what he had run into and seeing nothing. Thinking he had been felled by an invisible opponent, he drew his sword and swung it all around him, then promptly tripped and fell as Steiger's prone body materialized between his legs. The archer screamed, dropped his sword and came as close as a man could come to breaking light speed.

Hercules ran hard, heedless of the arrows raining down upon him. He reached the *Argo,* flung the golden fleece on board one-armed and then unceremoniously hoisted Medea up over his head and tossed her into the waiting arms of Argus. He tossed her a bit too hard and Argus suddenly found himself flat on his back upon the deck, pinned down by an hysterical female. He dislodged her and dragged her to her feet and shook her, but she kept right on screaming. Unable to think of what else to do, Argus gave her a stinging slap across the face. The screams stopped instantly and for a moment her eyes went out of focus, then they went wide with shock and outrage.

"How *dare* you!" she cried, forgetting everything else in her fury as she hauled off and smashed her right fist into the shipwright's face. Argus staggered backward, momentarily stunned, as Medea cried out with pain and clutched at her right hand, then she remembered where she was and what was happening and started screaming once again.

"If one needs any proof of the capricious nature of the gods," muttered Argus, "one need only look at women." He drew back his fist and slammed it right into her jaw. She fell to the deck like a stone. "Do something with her!" Argus said to Hylas, then ran back to the tiller as the boy started to drag her unconscious body across the deck, out of the way.

Having disposed of Medea and the golden fleece, Hercules ran back to join the battle. The corpse soldiers were not as quick in their movements as were the Argonauts, but they were relentless. The Argonauts ran them through again and again, but still they kept on coming. A number of the corpses were riddled with arrows shot by several of the Argonauts, but they were undeterred and they continued pressing their frightening assault, moving forward slowly in a jerking manner and slashing spasmodically with their swords. Several of the Argonauts had fallen. Even more of the corpses had fallen, but they still kept on, dragging themselves across the sand. Only those that had their skulls split or their heads knocked off lay still, but the Argonauts were steadily being pressed back toward the sea.

Hercules didn't even bother to draw his sword. He plunged

into the battle, swinging both fists like bludgeons and rallying the Argonauts as heads popped off the necks of corpses with each blow. Belatedly realizing the effectiveness of the technique, the Argonauts aimed for the heads of the dead bodies and the tide of the battle began to turn. The beach around them resembled an explosion in a pathology lab. Argus had succeeded in pushing the ship away from shore and he now shouted to the remaining Argonauts to get on board. A number of them felled their lifeless opponents and turned to sprint across the beach and into the water, striking out for the ship.

Steiger felt as if he had slammed into a tree. He shook his head and tried to get his eyes to focus. They focused on Kovalos, crouching over him, and on the business end of a plasma pistol pointed directly at his face. Still groggy, Steiger counted three seconds. When he didn't dematerialize, he realized the fugue program had run its course. He also realized that he was in serious trouble.

"Drop the bows or your partner's had it!" said Kovalos, speaking in English. "And keep your hands away from those bracelets!"

Andre and Finn hesitated, then dropped their bows down on the ground.

"The quivers, too," Kovalos said. "And then the swords."

"Special Operations Group, I take it," Steiger said.

"Just lie very still, friend," said Kovalos. "I've still got your two partners to deliver to Interrogation. I don't really need you. You so much as twitch an eyebrow and you're dead."

"And so are you," said Steiger.

"Like hell," Kovalos said. "If you people had any serious weapons, you would've used them. You got screwed by your own cover. You think your friends can pick up their bows and fit their arrows faster than I can squeeze this trigger?"

"Man's got a point," Delaney said. "Okay, Mister, it's your move. What's the deal?"

"Deal?" said Kovalos. "You have to be kidding. The only deal you people get is staying alive unless you try something stupid. You've got nothing to deal with."

"What makes you so sure?" Delaney said. "I thought your people were pretty anxious about Project Infiltrator and its director."

"The psych teams will get everything they need out of you," Kovalos said.

"I don't doubt that," Delaney said. "Only by then, it'll be too late for the information to do them any good. And it won't get you any points. What's your rank? Lieutenant? Captain? There'd be a nice promotion and a commendation in it for you if you turned up information that could lead your adjustment team to your missing Infiltrator Project."

"That's your offer?" said Kovalos. "You'd sell out your own people?"

"No," Delaney said. "My people haven't got it. It's probably right under your noses and you don't know to look in the right place. Believe me, I'd rather the Special Operations Group had it back than leave it in the hands of the man who's got it now."

"That's a poor stall, friend, and it won't work," said Kovalos.

"Pity," said Drakov, from behind him, "he's telling the truth, you know."

Kovalos spun around, but he wasn't quick enough. Drakov fired point-blank into his chest and Kovalos screamed as the plasma enveloped him in an aura of blue flame. Steiger scrambled for the weapon that Kovalos had dropped.

"I wouldn't," Drakov said, aiming his pistol at Steiger.

Steiger held Kovalos' pistol pointed at Drakov. "One of us won't make it," he said.

Both Finn and Andre had recovered their bows and they held them drawn, aimed directly at Drakov.

"Arrows are just as effective as a plasma pistol at this distance," said Delaney.

"True," said Drakov, "but before you demonstrate that point, you might wish to take a glance behind you."

"Give it up, Drakov," said Delaney. "That one's as old as—"

"Finn . . ." said Steiger, his gaze fixed on a point behind and above them.

Delaney saw the expression on his face and looked behind him. His gaze slowly traveled up until his head was back as far as it would go.

"Finn?" said Andre, still covering Drakov with her bow, not taking her eyes off him for an instant. "What is it?"

"You don't want to know," Delaney said.

Staring down at him was a huge, impassive metal face. The bronze colossus towered above them like a skyscraper, the chiseled features beneath the war helmet expressionless, the solid bronze orbs that were the eyes motionless, fixed upon him by the forward inclination of the head. The bronze shield was about twenty-five feet in diameter and the bronze sword was large enough to demolish a small building with one stroke.

"I could not resist the final touch," said Drakov. "What is the myth of Jason and the Argonauts without Talos, the bronze giant?"

Steiger threw down the pistol in disgust. "Man," he said, "this just is *not* my day."

13 _____

"I'm disappointed in you, Mr. Delaney," Drakov said, mockingly. "Here I am helping you complete your mission and you were going to sell me out."

"Some help," Delaney said.

Andre was staring up at the immobile bronze giant. "*You* made this?" she said.

"I thought you'd be impressed," said Drakov. "Actually, an old friend directed the construction process. The laborers who performed the bulk of the less sophisticated tasks thought they were working for Hephaestus, the Greek god of the fire and the forge. Santos found it all very amusing, being a god."

"Santos Benedetto?" asked Steiger.

"The last of the Timekeepers," Drakov said, "except for myself, of course. If you care to wave hello, he's sitting up there in the helmet, at the controls of what I believe is the largest robot ever built. As I told you once before, the game continues. And we are still a long way from the endgame. The problem is what to do about you in the meantime."

Drakov glanced out over the water at the *Argo,* receding in the distance. "I'm afraid you've missed your ship. No doubt

marine for time travel. Now, it performed the same function for the robot inspired by Talos, the bronze giant of Greek mythology.

"It seems to be old home week," Benedetto said, looking down at them and grinning wolfishly. He looked older and even thinner, but beyond that, he hadn't changed. He still dressed habitually in black and his sharp features and neatly trimmed black beard gave him the look of a Renaissance assassin. His knowledge of cybernetics combined with his training in psycho-conditioning made him doubly dangerous and he had no scruples whatsoever. Once a passionate moralist, a scientist who had enlisted in the Temporal Preservation League out of a genuine concern over the Time Wars, he had gravitated toward the radical militants who had made up the Timekeepers. Terrorism had destroyed his ethics and he was reborn a consummate cynic without any hope or optimism. Drakov conceived his mad plans in deadly earnest, but to Benedetto, they were merely fascinating games, complex entertainments for his jaded appetites.

"We're going home, Santos," Drakov said.

"Before or after we take care of our intruders?" Benedetto asked.

"Our guests will accompany us," said Drakov. "I think they'd enjoy meeting the professor."

"I wasn't referring to our commando friends," said Benedetto. "I meant the two men who came in after you."

Drakov glanced up at him sharply. "*What* two men?"

"Really, Nikolai," said Benedetto, "you're becoming careless. Two men managed to slip inside before I could close the door. Talos isn't exactly state-of-the-art design, you know. Certain operations are cumbersome and they take some time. I told you we should have used nysteel construction."

"Translocate, Santos! Immediately!"

"As you wish."

He turned around and returned to the controls. A moment later, the V-20 warp disc suspended overhead started to glow. Drakov motioned the three agents over to the bed and indicated for them to sit down, then he sat in a chair across from them, in a position where he could keep them covered and at the same time observe the opening in the floor.

"If we've been penetrated by agents of the Special Operations Group," he said, tensely, "things might become a bit more interesting than I care for. We'll be better able to deal with the threat when we reach our home base."

"*Our* home base?" said Finn.

"Certainly," said Drakov. He smiled. "We are working together in this venture, are we not?"

"Where is 'our' home base?" said Andre.

"On a small island in this very time period, Miss Cross," said Drakov. "We shall arrive at the Greek islands well ahead of your former shipmates."

"How do you manage to hide a robot of this size on a small Greek island?" asked Delaney.

Drakov smiled. "I don't bother to try. I keep Talos right out in the open, standing astride the entrance to the harbor of Rhodes."

"The Colossus of Rhodes," said Steiger. "One of the ancient wonders of the world. Very nice. Only how does the population of the island react when he disappears every now and then?"

"They never notice," Drakov said. "A careful log is kept of each temporal transition Talos makes. We merely clock back in a fraction of a second after we have left." He frowned. "Whoever our friends below are, they are apparently hesitant to join us. They think to catch us as we go back down. So much the better. They will shortly find themselves caught squarely in the middle."

"In the middle of what?" said Delaney.

Drakov smiled. "You shall see. Santos, have we arrived?"

"We're here," said Benedetto, from above them. "I've got the hominoids standing by. Want I should let them in?"

"By all means," said Drakov. "We mustn't keep our two guests downstairs waiting."

Benedetto threw several levers and opened the door in the giant's ankle.

"This should prove to be amusing," Drakov said. He beckoned them to the opening in the floor with his pistol. "Why don't you lead the way?"

Delaney went down first, followed by Steiger and then Andre. Drakov went behind them, keeping them covered with his pistol. Benedetto remained behind. They descended the metal stair to the landing inside the hollow of the giant's chest. Below them, they could hear the sounds of battle. The report of plasma weapons being fired echoed up to them, accompanied by the screams of frenzied hominoids attacking the two men below them. Steiger ventured a quick glance over the metal guardrail. Below him, the interior of the robot lit up several times with the reflections of plasma blasts and he could see blue flame down there as figures burned, but as those who pressed the two intruders died, others replaced them. They heard more screaming and shouts and then the sound of booted feet on metal as someone came running up the steps toward them, moving fast.

"Drakov!" shouted Delaney. "We're going to have company in a minute."

"I can hear," said Drakov, calmly.

"So what the hell are we supposed to fight with?" said Delaney.

"Think positive, Mr. Delaney," Drakov said. "Perhaps my hominoids will catch up with whoever it is and kill them before they reach you. If not, why then you'll have to use your ingenuity. Don't be concerned, I'll cover you."

"Somehow I don't find that very reassuring," said Delaney. He glanced back at Steiger and Andre.

"Nowhere to go," said Steiger. "Someone's coming up toward us with plasma weapons and Drakov's behind us with a plasma pistol of his own. We're caught between a rock and a hard place." He glanced over the side. "And it's a long way down."

The running footsteps came closer, followed by the sounds of others pursuing from below. There were no more plasma blasts. Whoever was coming toward them wasn't wasting any time stopping to fire at those below.

"They're coming fast," Delaney said, tensely.

A figure came running up onto the landing just below them. Drakov fired over their heads and the heat of the plasma blast singed their hair as it passed above them and slammed into the inside wall of the robot, just ahead of the running man below them. He jerked back from the wash of flame as melted bronze dripped down the wall and the superheated guardrail just ahead of him started to sag.

"Drop your weapon!" Drakov shouted.

The man started to raise his pistol, then saw Delaney standing just above him and he froze.

"My God," he said.

"Drop it, I said!" Drakov repeated.

The pistol clattered to the metal floor of the landing, bounced, and skittered over the side to fall to the bottom of the robot's leg. Drakov kept his pistol pointed at the man, but it was Delaney that the soldier stared at.

"Jesus Christ," said Delaney, softly, staring at the man's face.

Andre didn't say a thing. She stood frozen to the spot, speechless, staring at the face of a man who couldn't possibly be alive, the face of Lt. Reese Hunter.

"The sight of you took about ten years off my life," said Hunter. "I saw you killed, torn to pieces, then some thirty seconds later, there you were standing right in front of me."

They were locked in a room in the cellar of Drakov's palace on the island of Rhodes. They were in almost total darkness, with the only light coming from a small barred window high above them, level with the ground outside. The window was out of their reach and too small to squeeze through, even if they could have reached it and defeated the iron bars.

The man who spoke, addressing his comments to Delaney, was Reese Hunter, and yet he wasn't Hunter. The Reese Hunter Finn and Andre knew had been killed in 17th century Paris, assassinated by the Timekeepers. This was his doppelganger, his twin from the future of the congruent universe. The face, the name, everything about him was the same, except that he was a captain in the S.O.G., the Special Operations Group of the Temporal Army of the congruent universe, their elite commando force assigned to deal with temporal disruptions, specifically to conduct the war against the universe from which the temporal agents came. They knew him, and yet they didn't know him. And he "knew" them, as well.

Finn Delaney's twin had been a member of the adjustment team, along with Captain Hunter, commanded by Major Kennedy, the man the temporal agents had known as Kovalos. They had been attempting to adjust the temporal disruption, thinking that the temporal agents were responsible, never suspecting that Drakov was behind it all. They had clocked several teams back and now only Hunter was left.

"Kennedy was going to signal the assault the moment the Infiltrators we had buried on the beach engaged the Argonauts," said Hunter. "We were going to hit from both sides. We were waiting for his signal when all hell broke loose. That damn giant robot clocked in right on top of us." He took a ragged breath. "The poor bastards were crushed. Finn and I were the only ones who got away. We tried to get back to Kennedy, up on the crest, and clocked in just in time to see him buy it. We couldn't see your faces from where we were. We didn't know what the hell was happening. We had no idea what Drakov was doing here. He was supposed to be working for us. Last time I saw him, he was updating the C.I.S. archives."

"C.I.S.?" asked Steiger.

"Counter-Insurgency Section," Hunter said. "New branch of our Intelligence service."

"The ones in charge of intelligence concerning us," said Andre.

Hunter nodded. "Anyway, we were trying to figure our next move when Drakov herded you three inside the robot. The minute I saw that, I knew he was the one responsible for hitting us, not you people. And we still didn't know who you were. Delaney decided to make a try for the door before it closed. Worst damn decision that fool ever made." He glanced at Finn. "Nothing personal."

Delaney smiled wryly. "Yeah, right."

Hunter leaned back against the wall and gave out a small groan. "Damn. Everything went wrong. We were going to jump you people as you came back down. We thought there was a chance we might have been spotted, but we figured what the hell, you had to get by us anyway, so it was worth a shot. We never put it together that Drakov was the one who stole the Infiltrator Project. The next thing we knew, that door was sliding open and they were coming in behind us, rushing up the stairs like an army of ants. We fired and fired and they just kept on coming. Delaney ran out of plasma charges and they got him. Tore him apart with their bare hands. I never saw anything like it."

Delaney shuddered at the thought of his twin from the congruent universe being slaughtered while he was standing on the stairs just overhead.

"I would've burned him to save him from that agony," Hunter went on, "only I had run out of charges, too. There was only one way left to go and that was up. I had an empty gun, but I thought maybe I'd have a chance to bluff you and get those horrors called off. And then I ran smack dab into you. I thought I was hallucinating. Christ, you're his spitting image. And Andre. Jesus, you were dead as well, and there you were."

"What happened to 'me' in this universe?" Andre asked, hesitantly.

"You bought it on an adjustment mission," Hunted said. "Priest never got over it."

"Lucas?" Andre said, feeling as if a cold hand were closing around her insides.

"Your husband," Hunter said. "Or rather, *her* husband. Our Andre Cross, that is. Only she wasn't Andre Cross in our timeline. Her name was Andre de la Croix."

Andre swallowed hard. "That used to be my name," she said. "I changed it."

Hunter nodded. "Hell of a thing, isn't it? And you have a Lucas Priest, as well?"

"Had," Delaney said. "He died on our last mission."

"So did ours," said Hunter. "He was waiting for it, I guess. He never came back from the last one. From what I heard, it was a real killer. You people got us good."

Delaney had no response. What could he say, that he was sorry? The situation was difficult enough as it was without his telling Hunter that he was the one who had killed their Lucas Priest. Andre felt numb. In their own timeline, she had always felt very close to Lucas Priest. In the congruent universe, her twin and that of Lucas had married. It might have happened to them, too, had her Lucas lived long enough. She could not get the image of Hunter's Lucas Priest out of her mind as she stood before her in 19th century Afghanistan, pointing a laser at her chest. She was the enemy and he should have fired, but he had hesitated. There had been a tortured look upon his face as he had briefly lowered the laser, then raised it once again, resigned to what he had to do. That moment's hesitation was what killed him. He had said, "Forgive me, Andre," then just as he was about to fire, Delaney had bayoneted him from behind. She hadn't understood what happened then, why he had hesitated. Now she knew and she wished she didn't.

"So there's a Reese Hunter in your timeline, as well," said Hunter.

"Was," said Delaney.

"Was?" said Hunter. "I see." He shook his head. "Man, that's strange. It's like being told I died."

"Tell me about it," said Delaney.

"Yeah, it's a macabre situation, pilgrim. I keep having to remind myself that you're really not my partner, just like you're probably having a hard time remembering that I'm not the Reese Hunter that you knew. What was he like?"

"He was a lot like you," Delaney said. "Hell, he *was* you, only his history followed a slightly different path. He was an officer in the Airborne Pathfinders who became separated from his unit in 12th century England."

"Christ," said Hunter. "The same thing happened to me."

"Only you apparently came back," Delaney said. "Our Hunter decided to go underground."

Hunter chuckled. "I thought about it. Almost did it, too. It was tempting as hell. How'd your boy make out?"

"Pretty well," Delaney said. "He had quite a setup for himself back there in Sherwood Forest. Built himself a cabin and stocked it with all sorts of goodies from various different time periods. He had all the conveniences. Sound system, generators, microwave oven, briar pipes, smoking jackets, various kinds of ordnance, fine wines . . . The locals believed he was a wizard and he played up the idea to keep them from bothering him. Grew his hair long and dressed up in some kind of crazy silk robe from Japan with dragons on it. Then he got mixed up in one of our missions. Complicated story."

Hunter glanced at Andre. "He bring you back from the 12th century?"

"Yes," she said. "How did you . . . oh, of course. But we went to 17th century Paris first. That was where he . . . died."

Hunter sighed. "Glad I never went to Paris," he said. "We clocked straight back home. Christ, it's really something. Alternate universes, almost exactly identical. And we're at war."

Delaney remained silent.

"Look," said Hunter, "if you don't want to answer this one, just forget I asked, but I've always wanted to know something. Why'd you people start this? I realize you're only grunts, like I am, so maybe you don't really know, but it strikes me that there had to be a better way. All right, so the confluence phenomenon was endangering both our timestreams, but maybe if we got together, we could've figured out a way to lick this thing. But after what you did—"

"We didn't know," said Steiger.

Hunter sighed. "Well, I guess I sorta figured that. Hell, it wasn't your decision. You people are just soldiers, like me."

"You don't understand," said Steiger. "I meant we really didn't know. Until your people attacked us in 19th century Afghanistan, we didn't even know that you existed."

"Come on," said Hunter. "Is that really the line they fed you? Your people bombed the hell out of us. You wiped out entire colonies, killed millions of people—"

"And we didn't even know we were doing it," Delaney said. "He's telling you the truth. We have a temporal nuclear device known as a warp grenade. It allows you to utilize a specified portion of a highly controlled nuclear explosion and it clocks the surplus energy through an Einstein-Rosen Bridge out into space somewhere. We thought we were disposing of the surplus energy in the Orion Nebula, but apparently sending such massive amounts of energy through space warps somehow affected chronophysical alignment. We were clocking nuclear explosions into your timeline and we didn't even know it."

Hunter stared at him. "Are you serious?"

"I can't make you believe me, Hunter, but what I told you is the truth, I swear it."

Hunter sat silent for a long moment. "Hell, ain't that a kick in the head?" he said, his voice heavy. "The most dangerous war in the history of both our timelines and it got started by accident."

"Well, we were the ones to start it, even if it was an accident," said Steiger, "but your people are the ones who have a chance to end it."

Hunter snorted. "Not bloody likely, pilgrim," he said. "You want to know what kind of hatred the people in this timeline have for you? You know what kind of image you people have here? You guys are the living incarnation of evil, according to the politicians and the media. Mass murderers without a conscience. Imperialist warmongers determined to drive us straight into temporal chaos or oblivion to safeguard your own timeline. The only way to deal with you is through force, because that's all you understand. Nobody believes you'll negotiate. And nobody really wants to try."

"Is that how *you* feel?" Andre said. "I'm not hearing any hatred in your voice."

"Yeah, well, I'm not a civilian," Hunter said. "And I didn't have anybody in the colonies that were destroyed. I'm just a military man." He paused. " 'War is much too serious a thing to be left to military men.' A fellow named Talleyrand said that and everyone believed him. Unfortunately, Talleyrand was an asshole.''

"Politician, wasn't he?" said Steiger. "I think I met some of his relatives."

"For what it's worth," said Hunter, "I don't hate you people. That would be something like hating your own reflection in a mirror. But then, nobody consults me about things like that. Anyway, I guess it's over for us now. It's just as well. I've had about enough."

"It isn't over yet," said Steiger.

"Isn't it?" said Hunter. "Take a look around you, pilgrim. I don't think we'll be getting out of this one. Compared to the head of Project Infiltrator, Drakov is downright civilized. You think Drakov's got toys in his attic? Wait 'til you meet Dr. Moreau."

14 _____

It was an incongruous room to be found in a palace in ancient Greece. The floor was parqueted wood covered with a Persian carpet. The furnishings were late Victorian. The wine decanter on the sideboard held a Margaux made from grapes that would not grow for several thousand years. The cork-lined wooden humidor upon the desk contained tobacco blended from plants grown in a country that would not be discovered for centuries. The briar pipe held in Drakov's hand had been made by an English craftsman whose ancestors were at that moment painting their backsides blue and worshiping the trees.

In a land that would be the cradle of civilization, at a time when that cradle had not yet been constructed, in a universe that was familiar and yet alien to him, Nikolai Drakov had created an environment that belonged to no one time or place. It was an environment that suited him, a man who belonged to no one time or place himself. It did not, however, suit the man who paced back and forth across the room, doing his best to control his temper and failing in the task.

"You are being unreasonable, Moreau," said Drakov, momentarily wreathed in a cloud of aromatic pipe smoke.

"Everything is under control. Sit down and relax. Have a glass of wine. It will help steady your nerves."

Moreau stopped his pacing and stood in front of Drakov stiffly, his arms held tightly against his sides, his hands balled into fists. He was a small man, slightly built, with a high forehead crowned by a thick shock of unruly gray hair. His eyes were a very pale blue and he had grown a thick, luxuriant gray beard since leaving his own time. He was dressed in a white laboratory coat, a stark contrast to Drakov's elegant smoking jacket in black and red brocade.

"My nerves are not in need of steadying, thank you," said Moreau. "I am not nervous. I am *not* being unreasonable and everything is *not* under control. When I agreed to join you in this venture, you gave me certain assurances and you are failing to live up to your part of the bargain."

"And in what way have I failed, Professor?" Drakov said, evenly.

"In more ways than one," Moreau replied. "You are being careless, Drakov. Your monumental ego is placing this entire project in jeopardy. It seems as if you have gone out of your way to advertise our presence in this time period. Did you think the Special Operations Group would fail to notice? And now taking those temporal agents prisoner and bringing them here—the risk is simply unacceptable. You've told me yourself that these very agents have defeated you several times before and yet it seems you've failed to learn from the experience."

"Go on," said Drakov, his voice sounding dangerously calm. "You said I've failed to respect our bargain in more ways than one. What else?"

"You have displayed nothing but callous disregard for my creations," said Moreau. He put his hands on the edge of Drakov's desk and leaned down toward him. "I took my project away from the Special Operations Group because they insisted upon treating my hominoids as some sort of inferior sub-race. I did not devote half my life to this project merely to turn out genetically tailored mongoloids for the Special Operations Group to use as cannon fodder. I set out to create beings specifically designed to perform tasks and survive environmental conditions hostile to ordinary humans. I meant for them to work together, for hominoids and humans to complement each other in order to achieve a more perfect society. Yet fools and paranoid bureaucrats saw them only as slaves, creatures to be inhibited in their development so that they

could not become 'competitive' with humans, to have their
pain centers blocked and their minds programmed so that they
could fight like automatons. I thought you were different.
You made me believe that you were sympathetic to my goals,
but you are no different from the others. Forty-seven of my
hominoids were killed by those two S.O.G. agents when you
sent them into that idiotic robot of yours. And for what?
What did you accomplish? You killed one and took the other
prisoner. Was that worth forty-seven lives?"

"Are you finished?" Drakov said.

"No, not quite. I insist that we move the headquarters of
this project at once. It has become far too dangerous for us to
remain here. I also demand that the prisoners be removed. Get
rid of them. Clock them out to some other time period. Their
presence here constitutes a serious threat to the project."

"*You* insist?" said Drakov. "*You* demand?" He rose to his
feet, towering over the professor. "You arrogant pismire!
You dare to dictate terms to me? *I* was the one who seized the
Infiltrator Project from the Special Operations Group. *I* was
the one who took a glorified university professor away from a
government sponsored research project and gave him the opportunity to play at being God! Without me, you are nothing!"

"And without me," Moreau said, his voice barely under
control, "you don't have the hominoids."

"You delude yourself, Professor," Drakov said. "I could
easily have compelled your unquestioning obedience through
psycho-conditioning from the very start. Santos is quite expert
in such matters. I did not do so because I did not wish to risk
damaging your creative faculties. However, do not make the
mistake of thinking yourself indispensable. Do you think I
have been merely sitting on my hands all this time? I have been
watching you most carefully. Watching and learning. I am a
highly intelligent man, Professor, but I am not a genius, as
you are. I could never have created the hominoids myself, but
given the creative spark you provided, I could learn to imitate
the process. I do not pretend to have acquired all of your ex-
pertise, but I believe that I can create hominoids of my own
now without any help from you."

"And you call *me* arrogant?" said Moreau, sarcastically.

"Here," said Drakov, picking up a file from the desktop
and tossing it to him. "See for yourself."

"What is this?"

"Don't you recognize it, Professor? It's a status file on a new generation of hominoid. I have done this one exactly as you have done yours, only I wasn't going to tell you about it quite this early. I was going to save it for a surprise."

Moreau leafed through the file quickly, his eyes growing wider as he read it. "You can't be serious! This is some sort of joke."

"It's no joke, Professor, I assure you. By the way, please feel free to point out any errors you feel I might have made. After all, I am only the apprentice while you are the master."

"I don't believe it!" Moreau said. "You couldn't possibly have done this. It's beyond your scope, beyond all your abilities—"

"If that is, in fact, the case," said Drakov, "then it should show up in the status file. Does it? It is too early yet to tell how it will perform when it matures, but tell me, how does it look on paper?"

Moreau was shaking his head slowly. "This is monstrous!" he said. "Creating hominoids such as the titans and the harpies is one thing, but this is precisely what the government officials were most frightened of. This *is* a species that would compete with humans!"

"So you acknowledge that I have done it, then?" said Drakov. "That it is not, after all, beyond my capabilities?"

Moreau moistened his lips. "On paper, I must admit that it looks feasible," he said. "However, you have merely taken the first step. Still, I see that I have seriously underestimated you. I must congratulate you. Obviously, you are not as ignorant of the science of genetic manipulation as I thought. I cannot believe that you have learned all of this from me in so short a time."

"Now you underestimate yourself, Professor," Drakov said. "You have been an excellent teacher. However, you are quite correct. I am not an entirely unversed layman. Knowledge is power and power is a passion with me. To one who has lived as long as I have, and to whom time poses no barriers, it is not difficult to accumulate vast amounts of knowledge. I have spent years of study in preparation for this."

"You never told me," said Moreau.

"You would have been more guarded with me if I had," said Drakov. He poured Moreau a glass of wine. "It is pointless for us to quarrel, Professor. True, I have used you, but then you also have used me. In that sense, our relationship has been quite symbiotic. Look at all we have accomplished. I do not blame you for your concerns, but then you do not see the full scope of my plans. You do not have access to all of the details. I have learned long ago not to put all of my eggs into one basket. True, I have taken risks, but believe me, they have been well within the parameters of acceptability. I can understand your being protective, but you are being too conservative."

"Conservative?" Moreau snorted. "That's a new one. I have been called mad, but never conservative."

"That is because the people you have dealt with are little men," said Drakov, "and little men have little vision. I am not a little man, Professor. And my visions are panoramic."

"And you have really *done* this?" said Moreau, tapping the file. "This wasn't just an exercise? You have really taken this to the gestation stage?"

"That one and several others, as well," Drakov said. "But I could never have done it without you. As I have said, you are the genius. I am merely a clever imitator."

"And where will you go from here?" Moreau asked. "To what use do you intend to put this . . . this creature?"

"It shall be brought along in a manner similar to all the others," Drakov said, "only this one shall be allowed to develop to its fullest potential, even beyond what we have achieved with the centaur. And what we have learned here with our little exercise in altering historical scenarios and making myths reality will be applied with this creature and others like it in my own timeline. I will clock it back to the appropriate time period, Professor, and then I will set it free."

The heavy bolt on the other side of the door was slowly drawn back and the temporal agents were on their feet in an instant. As the door started to open, Delaney grabbed it and pulled back on it hard, yanking the person on the other side into the cell. The others were standing poised to attack, but there was only the one man whom Delaney had knocked to the floor. He held his hands out in front of his face to shield himself from further blows.

"Don't!" he cried. "I've come to help!"

"Moreau!" said Hunter.

Delaney let him up.

"Here," said the professor, reaching inside his jacket and

removing several warp discs. "Take these. Quickly. You must escape at once."

"What is this?" Hunter said. "I thought you and Drakov were in this thing together. Why are you doing this?"

"Because I must," Moreau said. "I've been a fool, thinking Drakov would help me prove the worth of my creations, demonstrate what they can be capable of doing, but he has perverted all my work, stolen the fruits of all my labors and now he plans to do something so monstrous that I cannot even imagine what the consequences will be if he is not stopped."

"How do we know you're telling the truth?" said Steiger.

"I have given you the means to escape and bring soldiers here to stop him," said Moreau. "You must do it now, immediately, before it is too late."

"You weren't so concerned when you were helping him create a temporal disruption," Hunter said. "What's so terrible that you suddenly developed a conscience?"

"It's true," Moreau said, "I was angry, embittered, determined to make them pay for turning my creations into mindless slaves, but this . . . what he plans is unthinkable. It's madness. I have to stop him somehow."

"I think you've done enough, Professor," Hunter said. "The Special Operations Group will stop him. You're coming back with me."

"I don't think so," Steiger said. "I'm afraid we can't let you take him, Hunter."

"Well, I'm not about to let *you* take him, pilgrim," Hunter said.

"I guess the truce is over," said Delaney.

"Moreau's coming with me," said Hunter. "And if I have to take you out to do it, I will."

"All three of us?" said Steiger.

"You fools!" Moreau shouted. "There is no time for this!"

"Get back behind me, Professor," Hunter said, reaching out quickly and pulling Moreau behind him.

"Don't make us do this, Hunter," said Delaney.

"Sorry, Finn," said Hunter. "I've got my duty. If you want him, you're going to have to come through me to get him."

"No one's taking me anywhere!" Moreau said. "Fight like dogs for all I care! I will do what must be done myself!"

He disappeared.

"Finn, he's clocked out!" Andre shouted.

Hunter turned around and Steiger hit him with a flying tackle. They fell to the floor, but Hunter recovered quickly, striking Steiger in the temple with his elbow and throwing him off. Delaney was on him before he had fully regained his feet and he slammed him against the wall. The breath hissed out of Hunter, but he brought his knee up into Delaney's groin and smashed a hard right into his face, then reeled back from Steiger's right cross to his jaw, ducked beneath his left and drove his own fist into Steiger's solar plexus. He followed it up with an uppercut to Steiger's chin and then turned toward Andre just in time to catch a spinning wheel kick to the head. Her heel connected with his temple and he staggered back, bounced off the wall and fell to the floor.

"Son of a bitch hits hard," said Steiger, rubbing his chin. Delaney was still doubled over, clutching his groin. "You okay, Finn?"

"I'll live," Delaney managed to reply, though his voice was a bit high.

"Nice work," Steiger said to Andre.

"You two are slowing down," she said. "You should work out more often. What do we do with him now? We can't just leave him here."

"No, and we'd better get out while we still can," said Steiger. He bent down over Hunter's warp disc and started programming coordinates. "I think we're going to need some help. We'll clock him back with us and turn him over to Curtis. Then we bring the Rangers back with us and hit this place with everything we've got."

"Major Curtis!" the sentry shouted.

Curtis came running. From the direction of the river, four people dressed in ancient Greek costume were coming toward him. Two of them supported a third between them, with his arms over their shoulders.

"Hold your fire!" Curtis shouted.

"Got a prisoner for you, Major," said Steiger. "Capt. Reese Hunter of the Special Operations Group." They dropped Hunter to the ground at Curtis' feet.

"Well done," said Curtis. "Mission accomplished?"

"Not exactly," said Delaney. "We've got a problem. A big one. Hope your boys are ready for some action, Major."

"The whole thing was a setup," Steiger said. "The opposition got suckered in as badly as we did. Our old friend Drakov is behind it all. He's using the congruent universe as a staging area to launch an attack on our timeline using beings created by genetic manipulation. We've just come from his base. We're going to have to go back and hit it before he has a chance to move his operation. Hit it hard."

Curtis was all business. "Sgt. Peck, Corporal Willis, take charge of the prisoner. Lt. Nelson, clock out to Galveston and get the strike force mobilized and back here on the double. Pick up your attack coordinates from Col. Steiger." He spoke into his communicator. "Condition Red," he said. "Repeat, Condition Red. We're going through. Unit will assemble at the picket lines on the double. Move it!"

"Look out!" Peck shouted.

As they had started to help Hunter to his feet, he had uncorked a haymaker into Willis' midsection and now he and Peck were rolling on the ground, struggling. Nelson aimed her plasma pistol at the pair.

"Hold it!" Curtis said. "You'll hit Peck."

Peck had rolled over on top and was trying to pin Hunter to the ground, but Hunter brought a knee up sharply and Peck grunted and went limp on top of him. A second later, Peck wasn't on top of Hunter anymore. Hunter had disappeared and Peck dropped about a foot to the ground onto the space where Hunter had lain.

"What the—" Nelson said. "He got Peck's warp disc!"

"Never mind," said Curtis. "It was set for HQ. He'll have a nice surprise when he clocks in. Get some battle gear for these people, move it! You're busted to corporal, Peck. Private Willis, on your feet! Fall in!"

The Rangers began to clock in at the picket line, ready for battle.

Moreau ran through the clean room of the laboratory, smashing racks of petri dishes and destroying the equipment. Tears ran down his cheeks as he obliterated his life's work, killing his creations before they ever had a chance at life. He knew that somewhere in here, hidden among the others, had to be the creature Drakov had created and he had to make certain to destroy that one above all others. Once that was done, he intended to kill Drakov, even if at the cost of his own life.

Nothing mattered anymore except the ending of it all. He had devoted years of painstaking research and experimentation, sacrificed everything to his work, suffered the derision of his colleagues and the insults of petty bureaucrats and government officials who referred to him at best as "the mad professor" and at worst as a monster without a conscience, "the modern Mengele." He had sought to improve the human condition, to broaden the capabilities of the race, and they had vilified him for immorality, accused him of playing God with human reproduction even while they backed his work and used his developmentally stunted creations as if they were android slaves. They had never given him a chance to allow his creations to develop to their full potential, partly out of fear and partly out of a self-serving justification—it was all right to treat them as sub-human so long as they were not fully developed.

The hominoids were never allowed a chance to stand on equal footing with humans and now they never would receive that chance. It was over. His life's work, wasted.

"That will be enough, Moreau!"

Moreau turned to see Drakov standing at the entrance to the clean room, a laser pistol held in his hand.

"You're too late," said Moreau. His voice broke. "I've destroyed them all. I began with the gestation room and once I smashed all the artificial wombs, I finished the task here. There is nothing left. Nothing."

"You're wrong, Professor," Drakov said. "I told you before, I learned long ago not to put all of my eggs into one basket. Did you think this was my only laboratory? You have destroyed all of your own work. My own creations are being kept elsewhere. In fact, the one you were so concerned about has already been born. Even as we speak, it is in its time cycle of maturity. You are the one who is too late, Professor. When the Special Operations Group arrives, they will find three dead temporal agents and the corpse of one of their own people. Your body shall be here, as well. I imagine that Capt. Hunter will receive some sort of posthumous decoration for having single-handedly, at the cost of his own life, eliminated the threat to this timestream. You see, Professor, it all dovetails neatly. What you have done here will only lend credibility to the scene I will create."

"Only it doesn't dovetail quite so neatly, Nikolai," Moreau said. "You will not have any corpses with which to stage your scene because I have released the prisoners and they are long gone."

"You've done *what*?" said Drakov.

"They'll know now who was responsible for this," Moreau said. "and the only corpse they find here will be yours!"

He hurled a glass specimen jar at Drakov. Drakov jerked his head aside and fired as the jar smashed against the wall behind him, but his shot went wide and Moreau was on him in a flying leap. The laser flew out of Drakov's grasp and skittered across the floor, beneath one of the counters. They fell to the floor, Moreau on top, his fingers digging into Drakov's throat. Drakov dislodged him effortlessly, rolling him over and reversing their positions.

"You fool," said Drakov, pinning him down. "I have three times your strength!"

Moreau's hand clawed for Drakov's eyes. Drakov grabbed it, twisted Moreau's wrist, and broke it. Moreau cried out with pain. Drakov drew back his fist and smashed it into Moreau's face, once, twice, three times—and then the wall exploded.

The Rangers fanned out as they clocked in, circling round the palace complex from both sides and firing their weapons as they ran. The plasma blasts whumped against the walls, imploding them and bursting into washes of blue flame. A black garbed figure came diving out of one of the second-story windows as the palace erupted into flame. He hit the ground in a hard and awkward roll and came up running, favoring his side and holding his left shoulder as he ran.

"Benedetto!" Delaney shouted. "Come on, he's heading for the robot!"

"For the what?" yelled Curtis, but Delaney was already sprinting after Benedetto with Andre running behind him. Deciding that two of them were sufficient to catch one man, Curtis turned his attention back to the assault. They were only a handful, one small unit, and they had to hit hard and keep on hitting hard until the Temporal Counter-Insurgency battalion clocked in from Galveston and came through the confluence to reinforce them. With any luck, they'd already have the job done by the time the T.C.I. strike force came on the scene. They had to get in and get out fast. The last thing they needed was for S.O.G. units to show up.

As Curtis and his squad moved in, a howling mob of half-naked men came streaming out from the compound, bearing down on them. Curtis blinked several times. They seemed to have about six arms apiece.

"*Fire!*" Curtis shouted.

His squad opened up on the attackers. They kept on coming, living torches running at them until they fell to the ground as lifeless hunks of charred meat.

"Sir," said one of his men, "did those guys have—"

"Never mind," said Curtis. "Just fry anything that moves."

"Or flies?" the soldier said.

Curtis looked up. "What in the name of . . ."

Screeching like banshees, the harpies came diving down, talons extended.

Moreau struggled to his knees, his face a mask of blood. Drakov was gone. The entire side of the building was demolished and the laboratory was in flames.

"All for nothing," Moreau said, wiping the blood away from his eyes with his one good hand and gazing about him through the smoke at all the ruin. "Drakov!" he shouted. *"Drakov!"*

The flames were coming closer and he crawled away, coughing from the smoke.

"You should have killed me, Nikolai," he said. "You should have killed me while you had the chance."

He struggled to his feet and lurched out of the laboratory into the hall. He could feel the plasma blasts slamming into the building and he knew there was very little time left. He staggered into Drakov's quarters and half collapsed onto his desk. He pawed through the papers, finally finding what he sought. He tucked the files beneath his arm and rummaged through the drawers, seeking the spare warp disc he knew Drakov kept there for emergencies. He knew it would be programmed with escape coordinates. He had little doubt that Drakov had already made good his escape. Wherever he had gone, Moreau would follow.

The entire room shook as a plasma blast hit the outside wall and the ceiling fell in. Moreau's hand closed around the warp disc as the debris struck and knocked him to the floor. The whole room was in flames. Half buried under the wreckage, wincing from the pain in his broken wrist, Moreau reached for the controls.

The fall had broken Benedetto's shoulder, but it hadn't slowed him down much. He knew well what to expect from the soldiers of the Temporal Corps and there was no chance to clock out. When the plasma blasts had hit the building, he was blown right through the window and the fall, in addition to breaking his shoulder, had shattered his warp disc. The only chance he had left now was Talos.

Trying to ignore the pain, he sprinted hard for the harbor. He glanced over his shoulder and saw two figures running after him. He swore and redoubled his efforts, but they were gaining on him. A plasma blast exploded on the ground to his left. Seconds later, another one hit to his right, directly ahead of him. They had him bracketed. The next one would find its target. He started to run serpentine to throw off their aim. It was the only thing to do, but it resulted in their closing the distance between them.

He reached the giant robot straddling the harbor, with plasma fire exploding all around him. One blast hit right next to him, close enough to throw him to the ground and set his clothes on fire. Gasping with pain, he ripped off his burning shirt and threw himself through the doorway in the robot's ankle, stabbing with burned fingers at the controls which would shut it. As it started to slide to, two plasma blasts struck it in rapid succession, the wash of blue flame coming through the slowly closing opening. He threw himself back just in time. Several more blasts hit the door and he saw molten bronze flowing at the bottom of the crack. There was no way out now. He was sealed in.

He half ran, half staggered up the metal stairs toward the control room, pulling himself along with his right hand grasping the railing. "Bastards!" he swore, as he climbed the stairs, "fucking bastards!"

Finn and Andre fired charge after charge into the door in the giant robot's ankle. They saw the bronze soften and start to flow, but even the intense heat of the plasma charges was not enough to blast the door open.

"It's no good," said Delaney. "The door's melted shut."

"Then he's not going anywhere," said Andre.

"Don't bet on that," Delaney said, tersely.

From inside the robot, they heard the sounds of machinery and hydraulics starting to move.

Curtis had posted guards around the perimeter of the transit area, but he needn't have bothered. The terrified population had fled in terror from them. The ground was littered with the corpses of Moreau's creatures and with the bodies of several of the Rangers who had been killed in the suicidal attack of the harpies. Drakov's ruined palace was ablaze. It was all over by the time the first wave of the T.C.I. strike force battalion started to clock in. Curtis approached Col. Cooper, the commander of the strike force.

"Looks like you people didn't need us," Cooper said. "You seem to have the situation well in hand."

"We had no idea what kind of resistance we might have encountered, Colonel," Curtis said. "There was a —"

"Jesus H. Christ on a crutch!" said Cooper, looking beyond him. "What in the hell is *that*?"

Curtis turned around. "Holy shit!"

Finn and Andre were running at top speed toward them, while behind them, gaining with every massive stride, was Talos. The bronze giant, with Benedetto at the controls, was moving slowly, awkwardly, but with the length of its strides, it didn't need to move fast. Servomotors within it whined with each giant stride. The huge arm lifted the bronze obelisk of a sword.

"Skirmish line!" Cooper shouted out to his battalion. "Fire at will!"

A hundred plasma rifles opened up on the advancing robot, wreathing it in an aura of blue flame and blackening the bronze. Benedetto was blinded by the plasma fire, but he remained at the controls, keeping the robot advancing toward the soldiers. He felt the intense heat building up as the relentless barrage continued. The bronze began to soften.

"I knew I should have installed cannon in this ridiculous contraption," Benedetto said, grimacing with pain. The controls were growing hot to the touch. "I'm going to be cooked alive like some damned lobster." He slammed a control lever forward, but the robot arm holding the sword remained immobile, the servomotors damaged by the plasma fire. "Damn it!" Benedetto swore. He reached for the level controlling the arm holding the shield.

"Maintain fire!" Cooper shouted as the strike force and the Ranger unit poured everything they had into the robot. Molten metal was now running down its exterior like hot wax flowing down a candle. The robot's impassive features sagged. Molten bronze fell to the ground in globs with each step it took.

Inside the control room, it was like an oven. The interior walls were starting to glow red. Benedetto's skin was turning red and blistering. His hands were being crisped as they

confluence, the better I'll like it. Our report's going to look
bad enough as it is. If General Forrester finds out about this,
he'll hand our asses to us.''

"Look down there," said Andre, pointing to an area where
the framework of a ship was being erected. "Isn't that
Argus?"

"So it is," Delaney said. "Come on."

The shipwright was astonished to see them. "Fabius!
Creon! Atalanta! By the gods, we thought you were dead!"
He clapped his arms around each of them in turn.

"We came close enough to Hades, old friend," said Delaney. "We managed to escape the dead warriors of Colchis,
but when the ship left without us, we had to make our way
back over land. It was a long, hard journey, but we had to
come back and find out what became of all of you."

"It has been a long time," Argus said. He shouted to one of
his workmen. "Demetrios! Take over for me! I will return
later." He turned to the temporal agents. "Come, we will sit
down to dinner and we shall have some wine and I will tell you
all about it."

Inside the modest house close to the wharves, they sat and
listened as Argus told them what became of the Argonauts
after they left Colchis.

"We thought we had made good our escape from Colchis,"
Argus said, "but Aietes sent his fleet to pursue us. For days we
fled from them, but they kept on closing the distance between
us until finally we saw that we could not escape and we would
have to fight. But Medea tricked her brother, Apsyrtus, the
commander of the Colchin fleet, into coming ashore with all
his captains and sitting down to a parley. She made him promise to let us go if we gave up the golden fleece without a fight,
but while she met with her brother and his captains, we had
already come ashore. We fell upon them and killed every last
one of them, just as Medea had planned. Then, before the
Colchin fleet could recover from the loss of its commanders,
we slipped away from them in the dead of night. When Jason
saw Medea standing there, covered with her brother's blood, I
tell you, such a look came upon his face that it was as if he
were seeing her for the first time. His passion cooled somewhat after that.

"We sailed on until we came to the island of Circe, the sister
of King Aietes. Medea insisted that we stop there and we could

not see why, but it seemed a pleasant island and Jason wished
to please her. We came ashore and supped at Circe's table. I
tell you, such a woman I have never seen before and hope
never to see again. All the gold and gemstones in the world,
and she wore many, would never make up for such ugliness. A
fat, pustulant old hag she was, and such a smell came off her!
I tell you, one look at that woman could turn a man into a
swine!

"Well, there we sat, trying to avoid gazing at her so that we
could keep down our food, and Medea begins to rail at her, to
shout about all the abuse that she had suffered at her hands—
and I never did quite understand what this abuse was, unless it
was that as Aietes' sister, she stood higher than Medea at the
Colchin court—and to shout how she would be far greater
now that she would be queen in Iolchos with the golden fleece.
Well, not surprisingly, Circe did not take kindly to this loud
display and she drove us from her table and her island, both.
So, we set sail once more, Jason even more silent than before.
But not Medea.

"She began to make plans for the palace we were to build
for her in Iolchos and she had me design a pleasure barge upon
which she would cruise between the islands. Well, then a storm
came and kept us busy and her quiet for a time. Of course,
when the storm had passed away, she blamed us for her dis-
comfort and demanded that we provide smooth sailing from
then on. Still, we all tried to be patient.

"Well, we did not encounter such adventures upon our return journey as we did when you were with us, only that there
were other storms which we survived—thanks to the lessons
you had taught me, Fabius, about sailing in a storm—but then
when we were drawing close to home, we came upon an island
where we found the fallen body of a giant made from bronze.
The bronze was molten, as if this giant had been placed within
some fantastic forge and then left out upon the ground to
harden once again. His sword was raised, as if he had been
fighting for his life, but the flames which had been cast at him
overcame him. There was also a ruined palace on this island, a
palace which had been razed to the ground by fire, and we
learned from the people of the island that a powerful god had
lived there once, and that this god had somehow offended the
other gods so that they came and fought with him and there
was a mighty war in which this god of the island was defeated.

"Jason took all this to be an omen and he turned to Idmon and asked him what it meant, if it was possible that these gods had fought over our voyage. He asked Idmon if he had any premonitions about what his future held in store for him. Idmon tried to look into the future, but as you know, Idmon does not always see things clearly. He looked disturbed and told Jason that he had an intuition that Jason would be happy, but he did not see him upon the throne of Iolchos. At this, Medea lost her temper and called him an old fool and other things more vile, insisting that of course Jason would be on the throne in Iolchos, how else could she live but as a queen. Jason said nothing. It was on this island, also, that Hercules and Hylas parted company with us. Hercules looked disturbed when he heard about this god who had once lived upon the island and he said that there was a strange feeling he had about the place, a sort of kinship to it, and he would stay there for a while, rest from the voyage, and then travel on with Hylas to seek his fate and fortunes elsewhere. We wished him luck and sailed on as he and Hylas waved to us from shore. I have not seen either of them since.

"We stopped once more at Pelion, but when we went ashore, we found no trace of Chiron. The cave was just as we remembered it, but the centaur was no longer there. It was deserted. Jason was saddened by this. We waited for a long time, but Chiron never returned and finally we continued on.

"And then, the night before we were to make safe harbor here in Iolchos—for I knew we were already in familiar waters —a most peculiar thing occurred. Medea had taken to sleeping with the golden fleece and while we were anchored offshore for the night, in a protected cove not far from Pelion, I was awakened with the others by a fearful noise. It seems that Pelias had placed a spy within our midst and that spy was none other than Orpheus, the last man I would have suspected, even had I thought there was a traitor among us. He had been promised a great reward and a post as the poet at the court of Pelias if he could contrive to sink the ship or to kill Jason or to somehow stop him from fulfilling the conditions of the quest.

"Well, Orpheus did not have the stomach for committing murder, so he had waited to see what would occur that would give him an opportunity, yet he did not act because, he claimed, he had come to look upon us all as friends and, I think, although he did not admit it, because he was afraid. Yet

now that the time had come when we would be sailing into
Iolchos on the next day, he knew he had to act or else forfeit
the reward. He did not believe that Pelias would honor the
promise he had made to Jason and he believed that all of us
would be set upon and killed if we came back to Iolchos with
the golden fleece.

"While Medea slept, Orpheus had stolen into the cabin and
taken the golden fleece. But it was heavy, as you know, and in
dragging it out of the cabin, he made some noise and woke
Medea. We found them both on deck, with the golden fleece
between them, Medea screaming like as not to wake the dead
and beating him about the head and shoulders with such
fierceness that it was all poor Orpheus could do to cover his
head and shield himself from her. Well, when we found them
that way and Theseus pulled Medea off him, Orpheus cried
and confessed everything to us. Medea demanded that we kill
the traitor and Theseus looked to Jason to see if that was what
he wished, but Jason said not a single word. Instead, he bent
down, and with a great grunt of effort, picked up the golden
fleece and threw it overboard.

"For a moment, we were all too stunned to move or speak,
but then Medea let out a scream that was, if possible, even
louder than before. She lost her head completely and demanded that Jason dive for it and bring it up, as if he was capable of such a thing. And to our amazement, Jason un-
buckled his sword and stood upon the railing, ready, it
seemed, to do exactly as she wanted. He leaped over the side
but instead of diving for the fleece, he struck out for the shore.
At this, Medea went wild and sought to grab a bow, so that
she could shoot an arrow after him, but Theseus, whose patience is not great, struck her a blow and felled her to the deck,
telling her that if she wanted the golden fleece, she should dive
for it herself. And then he, too, leaped over the side and struck
out after Jason.

"And there it ended. A most peculiar conclusion to the
story. We made port the next day and the Argonauts dis-
banded, each going their separate ways, yet no one com-
plained that the journey was for nothing. I know a number of
them stayed in Iolchos for a while, and several still remain
here, telling stories of our journey in exchange for drinks and
meals. I have heard some of those stories and, like the tale
Orpheus had told, they grow better with each telling. Orpheus

never received his reward from Pelias, who claimed to know nothing of any such arrangement. He left Iolchos and I doubt he will return again. Theseus, I have heard, returned to Athens and of Jason, I have heard nothing at all. Idmon lives nearby and still makes his living as a soothsayer. He comes to see me on occasion and he tells me that he feels his intuition was correct. Jason did not sit upon the throne in Iolchos, but wherever he has gone, he has found happiness.''

"And what of Medea?'' asked Delaney. "What became of her?''

"She found herself without a palace or a throne, without the golden fleece, and with no protector in a strange city where she knew no one. She was frightened at this prospect, so she found a man to take her in. This man was not a wealthy or a powerful man, but he knew how to handle a proud woman and was not so vulnerable to her beauty as younger men would be. In time, Medea became humbled and her nature grew much more agreeable." He turned. "Woman! Where is dinner? Our guests are being kept waiting!''

"Coming, Argus,'' said Medea, entering from the kitchen, carrying a tray.

The three agents sat in Forrester's den, surrounded by books and memorabilia from previous missions. On a low table before them was a bottle of Irish whiskey and a small tray holding glasses. Forrester sat across from them in his reading chair, smoking one of his antique Castello pipes and studying their report. When he finally put it down, he sat silent for a long while before speaking.

"Clocking back to Iolchos afterwards was risky,'' he said, staring down at the carpet, "but it did produce some useful intelligence.'' He nodded. "You were correct to do it and include it in your report.''

He pursed his lips, thinking. "I don't know whether to call it a successful mission or not,'' he said at last. He sighed. "A disruption *was* created, though it was mostly not your doing, and the S.O.G. will have their hands full attempting to adjust for it, but Drakov and this professor have apparently escaped. Major Curtis reported that their bodies were not found in the ruins, though it's possible they were burned. Still, knowing my son . . . I wish I'd killed him when I had the chance, God help me.''

His face looked grim. "The S.O.G. will probably try to hunt down Hercules, as well as Jason."

"I hope they make it," said Andre.

Forrester frowned, then his face cleared as he understood her meaning. "Oh, the hominoids, you mean." He nodded. "Fascinating creatures. I see you've made a number of unsubstantiated statements here. . . ."

"That's because there was no way to substantiate them, sir," Delaney said. "All we can do is guess. We figure the reason the Argonauts were drugged at Lemnos is because Drakov wanted to separate us from them there, or at least verify who was really who among the Argonauts. Maybe they were drugged because we broke out of that cell before he had a chance to get there. I'm inclined to think he meant to get us. During our fight with the harpies, one of them tried to carry Andre off. We're also guessing about the Dalion women who were carried off by the titans. It's possible they were required for Moreau's experiments. It's even possible they became the harpies. On the other hand, the hominoids were essentially human, or at least human-based life forms. The titans were extremely primitive, but I'm assuming they still had human urges. Now none of these things have any particular significance, except for our comments concerning the storage room on Lemnos where Creed discovered the inactive hominoids."

"And incorrectly assumed them to be androids?" Forrester said.

"Yes, sir," Steiger said. "There are two significant points there, again, neither of which can be substantiated, but the circumstantial evidence in their support is strong. Drakov told us they were early prototypes of hominoids made for S.O.G., a number of which he had stolen. That, combined with the fact of the dead warriors, strongly suggests that S.O.G. still has a significant inventory, if you will, of these early prototypes. And my discovery of them in the storage room on Lemnos supports our conclusion that they can be deactivated. Since they are not androids, but organic beings similar to ourselves, we think this deactivation is probably accomplished by placing them into some sort of deathlike coma, like suspended animation. The interrogation of our prisoner should give us more conclusive information."

"I'm afraid that won't be possible," said Forrester. "Capt. Hunter has escaped."

"Escaped?" said Andre. "How?"

"Well, more to the point, he was never placed in custody," said Forrester, wryly. "No one at HQ was aware that a prisoner was clocking in, so he managed to bluff his way past the transition station personnel and disappear along with his stolen warp disc."

"I'll be damned," Delaney said. "And now he's loose somewhere in our timeline."

"Yes, but at the moment, we have more pressing concerns," said Forrester. "I'd like to get back to your report. What about those nysteel birds that attacked the ship?"

"It's possible that they were Drakov's," Steiger said, "but he never mentioned them and they never showed up during the battle on Rhodes. That's what makes me think they were S.O.G. drones, equipped with nysteel projectiles and programmed not to kill certain members of the crew. They had to keep Theseus and certain others that were important to their historical continuity alive. That's why they couldn't make a direct hit on the entire ship."

Forrester nodded. "And the same applies to the so-called 'dead warriors.' Specifically programmed not to kill certain members of the crew. Which is why I find your final comments about Jason very interesting. When you mention that he apparently acted counter to his programming in throwing the golden fleece overboard, you have in parenthesis the words, 'developmentally related?' What precisely do you mean by that?"

"Again, this is getting into conjecture," Steiger said, "but we're assuming that there was a programmed imperative in the Jason hominoid. It seems to be a fairly safe assumption, but we don't know for sure what that imperative might have been. Obviously, he was programmed to *be* Jason and to act accordingly, but there's no way of knowing precisely how that imperative was couched, so we don't know just how far his actions ran counter to his programming."

"There's also the fact that it's not as if we're talking about an android here," Delaney said. "Jason was purely organic, essentially a cloned human being raised under highly controlled conditions. Drakov implied that the generation of hominoids Jason came from was the most advanced one. Perhaps the level of development was responsible for the independence of the action. Jason might have been naive and emotionally simplistic, but he nevertheless had a fully developed personality. And then Moreau seemed to have a highly protective attitude toward his creations, so that could have been a factor as well. He may have specifically programmed them to allow them a certain amount of independent thought and action, especially the more advanced ones.''

Forrester nodded again. "That about covers it, I guess. Unfortunately, it still leaves us with a number of unanswered questions. Archives Section isn't going to be very pleased. I notice that you never addressed the issue directly, but there are a number of implications here between the lines that are going to give them real headaches. Specifically, there's still the question of trans-temporal influence. It doesn't seem probable that the earthquake responsible for the 'Clashing Rocks' was arranged in any way, and yet the event fits the myth precisely. *Our* myth. And what was Drakov planning for this timeline that made Moreau turn against him? That has to be our single, overriding concern right now. And I'm afraid it may tie in directly with the question of trans-temporal contamination.''

Delaney frowned. "What do you mean, sir?"

Forrester stood. "I'm referring to the fact that Moreau's body was never found. And to the fact that he is the creator of the hominoids and that his name happens to be Moreau.'' He scanned his bookshelves. "There is a book here I think you should read.''

He took down a leather bound volume and handed it to Delaney.

"The Island of Dr. Moreau," Delaney read from the cover, "by H. G. Wells?"

"I think you'll find it very interesting," said Forrester, "and highly disturbing, in light of your recent experiences. Perhaps it's only a coincidence. Perhaps it's also only a coincidence that Wells also wrote a novel called *The Time Machine.*''

"Those would be two very interesting coincidences," Steiger said, uneasily.

"Yes, they would indeed," said Forrester. "I realize you've just returned from a mission, but I'm afraid I'm going to have to send you out again almost immediately. Drink up. I want you to get a good night's sleep. You'll be clocking out at oh-six-hundred. I think you three should have a long talk with Mr. H. G. Wells.''

* * *

Drakov stood alone in the dark, dank cellar of the ruined castle. He held a torch in his left hand and in his right, he held a small electronic box.

"It seems as if we have come full circle, my friend," he said, looking down. "It began in a ruin much like this one, in Ruritania. In the cold, damp corridors of Zenda Castle, where I first encountered the temporal agents. And it is a fitting environment for your beginning, as well."

He pressed a button on the tiny box, activating the implant that would revive the creature from its deathlike sleep.

"You shall give them nightmares," he said, chuckling. "And you shall only be the first of many."

He put the black box back inside his pocket, activated his warp disc and disappeared. For a moment, all was silent in the cellar of the ruined castle, and then a hand came out from beneath the coffin lid.